MAXINE MORREY has wanted [...] can remember and wrote her first [...] for school when she was ten.

Years passed and she continued to write but life often got in the way. She has written articles on a variety of subjects, as well as a local history book and in 2015 she won a contract for her Christmas romcom, *Winter's Fairytale*. Since then she has written many more 'romcoms with depth' and wants to encourage everyone to 'Read Yourself Happy'.

She is the bestselling author of *Things Are Looking Up*, *#NoFilter*, and the Kindle UK top ten read, *The Christmas Project*, among others.

In 2024, her book *You've Got This* won The Romantic Comedy Award at the Romantic Novelists' Association award ceremony in London.

When not wrangling with words, she loves to read, sew and listen to podcasts. She can also often be found out on a gentle walk in nature, camera in hand.

You can find Maxine on Instagram @scribbler_maxi.

Also by Maxine Morrey

No Place Like Home
Winter's Fairytale
The Christmas Project
Around the World with My Ex
The Best Little Christmas Shop
Second Chance at the Ranch
Coming Home to Wishington Bay
#No Filter
My Year of Saying No
Winter at Wishington Bay
Things Are Looking Up
Living Your Best Life
You Only Live Once
Just Say Yes
You've Got This
Just Do It
Be Your Best Self

The Best Little Christmas Shop

MAXINE MORREY

HQ

ONE PLACE. MANY STORIES

HQ
An imprint of HarperCollins*Publishers* Ltd
1 London Bridge Street
London SE1 9GF

www.harpercollins.co.uk

HarperCollins*Publishers*
Macken House, 39/40 Mayor Street Upper,
Dublin 1 D01 C9W8
This edition 2025

1
First published in Great Britain by HQ,
an imprint of HarperCollins*Publishers* Ltd 2017

ISBN: 9780008808631

Printed and bound in the UK using 100% Renewable
Electricity by CPI Group (UK) Ltd

MIX
Paper | Supporting
responsible forestry
FSC™ C007454

This book contains FSC™ certified paper and other controlled sources
to ensure responsible forest management.

For more information visit: www.harpercollins.co.uk/green

For José

Chapter 1

I dropped my bag on the floor, flopped facedown onto my childhood bed, and let out a groan. This was so not how it was supposed to be. But then I'd learned there were some things in life that, no matter how much you planned or wanted them, just weren't to be.

Letting out a sigh, I wriggled over onto my back, staring up at the ceiling blankly for a moment before dragging myself up and wandering over to the squishy sofa that sat beneath the window, snagging my furry slipper boots on the way. Plopping down into the softness, I pulled the boots on before turning to look out of the window. Folding my arms across the back of the sofa, I leant my chin on them and peered out into the last vestiges of daylight.

My room was separate from the rest of the house – a self-contained studio flat above the garage that my parents had created for me in my early teenage years, providing an escape from my three brothers. Not that we didn't get on – I was lucky in that respect. But a girl still needs her own space and, more importantly, her own bathroom. The fact that Mum often used to come and sit with me clued me in to the idea that I wasn't the only one using it as respite from all that testosterone.

Mum and Dad had always wanted a girl. They never planned

to have four kids, and I was definitely a last-ditch attempt, so there was some relief when I popped out. From the time I was born, I'd been dressed in, and surrounded by, more pink than was really acceptable, even for a very girly girl. And therein lay the problem. I was, very definitely, not the girliest of girls. I could have the prettiest dresses and the cutest little bunches, but still came home covered in mud, with scrapes on my knees and a big grin on my face.

To their eternal credit, Mum and Dad had never tried to force me into doing something I didn't want to, or stop me doing the things I did. Trailing along after my brothers – Matt, Dan, and Joe – up to their elbows in car parts, wood, oil and mud, I was at my happiest. It was hardly a surprise then that my choice of career wasn't traditionally feminine either. After years of working my way up, I had been well on my way to becoming Chief Engineer for the number one driver in the Formula One team I'd worked for. But 'had been' was definitely the operative term.

My eyes drifted to the corner of the sofa where my old, much-repaired teddy bear lounged comfortably. I reached out and pulled him to my chest, folding my arms across him as my mind drifted back over the past year. I'd spent the best part of it trying to find another place that fit me so well as the Formula One world had, but nothing felt quite the same.

I was therefore, at present, unemployed. I'd been lucky enough to have never been in this position before and it was a distinctly odd feeling and definitely not one I was comfortable with.

I let my gaze drift down to where weak, cloud-shrouded moonlight was now highlighting the bare branches of the huge honeysuckle bush that sat beneath the window. In the summer, its heady, intoxicating scent would drift up and fill the space. Now it just looked spiky, bare, and barren. There was a knock at the door and I rolled my head to see my eldest brother, Matt, enter carrying my case and another smaller bag.

'Where d'you want these?'

I shrugged. 'There's fine. Thanks, Matt.'

He gave me a glance, ignored my instructions, and carried the luggage across the room, laying them next to the off-white French-style wardrobe and chest of drawers.

'Any chance of a cuppa?'

I let out another sigh and dragged myself off the sofa and over to the tiny kitchenette. It had rarely been used for anything more than a sandwich and endless cups of tea and hot chocolate because, although I might have wanted a little independence all those years ago, I also knew that my mum was the best cook in the world.

Big family dinners were our thing. It didn't have to be a special occasion. The everyday was special in our house. It was fun, sometimes noisy – OK, always noisy – with plenty of discussion and a lot of laughter. I think that's why I'd enjoyed the team atmosphere of work. We'd got on well and, being away from my own family so much, it had provided me with a surrogate one.

I boiled the kettle and pulled a couple of mugs out of the cupboard while Matt grabbed a pint of milk from the mini fridge that Mum had clearly stocked up earlier in the day.

'I'd ask if you're glad to be home but it's pretty clear from your face that you're not,' Matt said as he plopped milk into our tea.

'What?' I looked up at him, genuinely horrified. 'Of course I am!'

'OK.' He took a slurp, watching me over the rim of the mug. 'But you are aware you've got a face like a slapped bum?'

I rolled my eyes at him, picked up my mug, and took it back to the sofa, pulling the handmade quilt draped across the back of it over my legs as I sat down. Matt sat next to me, his mere presence calming me as it always had. He and I had always had a special bond. As the eldest, he'd seen it as his job to take care of all his siblings, but especially me as the youngest and as a girl. It didn't matter how many times I tried to tell him not to treat me differently, I always got that little bit of extra attention from

3

him. And secretly I loved it. Whatever happened, I always knew Matt would have something wise and comforting to say.

'So, guess you're really stuffed on your career then if you're home?'

All right. Maybe not always.

I gave him a stony look. 'Thanks for that.'

He shrugged and took a sip of tea. 'I'm sure you've got a plan. You always do, no matter what life throws at you.'

I lowered my eyes and watched a traitorous tear splosh into my drink.

'Lex?'

'Hmm?' I kept my gaze lowered.

Out of the corner of my eye, I saw Matt put his mug down to the side of the sofa and reach out to take mine. I made a half-hearted attempt to hang on to it for a moment but gave up. I was tired. It had been a long day of travelling and really, I was just tired of all of it, of putting on a brave face for everyone, pretending that everything was under control when the truth was quite the opposite. Matt tilted and dipped his head, forcing me to look at him.

'What is it?'

I just shook my head. 'I don't have a plan, Matt. I've tried everything. No one wants to take me on. As far as they're concerned, I bailed on the team and broke my contract, and all the previous years of utter and absolute commitment mean absolutely nothing. I've tried everything I can think of. I thought normal stuff would be OK but just doing MOTs and basic repairs nearly sent me insane within a couple of weeks. I don't have a clue what to do now. I'm effectively homeless, jobless, and appear to have entirely burned my bridges in the racing world. You're right. I'm stuffed.'

Matt took a deep breath, reached over one brawny arm, and scooped me up against him, wrapping the other one around me as I flopped dejectedly onto his chest.

'You're not stuffed. Something will work out. It might not be what you originally had in mind but that doesn't necessarily mean it won't be just as good. And you're neither homeless nor jobless. You've got a home here – and you always will have. You're not jobless either. The shop opens at nine tomorrow morning and there's a tonne of Christmas wreaths that need to be made up. Since we got featured in that fancy magazine, the orders have shot up. We're all chasing our tails trying to keep up with the demand and get everything out in time. I know you're not thrilled to be home, but we're thrilled you're here.'

'Only because you're short-staffed,' I grumped.

Matt gave me a squeeze. 'Don't be a grouchy arse. You know that's not the only reason. It's nice to have you here. We all miss you.'

My eyes started filling again. 'I missed you all too.' I shoved myself up and turned back to face him. 'And please don't think I'm not happy to be home. I am. You know I am. I guess it's just in different circumstances than I thought it might be. I feel a bit like … I'm not sure who I am right now.'

Matt gave a half laugh. 'Lexi. You are you. You're not, and never will be, defined by what job you do. You're fun, intelligent, and apparently some blokes think you're sort of pretty so—'

I stuffed a cushion over his face and he waggled his arms and legs about comically. I found myself laughing properly for the first time in what felt like months. In fact, it probably was months. I brought the cushion down, and Matt took big, dramatic breaths, his eyes wide.

'You daft sod.' I leant in on my knees and gave him a big hug. 'Thanks, big brother. I really missed you.'

Matt dropped a kiss on top of my head. 'I know you did. I'd miss me too.'

I sat back and shoved the cushion at him. He grabbed his tea and finished the last of it before picking up both the mugs and rinsing them out in the tiny sink.

'Come on. Mum's got a lasagne big enough to feed the whole

village over there. Everyone else should be here by now too.'

I hesitated in the quick brush I was giving my hair as part of an attempt to pretend that I was totally put together and hadn't just been having a blub. Not that it mattered. They'd all see straight through me anyway. Just like Matt was doing now.

'Whatever it is you're thinking, don't,' Matt said.

'They're going to think I'm a failure. That I should have made better decisions.'

'Lex. They're not. Not one person thinks that. At least not one person who matters. You made the only decision you could.'

He was right. Deep down I knew that. Not that it made things any easier.

'Stop thinking about it now. It's done. And I'm hungry so stop faffing and come on.'

I tossed the brush onto my bed and headed for the door. 'Nag, nag, nag,' I mumbled as I passed him, neither of us bothering to hide the big grins on our faces. As much as it was scary in one way, it felt unbelievably good to be home.

Chapter 2

A week later I was still up to my eyeballs in Christmas wreaths and in full realisation of what Matt had meant when he'd said orders had soared. The Four Seasons had started life as a quirky little gift shop many years ago – opened by my newlywed parents. It had a USP before that was even a thing in that it followed the seasons. In summer, it was stuffed to the roof with bunting, picnic blankets and baskets, tiki lamps, parasols, and everything else you could think of, and plenty you hadn't, for a perfect summer's day.

But now, in the grips of winter, it was overflowing with Christmas-related goodies and a warm, cosy ambiance. This was enhanced by a massive tree that had only just fit in the door and was topped off with classy but festive instrumental music playing softly in the background.

Much of the stock was locally made, some by my family, others by friends, and the rest sourced from artisans both here and abroad. My parents had always loved discovering and nurturing new talent, although since Dad's heart scare a couple of years ago, they'd stepped back and my brothers now took it in turns to do the travelling for this side of the business, cramming it in around everything else, including their families.

From a little shop in the village, over the last forty years, the business had grown into a very successful online one too and my brothers still had more plans for it.

The shop was part of my childhood, part of the fabric of my life. I'd actually taken my first steps in it, and growing up, I'd help choose new stock for the next season. Talking shop was never banned at our dinner table. It was positively encouraged. My brothers and I had been chief toy testers for many years and now my nieces and nephews had taken over that mantle.

Even though my own career had taken me out of the country for over half the year, my family had always made sure I was still included as much as I had the time for. Mum would email me a few pictures, or send me some product samples, asking what I thought. Depending on my mood, and how far away from home I was at the time, it was sometimes a bittersweet experience. I loved that they made a point of keeping me involved in any way they and I could manage, but I knew that had I been closer, I'd have been sat around the big, timeworn pine table discussing that same product with my family in person. Laughing, teasing, talking. And the truth was, I'd never stopped missing that.

Running a business was hard work but the shop had grown along with our family, and as such, it was almost another family member. Even when it took nearly every minute of our time, we loved it. And, much to my surprise, I now found myself sat back behind the project desk next to the till and experiencing exactly what Matt had meant about orders having shot up.

I put aside a completed wreath, gave a glance around my currently quiet surroundings, smiling at the warm fuzzies it set off somewhere deep in my soul, and began work on the next one.

Winding mistletoe around the main structure, I held it up, eyeballing it and sussing where the holly would go. The process was remarkably soothing and although I'd been doing much the same thing for the past week, in between serving customers, I'd felt some of the tension I'd been carrying around for a long time very slowly begin to ebb out of me.

Creating was good for the soul, my parents had always said, and although I'd been taught some basic skills, I'd always been more interested in tinkering with the old Jag Dad had in the garage below my room. It was one of those projects he always meant to get around to but never had, and then his heart attack had happened. It had been a huge scare for all of us. Dad had always seemed full of life and indestructible – big and broad like my brothers – but his heart attack had brought us down to earth, and now we all fussed him probably a little too much for his liking.

Thank goodness he'd been sensible, and my parents took the opportunity to step back from the business, leaving much of the day-to-day running to Dan and the others. And leaving the Jag to me. But it was still sat in much the same condition as when he'd given it to me. I just never seemed to get the time to do anything on it. When I did get to visit home, I wanted to be with my family and friends, catching up on everything I'd missed, not stuck out on my own in a chilly garage. As much as I loved cars, and that Jag particularly, I loved my family more.

Who knows? Maybe now that the career I'd worked so hard to build was swirling around the plughole, I might finally have the time to do something on it. Not exactly the way I'd planned for things to go but still. Although I loved the shop and had worked in here since I could remember, possibly as more of a hindrance than help in my early years, I never thought for a moment that I'd be sat back here in my thirties. A sharp jab in my thumb from a particularly robust holly leaf brought me painfully out of my reverie.

'Oh f—' I glared at the leaf now firmly attached to my digit. And then I looked over it and directly into the wide, soft grey eyes of a little boy around five years old who was regarding me curiously. Behind him was a pair of long, indigo-denim-clad legs. My gaze followed them up, and I found myself on the end of an intense stare from a similar pair of eyes.

But these were a much stormier grey, set in the ridiculously good-looking face of a man I assumed to be the boy's father. I cleared my throat and swallowed my words, making a mental note to get one of my brothers to fix a bell to the back of the door as soon as possible.

'I'm sorry. I didn't hear you come in.'

The man quirked a dark brow almost imperceptibly. 'Evidently.' His expression was firmly set to unamused. I gave him a fixed smile and looked back to my desk, hoping he'd leave to go and practise his ninja shopping skills elsewhere. The young boy's eyes were focused on my hands as I picked up the holly again, a little more carefully this time.

'Come on, George, let's—'

'What are you doing?' George asked, seemingly not hearing his father and sitting the teddy he'd been holding on the table at the end of my supplies so that he could observe too.

I smiled at them both, almost expecting the father to repeat his request to leave, but he remained silent, evidently happy to let George's curiosity be fulfilled and probably aware that the glare he'd given me moments earlier was enough to stop me even thinking about swearing again for the rest of my life. Well, at least until they left anyway.

'I'm making Christmas wreaths for people to hang on their doors.'

His eyes widened as his fingers reached out and touched the mistletoe. 'It's real?'

'It is. Mind the holly though. That can be a bit spiky.' I risked a glance up through my lashes and met his father's eyes, a glimmer of a smirk on a mouth that some might call tempting. I'd probably call it that too but I already had way too much to worry about.

'We had one like that last year but it was plastic.'

'Some of those can be very nice too.' I smiled.

'Not as nice as yours,' George said, moving to peer around me at the others he had now noticed hanging behind, ready for shipping out later.

'Thank you.'

George came around the front of my desk again and watched for a moment as I continued to work. His father had taken a couple of steps away and was now looking at the rows of chutney, fudge, and other delicious temptations on the shelves to my right.

'I do like your bear,' I said to George. 'Does he have a name?'

'He's just called Bear.'

'That sounds like the perfect name to me.' I gently took Bear's paw and shook it. 'It's very nice to meet you, Bear.'

George giggled. 'I'm George.'

I shook his hand in the same way. 'My name's Lexi. It's very nice to meet you too.'

George smiled. 'This is my daddy.'

'Hello, Daddy … I mean …'

Oh God, that sounded so weird!

He put his hand out. 'Cal is fine.'

I nodded and took it, aware that I now had cheeks as red as the wooden painted elves swinging their little rope legs off the shelf behind me.

Unaware of my embarrassment, George turned his attention back to his teddy. 'Bear's got a poorly head.'

'Oh! Oh dear. Yes, he does look a little sorry for himself. Did he have an accident?'

George pulled his toy back off the table and cuddled him around his squidgy middle, the teddy's head hanging decidedly lopsided and looking dangerously insecure as the little boy nodded in response. 'Yes. I accidentally shut his head in the car door and it came off when I walked away.'

'Oh!'

He pulled his mouth to the side. 'I know. I was very upset but Daddy mended him for me.' His little hand snaked into his father's large one and he looked up, pride on his face. I smiled at them both and noticed a slight flush on the man's cheeks as he looked down at his son. A feeling I didn't want to deal with

11

began creeping into my brain and I squinched it down before it could take hold.

'Come on, George. Let Lexi get on with her work now and come and help me choose some decorations for the tree. We'll take another look at Bear later and see what we can do.'

George gave me a smile and moved his bear to his free hand. The bear's head lurched again and I winced, half expecting it to plop off and roll across the pale sanded floorboards of the shop. Luckily it stayed in place but I didn't have great hopes for that state lasting very long. I chewed my lip for a moment.

'Do you have any brothers or sisters?' I asked George.

He shook his head. 'No. But I'd like some!'

I swallowed a grin. With a dad who looked like that, I was pretty sure the odds were quite favourable on that front. I glanced up and met a wary gaze.

'I have three brothers,' I began as the little boy listened, 'and when we were younger, sometimes we would argue and occasionally my teddy would get caught in the middle of it.'

'Was he trying to stop you arguing?'

'Umm … yes, I think he probably was.' I risked a look up at the man. The storm had gone from his eyes now and a hint of amusement played there instead. 'Anyway, sometimes my teddy would be in need of a bit of repair, so I ended up training as a Teddy Bear Surgeon. I am, in fact, fully qualified.' From the corner of my eye, I saw that delicious mouth quirk again.

'You are?' George asked, his eyes widening.

'I am.'

This wasn't exactly too far from the truth. All right, I didn't have paper qualifications but I'd had plenty of practice. My youngest brother, Joe, had gone through a phase of yanking off bits of my bear whenever we were arguing. We were the closest in age and the most likely to get into a big barney. After repairing Ted three or four times, my mum had given up and said that if we were going to destroy things, we were also going to have to repair them.

So, I'd learned how to sew and my teddy, although slightly wonky, was definitely more robust when he went in for the next round.

'Do you think you could help Bear?'

'George, I'm sure she has plenty to do already—'

'It's really no trouble,' I interrupted. 'I mean. If you don't mind. I quite like to keep my skills fresh so you'd actually be doing me a favour.'

Cal hesitated. 'I'm not sure—'

But George was already handing me the teddy. I met his dad's eyes as I took it. I could see he was still uncomfortable about a relative stranger doing something for him. He obviously wasn't local. If he'd been from the village, he'd have realised this was all part of normal life here. Unlike many places, the village had managed to retain its closeness and community. And while it was hard for people not to know everyone else's business, it was generally in a kind and considerate way rather than gossip. Of course, there was always a bit of that too – the villagers were human after all.

I looked the toy over and made a couple of 'hmm-ing' noises before returning my attention to Cal and George.

'It's good news, you'll be glad to hear. Definitely nothing serious. He's already had some excellent surgery.' George giggled and beamed at his dad. Cal's face remained impassive but I saw his Adam's apple bob briefly. 'He really only needs a tiny bit more. If you two want to have a look around the shop, he'll be fully recovered and waiting for you when you come back. If you want to go ahead with the procedure, of course.'

'Can we, Daddy?'

Cal gave me a look and a tiny shake of his head, but I could see the faintest of smiles on his lips.

'If Lexi doesn't mind, then yes, of course. As long as you're going to help me choose the decorations now. I'm not sure I can decide all by myself.'

'Of course I'll help you. Don't worry.' He kept hold of his

dad's hand as he looked at me. 'You'll look after my teddy, won't you, Lexi?'

'As if he were my own, I promise.'

'Come on, George. Surgeons need peace and quiet to work in. Let's start with finding you an advent calendar, shall we?' Cal led George away, throwing me a quick, grateful glance over his shoulder as he did. I gave him a nod and reached into the drawer of the old wooden desk I was sitting at and pulled out a biscuit tin. Opening it, I rummaged around in the sewing supplies it stored to find a cotton that matched the fur of the bear and then set about threading up a needle. Steadily I worked around the bear's neck, squinting at him occasionally and trying to ensure his head was level so that he wouldn't be for evermore looking askew at the world.

Finally, I gently took out the larger, uneven stitches that had been put in at the time of the original incident, the love they clearly represented more than making up for what they lacked in skill. By the time Cal and George came back to the desk, laden with items, I'd not only repaired Bear but also whipped the scarf off a toy we had on sale to finish him off properly. Luckily, I knew the maker of the scarves and would put in an emergency order by text once my customers had gone.

'Bear!' George cried as he saw his teddy casually lounging on the table that held the till. 'Daddy, he's got a scarf too, and it's the same colour as mine!'

Cal smiled. 'You really shouldn't have. How much do I owe you?'

'Ha! I'm good, but I'm not that good. I'll have to ring them up first,' I said, pushing my chair out to get to the till, leaning over for his basket as I did so.

'No, I meant for the repair' – he tilted his head – 'and his new scarf.'

'Oh!' I shook my head, frowning. 'Nothing.'

'No. I must. It's taken your time when you obviously have

plenty to do anyway. I'd like—'

'Really. It was my pleasure. There's no charge.'

Cal was a good head and half taller than me but I'd grown up with three brothers and spent my entire career in a male-dominated world. I knew how to make a point when I needed to. Matt called it The Tone. Even without this inside knowledge, Cal clearly got the idea I wasn't prepared to argue the point any further.

'Well then, thank you. Sewing, admittedly, is not my forte.'

I smiled. 'Then that makes two of us. You did a great job, honestly. There are plenty of people who wouldn't even know where to start! And George thinks you're a superhero so don't be too hard on yourself. Honestly, I've just tidied it up a bit, that's all.'

Cal tilted his head at me. 'I've a feeling you're being more kind than honest, but I'll take it. Thank you, again.'

'You're welcome. OK, let's get your purchases sorted, shall we? I think all this shopping has tired someone out.'

Cal turned in the direction of my nod to where George was now curling up on one of the faux fur beanbags, his fingers wrapping around the bear's scarf distractedly as his own eyelids drooped heavily.

'Oh crikey, hang on, I'll just get him—'

I caught Cal's sleeve. 'Don't. He's not doing any harm. Just leave him while we're sorting this out.'

'But isn't that your stock?'

'Yep. But it's made for sitting on.'

'Once it's paid for.'

'Look.' I turned George's dad around by his arms. 'You've clearly taught him well. He's even taken his shoes off. He's fine. The stock is fine. Relax!'

Cal looked down at me and I realised I was still holding his arms. I dropped my hands quickly and shoved them into the pockets of my jeans.

'Things are very different here from London,' he said, his

expression relaxing.

'Yes. They are. Which is a good thing, I think.'

'Definitely.'

'OK. Let's see what we have.' I started ringing up Cal's purchases, wrapping the breakables, and stacking things carefully in a couple of boxes to make it easier for him to carry and transport back home.

'Have you got a long journey back?' I asked as I rang up the final total, glancing over at the now sleeping George.

Cal gave me a quizzical look as he dipped a hand inside the padded jacket he wore, retrieving a wallet from the inner pocket and pulling out a credit card.

'No. Not far at all.'

'Oh! Sorry, I assumed you were down from London when you said that about it being different here from there.' I handed him the card reader and he put the card in as he answered me.

'We used to live there.'

'Oh.' Clearly he didn't want to share any more so I stopped my questioning and tried to remember that not everyone was as chatty as the locals. 'That's not reading properly. Do you mind?' He shook his head as I moved the reader around to face me and took the card out, switching it around so that the chip was in the machine. As I did so, he rolled his eyes at himself.

'My fault distracting you,' I said.

'Hardly.'

I dropped my gaze to the readout and took the comment at face value. Fair enough. Even if it was a bit blunt.

'I meant hardly in that it wasn't your fault, not that you weren't distracting. Not that I was …' He trailed off and I lifted my gaze to his. 'I think I'm just going to shut up now.'

I laughed. 'OK. Do you want to enter your PIN?'

'Very much so.'

I grinned, took the machine back off him, and waited for the receipt to chug out. I handed it over along with his card. As I did so, I noticed the name on it.

'Cal Martin?'

'That's me.'

'As in Xander's boss, Cal?'

'You know Xander?'

'He and Giselle are my best friends. I didn't realise you were The Cal.' I needed to have words with Giselle. She'd mentioned that her husband's boss was quite good-looking, but had left out the fact that he had eyes like a rainstorm, a mouth that suggested temptation, and from what I could see, a body that absolutely promised it.

'The Cal?' He laughed, a deep, throaty sound that he kept low in deference to his sleeping child. 'That sounds like quite a lot to live up to.'

'You know what I mean.'

'I do. When you said your name was Lexi, it did cross my mind that I'd heard the name but …' He hesitated. 'I didn't think you could be the same one because I was under the impression you were kind of a high-flyer and didn't live in the village. Don't you work in Formula One or something?'

'I used to, yes.' I'd intended to leave my explanation at that, but I hadn't banked on those eyes. When I lifted my gaze from where I had been fiddling with the credit card machine's cable, they were focused on me and I felt like I was the only person in about a five-mile radius. A thought, uninvited, flashed through my brain as to what that focus might feel like in a more … intimate … setting. Oh wow, probably best not to go there! Almost instantaneously, my cheeks flamed as I gave my thoughts a firm shove.

'I'm sorry.' He stepped back. 'I didn't mean to embarrass you.'

'Oh, no really. It's fine. It's not that at all.' *If only you knew …* 'I think I just got a little warm for a moment.' I flapped my hand a bit for emphasis, which only succeeded in making me feel like an even bigger idiot, so I shoved it back in my pocket again.

He smiled gently. 'It is nice and cosy in here. Certainly seems to suit some people.' We both looked over to where George was zonked out, Bear in one arm cuddled against him, the other flung out across the soft fur. 'I'd better get him home.'

'Oh wait. Don't forget this.' I placed one of the fresh wreaths I'd been making on top of one of the boxes. 'Your son seemed to really like them.'

'He did – you're right,' Cal agreed, reaching in his jacket for his wallet again.

I put my hand on his arm briefly to stop him.

'It's on the house.'

He frowned at me. 'You can't do that.'

'Yes, I can. It's my family's business and it's one wreath. Don't worry. It's not going to bankrupt us.'

'So you're Dan's little sister?'

I laughed. 'It's a long time since I've been called anyone's little sister, but technically, yes.'

He gave a brief head tilt. 'You are kind of little compared to your brothers.'

He had a point. I was.

Cal made an attempt to reach for his wallet again. 'I really would feel happier if I paid for this. You've already done too much for free.' He nodded at his son's toy.

I shook my head. 'Honestly, it made a nice change to do something different for a few minutes. You two brightened up my day so take the wreath as payment for that, if you like.'

Cal studied me for a moment, that gaze enveloping me once more. 'I'm not going to win on this, am I?'

I shook my head. 'Nope.'

'Xander did say you were a force to be reckoned with at times.'

'You mustn't believe everything Xander says.'

'So I'm also not to believe that you head-butted a kid much bigger than you who was bullying Giselle at school.'

I cleared my throat. 'I'd like to point out that we were seven and that I don't condone violence. But we'd already tried reasoning

18

with him. And have you ever seen Giselle cry? Even back then she was so feminine and delicate. It's heartbreaking! I did what I had to.'

'Fair enough. I also heard that the kid you nutted grew up to be the local policeman?'

I laughed. 'Oh, you do know all the gossip, don't you? Yes, he did. And he grew into a lovely man with a lovely family who totally agrees now that he was being a little … pain.' I checked myself in time and received a grin in return that did nothing to help cool me in the slightest. 'He says now that I was quite right to do what I did.'

'So you don't get speeding tickets even when you're parked then, or anything like that?'

'No. Thankfully!'

'I'm glad to hear it.'

'Right. I'd better get this little tyke home.' Cal bent and lifted the boxes and then as he approached George, he started bending his knees.

'You're going to drop the lot in a minute,' I said, coming up behind him. 'Here, I've got plenty of practice ferrying sleeping nephews and nieces to cars. I'll take him for you.'

'No.' His reply was so sharp that I actually took a step back. Cal turned a little more. 'Sorry, I didn't mean it to come out like that.'

I pasted on a smile, or at least half a one, and shrugged. 'No problem. I was just trying to help.'

'Yeah. I know.' He ran a hand through the dark hair. 'I know you were.'

'Let me take the boxes then.' I bent my knees to where he'd now put the purchases on the floor.

'No, they're pretty heavy.'

I blew out a sigh and stood, raising my eyes to him. 'OK. Look. One, I'm stronger than I look and two, one way or the other you're going to have to either leave George here while you take the boxes, or leave him in the car while you come back and get

19

them, and I don't think you want to do either.'

His lack of reply was enough.

'OK. So, you bring your son and I'll bring these.' I bent and scooped up the boxes, jiggled them into a better position, and peered around the side of the pile to see where I was going.

'Are you sure you're all right with those?' Cal asked as George flopped softly against his shoulder.

'Yes. So long as you're not parked miles away, I'm fine.'

'No, just down the road. Do you need to lock up or anything?'

'No, it's fine. Let's just get going, shall we?' The boxes were biting into my arms, and I wasn't about to show myself up by having to put them down again after I'd made such a song and dance.

Cal got the door and then led the way to a relatively new Land Rover Defender. He opened the boot and between us, him still with a sleeping child in one arm, we loaded the boxes into the storage area and wedged them in with a blanket and a coat so that they didn't tip. He closed the door and went around the side, deftly popping his son in and securing him into his seat.

'OK. Well, it was nice to meet you. Enjoy your purchases.' I smiled and made to head off back to the shop.

'Lexi?' Cal called.

I turned and waited as he took the couple of steps towards me. There was a faint scent of aftershave now that he was close. Woody, masculine. Very him.

'Look, I'm sorry if I snapped a bit at your offer earlier.'

'It's fine. I didn't mean to cross any lines. I apologise if I did.'

'No.' He threw a glance back at the car, as if to check it was still there even though we were only two feet from it. 'It's me. I'm still pretty new to all this.'

'All this?' I queried.

'People being kind, offering to help. Hell, even talking to one another for the most part.'

'Right.'

'I've hurt your feelings, which I would have felt a shit about

20

anyway but after your kindness today, I feel a double shit about it.'

'Honestly. Don't give it another thought. I'm not.'

'I think that's a big fib.'

I tilted my chin up in defiance. 'It's not, I assure you.' I think I was quite convincing until the big swallow I did gave me away.

A glimmer of a smile flitted across his lips. 'That's what I thought. Look, I … It's hard to explain. I just didn't want George suddenly waking and finding himself being carried by someone he didn't know then getting upset.'

'It's all right, Cal, really. You don't have to justify anything to me.'

'I think I do.' He was watching me and once again the world around me seemed to melt into nothing. I'd never met anyone who could make me feel like I was the only one in the room before – even outside. And the thing was, I was pretty sure he had no idea he was doing it.

I took a deep breath and looked away, feeling it to be the safer option. 'OK. Let's just agree that I didn't mean to cross a line and you didn't mean to bite my head off and move on, shall we?'

The glimmer became more of a smile. 'I think I'd like that.'

I smiled back. 'Me too.'

'Now get back inside before you freeze to death and I have something else to apologise for.'

I laughed, waved, and half ran along the narrow pavement before diving back into the warmth of the shop. As I did, Matt popped his head out from the back stockroom.

'There you are. Thought you'd abandoned ship.'

'No, not yet. Just helping a customer to the car with his purchases.'

'Good sale?'

'Yep. Very good actually. I threw in a wreath for free because his little boy liked them.'

Matt put a mug of tea down on the desk in front of me and I wrapped my hands around it.

'Ooh thanks, just what I need.' I took a sip and then realised he was watching me. 'What?'

'You. You make me laugh.'

I took another sip. 'Do I dare to ask why?'

'Well, you have this tough tomboy outer layer—'

'I do wear dresses sometimes, thank you.'

'You know what I mean. You give off this tough-girl attitude, your job is predominantly male—'

'My former job.'

'Stop interrupting for two minutes, will you?'

'Sorry.' I made a zipping motion across my lips.

'It makes me laugh that you try to make people think things don't bother you, that you're tough as old leather – and we both know that's not true. I just wonder why you always feel you have to do that. I can understand the work thing – why you don't want to be all girly there. But you're not as tough as you make out so why let people think that you are?'

'Because it suited me. I'm not pretending to be anything I'm not anyway. I'm just not all feminine and girly like Giselle. She cries and looks beautiful. I cry and look like a red-faced, swollen-eyed, blotchy mess. It doesn't quite have the same effect.'

'I'm not saying you have to cry all the time. God forbid. I'm just saying you're not as tough as you think you are … and that's OK.'

'Is there a point to this conversation?' I asked, staring into my tea.

'The family just wants you to be happy.'

I turned on the chair and folded my legs up into a crossed position. 'The family? You know we're not The Mob, right? And by happy, do you mean married?'

'Well, not immediately. And not at all if that's not what you want.'

'I did want – once. Remember how well that worked out?'

'So that means you keep yourself at a distance from everyone for ever?'

'It's a lot less hassle.'

'And a lot more lonely.'

'With a lot less heartbreak.'

'And a lot less chance at joy.'

I glared at him because I'd run out of arguments.

'Look. I'm not necessarily ruling it out but there was hardly a lot of opportunity before. Liaisons were frowned upon in the team and there was barely time for anything like that anyway.'

'Not entirely frowned upon.' Matt shifted position on the wall as he snagged another biscuit from the tin and frisbeed one to me. 'You were engaged to Marco.'

'He was their top driver and winning them the championship, not to mention millions in sponsorship. The rules didn't really apply to him so much. And I'd been working for a different team when we got together so they couldn't say a whole lot.'

Matt shrugged.

'Anyway. That's all a bit irrelevant now. Besides, dating is the absolute last thing on my mind right now. Trying to find another job is the priority.'

'Have you heard anything?'

'From Marco?'

Matt gave me an interested look. 'I meant job-wise but we can go with that.'

'Oh. No. I've got another enquiry out I'm waiting to hear back on but I don't know if anything will come of it.' I sighed and snagged another biscuit. 'I'm really good at my job but it's a small community. They all know what happened and as far as they're concerned, the years of commitment I gave were all wiped out by one action. I don't know if anyone will give me another chance.'

'They're idiots if they don't.'

I smiled at my big brother. 'Likely true.'

He gave me a wink, then scooped up my now empty mug. 'You know you've always got a job here, don't you? God knows we could do with the help.'

I nodded. I couldn't lie. The thought had crossed my mind more than once. The past year, being off the circuit had allowed me to get back more often and see my friends and family and I'd begun to realise just how much I'd missed it all. My friends, my family, even the shop. Matt rinsed the mugs in the sink and came back to lean on the wall.

'Have you heard from Marco then?'

'We've spoken a bit, yes.'

'And?'

'And it's fine. It's good. We're in a good place. A better place. Back to being friends, which is maybe where it should have stayed.'

'It was kind of a whirlwind.'

'Yep. It certainly was that. But at the time I thought it was the right thing. What I wanted. What he wanted.' I pulled my mouth to the side and gave my brother a look. 'Seriously not very good at the whole relationship thing, am I?'

'Aah, don't you worry. These things usually take two. And who knows? We might even be able to find a bloke to put up with you if you ever decided to stick around here. Stranger things have happened.'

'You know your comedic talent is wasted here, don't you?'

Matt opened his mouth to reply, and I rammed a bicie in it. 'Conversation closed.'

Chapter 3

'So! A little birdie tells me you met Cal?'

I was sat at the lime-washed pine table in Xander and Giselle's kitchen decorating gingerbread men while Giselle cooked something deliciously French for dinner on the hob of her pink Aga.

'Is that all right?' I asked, carefully tipping one of the biscuits towards her.

Giselle glanced over. 'Perfect! You know you don't need to check with me. We used to do these together for the shop all the time.'

I pulled a face as I squidged the icing down the bag a little more. 'I know. But I'm out of practice.'

'It's like riding a bicycle. It'll all come back.'

I gave my gingerbread man a neat side parting. 'If you remember, the last time I rode a bicycle with you, I ended up headfirst in a nettle bush.'

Giselle laughed. 'Oh my, I'd forgotten that. You were in such a state! I felt so sorry for you. It must have been agony.'

Gingerbread man got mittens. 'It definitely isn't in my list of top-ten favourite days, that's for sure.'

Giselle tasted the sauce and made a fluttering motion with her beautifully long, false lashes. '*Parfait!*' It always amused me how, even though she'd been over here since she was seven years old, there were times when she still dropped back into French. It wasn't forced or affected. I wasn't entirely sure she knew she was doing it. But I loved it.

'Good?'

'Very. Just needs to simmer a bit longer. Xander should be home any time so it should be about right.'

'Good, because it smells delicious and I'm starving. This ginger-bread man is lucky he's still got all his body parts.'

Giselle grinned and filled another icing bag before setting to work on the pile of biscuits that still needed dressing, ready for the shop.

'So … like I said, I hear you met Cal Martin?'

'I did. He came into the shop with his little boy. Although, I didn't realise it was him until he paid and I saw the name on his card.'

'Bit gorgeous, isn't he?'

I lifted my gaze and looked at her through my slightly overlong fringe. She waved her piping bag at me.

'What? Just because I'm married doesn't mean I'm not allowed to observe beautiful things. In fact, it's good for the soul. I just read an article on it. So?'

'So, what?'

Giselle squirted her piping bag at me so that a blob shot out and landed on my face.

'Oi!'

'Answer then!' She giggled as I felt around my cheek for the icing with my finger, found it, and ate it.

'What do you want me to say?'

'He said you had a nice chat and that you were quite the Santa's Little Helper.' She quirked a brow that was shaped, coloured, and tamed to within an inch of its life, yet still looked entirely natural. I made a mental note to drop into the local beauty salon and have a tidy-up.

26

'I'd say a chat was overstating it and I wasn't being "Santa's Helper", little or otherwise.' I flicked some icing back at her. 'There was no way that teddy bear's head was going to stay attached to its body for very much longer. I've repaired enough of my own – and my brothers' kids' toys – to know when immediate action is required. Plus, have you seen George? Can you imagine how heartbreaking that face would be as he watched his teddy's head fall off and roll into the road, only to be flattened by a passing car!'

Giselle was looking at me aghast. 'Well, for goodness sake, don't say that in front of him! I'm upset just thinking about it.'

'Sorry. Anyway, it's not going to happen. It's secured now.'

'He is a cutie, though. I agree.'

'Cal?'

Giselle raised an amused eyebrow. 'I was referring to George but if you like …'

'No. Carry on.'

'To be honest, both of them are. There's definitely been a clamour of play date requests since he moved to the village.'

'He is a sweet little boy and seems very well mannered too.'

'True. But I think the parent is a fair bit of the draw to be honest. A few of the mothers have been quite put out when his childminder has taken him to them instead, and I got a death glare once when I turned up with him. The woman tried to cover it up but not quite quick enough.'

'You took him to a play date?'

'Yes.'

'Wow. Cal must really trust you. George fell asleep in the shop and I offered to carry him the few steps to the car while he took the shopping, and he practically bit my head off.'

Giselle tilted her head a little and pushed out her bottom lip. 'Yes, he did mention that. Felt quite bad about it.'

I waved the comment away with my piping bag. 'It's fine. He apologised. It just shows how much he must value you to trust his son with you like that.'

'Well, I guess we've got to know him quite well since he moved here. At first, he wouldn't accept any invites but I can be quite persistent.'

'No!' I did a mock shock expression and Giselle squinted one eye and aimed her piping bag at me. I hid behind a naked gingerbread man.

'Anyway!' she said, grinning. 'Eventually he gave in and now he comes over for dinner a fair bit. George will snuggle up on the sofa with Sophia and is usually asleep within moments of his bedtime.'

Sophia was Xander and Giselle's incredibly cute cockapoo and was quite possibly the laziest dog in the world, so the fact that she would snag an opportunity to lie anywhere with another warm body didn't surprise me at all.

I lowered my biscuit shield. 'He did say something about not being used to people being nice or something. What was that all about?'

'Had a bit of a rough childhood, from what I can gather.' Xander's deep tones drifted through moments before he followed them in his socked feet.

I let my friends have their moment of greeting as I concentrated on giving my latest creation matching stripy hat, mittens, and wellies.

'All right, Muppet?' Xander said, and bopped a kiss on my temple. 'They look good.'

He reached his hand down towards the biscuit in front of me and I gently elbowed him away.

'Come on, just one.'

'No. They're for the shop. Plus your beautiful wife has made something delicious for dinner and you'll spoil your appetite.'

I knew for a fact that this was unlikely. Xander and I had been best friends since literally the day we were born and he'd been a dustbin from day one. It still amazed me thirty-odd years later that he could pack food away and not be the size of a house.

'She won't mind.'

'Yes, "she" will!' Giselle looked up from the pan she was now stirring, one hand on her hip.

Xander threw me an *oops* glance. 'Maybe after dinner then,' he conceded, winking at Giselle. 'Where's the dog?'

'Asleep on my feet under the table. At least I'm assuming that's what's keeping them warm.'

Xander bent down. 'Yep. Honest to God. I think we got a cock-a-sloth by mistake. I'm supposed to be greeted by a happy little dog, pleased to see me after I've had a long, hard day at work.'

'You've hardly been down the mines,' I said, concentrating on piping a smile.

'He's a tough boss,' Xander replied, purposely nudging me.

I sat back in the chair and fixed him with a look.

'Oh dear, look at that. Can't really sell that one, can you?' Before I could move, the gingerbread man was headless and half devoured.

I switched my look to Giselle. 'Honestly, I don't know how we put up with him.'

'Think yourself lucky you're not married to him.'

I did a theatrical shiver and Xander flicked me on the ear my hair was tucked behind.

'OK. Ow!'

'Honestly, I really hope this baby is a boy. I need some backup around here.' He pulled out a chair next to Giselle who had now sat back down opposite me, and he placed his hand on the ever-growing bump. I watched for a bit and then lowered my eyes back to my task. Even though these two were like family, I still felt a little intrusive in such moments and rather like one of the big, fat gooseberries Giselle currently had thawing in a bowl, destined for some delicious culinary fate.

'Right. That's the last one,' I said, putting the final biscuit on the tray and standing up to lift it.

'Here,' Xander said, getting up and coming over. 'I'll put it up here, just in case the dog ever discovers any energy. She'll have the lot of them.'

'Thanks.'

'Dinner's ready,' Giselle declared. 'Xander, would you pour the wine, please?'

Xander set about pouring wine for him and me and a soft grape drink for Giselle as she dished up the chicken. I sat at the table again, having been told there was nothing I could do, and enjoyed the smells swirling around me: the delicious aroma of dinner mixed with ginger and baking, plus the faint tang of soft roses from Giselle's perfume. I absent-mindedly thought about the expensive bottle Dan and Claire had bought me, which usually languished in a dark drawer, hoping to prevent evaporation. I really ought to get it out and actually use it, now that I wasn't wearing Eau d'Engine Oil every day.

I watched my friend as she expertly dished up the food, not splashing a drop, or missing a plate. Everything was perfect, elegant, beautiful. Just like her. I smiled and she caught me.

'What are you smiling at?'

'You.'

Giselle laughed. 'Why?'

'Because we're so different and I love that, but I also wish I could be more like you. If I was doing that, half the Aga would be covered and the dog would be having a field day.'

'Oh rubbish. You're perfect as you are. And you're totally capable of dishing up food neatly. I've seen you.'

Xander opened his mouth and then shut it as Giselle shot him a glare.

I laughed. 'It's fine. Whatever he was going to say was probably true.'

'Anyway, you have your own talents. Look at that time you fixed your date's car, even though it pretty much ruined that beautiful dress. Did you ever replace that by the way?'

I shook my head as I took another sip of wine. 'Nope. Not a

lot of call for it in my life right now.'

Or any time soon.

'And yes, I did fix his car, which resulted in him never contacting me again.'

'Oh, I'm sure that wasn't the reason,' Giselle said, then realised she was in a sticky position. 'I mean …' She put the plates down on the table and pulled a face.

'It really was the problem.' I waved her awkwardness away, filling her in. 'I ran into him a few months later in a pub. His very pretty, very feminine girlfriend nipped to the loo, and he mentioned that he had been planning to see me again right up until the moment I fixed his car. It was a "turn-off", I believe was the phrase he used.'

Xander shook his head. 'Idiot. Didn't deserve you then anyway.'

'No. Exactly,' I agreed with as much emphasis as I could before thanking Giselle and tucking in to the meal in front of me.

Chapter 4

'So, what was that about Cal not having had a very good childhood?' I asked Xander later, on my third glass of wine as I sat waving goodbye to my normal resolve to avoid gossip.

He topped up my glass then his own as he pondered his reply. 'He's not said a lot to be honest, has he, Gis?'

Giselle didn't need wine to enjoy a good gossip so long as it wasn't hurting anyone. 'Not really. From what I can gather he spent a lot of time in care.'

'Does he have any family?'

Xander shook his head. 'Nope. Just him and George.'

'What about George's mother?' I asked, snagging a couple of gingerbread men from the tray and handing one to Xander.

Giselle raised an eyebrow. 'Honestly. You two are as bad as one another.'

I beamed and fluttered my eyelashes at her innocently, then stopped when I realised it was making the room spin. Obviously, that was the reason. Absolutely nothing to do with the wine.

'Not interested in seeing him. The little one was a complete accident. She was pretty horrified to find out she was pregnant apparently. Some high-flying career type who absolutely didn't want to be a mother at that point. Actually ever, from what Cal intimated. I didn't like to ask too much, but he said they worked something out in that she'd go ahead with it all and once the baby arrived, he'd take full responsibility.'

'Tricky situation.'

'Mmm.'

I took another sip of wine. 'What do you think he would do if she turned up now?'

'I think he'd let her in, but I think he'd also be really careful. George is his world, and he'll do anything to protect him from getting hurt. But, either way, it seems an unlikely scenario to be honest. I mean, she resented the baby from the moment she knew about it. That didn't change even once he came into the world. I think Cal sort of thought she might have a change of heart once she saw the little one, but she definitely didn't.'

'That can't have been easy for him though. Raising a newborn on his own, with no family to help him? Did he have friends?' I said, a little intrigued, not to mention a tad in awe.

'It sounds like it was pretty much just him. He eventually found the childminder who's still with him now. Lovely lady. Widowed early and dotes on George. But I think Cal resisted even that for a long time. She came with him down from London. I think it's done her good too as she's met a lovely chap here. Derek, you know, from the plant nursery?'

I did know Derek. Ever so shy but a very sweet man who'd spent many years caring for his elderly parents who'd now passed away. It was nice to think that he'd met someone.

'Anyway, Cal was doing all this as well as trying to run a business. I think he finally realised he wasn't Superman. He had to ask for some help,' Giselle added.

'And now he probably gets all sorts offered here.'

'I should say!' Xander chuckled.

I slid my elbow along and jolted his. 'I didn't mean sexual help. I meant … general help.'

'But you wouldn't be averse to offering either?'

I made a 'pffft' noise of dismissal. 'That's the last thing I'm offering anyone right at the moment. My life is already a mess.' I put my head down on the table. 'I really don't need to be thinking about adding a bonk with Cal Martin into the mix.'

'Sorry. I did ring the bell ...' Cal's deep and disturbingly sexy voice drifted into my ears, and I fervently hoped that I was mishearing. The fact that, momentarily, both Xander and Giselle went suspiciously silent confirmed that I probably wasn't. *Oh God.* OK. It's fine. I'll just stay here and perhaps he won't notice me.

'Hi, Lexi.'

Bugger.

I dragged my head up off the table and shooshed my fringe with my hand.

'Hi!' I said, very casually as though I hadn't just been talking about bonking him when he walked in. I wondered if there was any way of persuading him to wear a cowbell in the hopes of avoiding three awkward encounters in a row.

'I hope I didn't interrupt anything?' he asked, his eyes scanning the table and our faces, lingering a little longer on mine with what I could clearly see now was a twinkle of mischief.

'No! Not at all. Sorry about the doorbell. I've been asking someone to charge it for the last week,' Giselle said pointedly, looking at Xander as she poured water into the kettle. He pulled a face as if suddenly remembering.

'Can you stay for coffee?'

As much as I loved Giselle and would do anything for her, I could also have quite happily throttled her right then.

Please say no. Please say no. Please say no.

'That'd be lovely, thanks.'

Damn.

'Martha's with George and he's already asleep. I was passing and just wanted to drop off the details of a couple of finds I've

34

discovered, to see what Xander thought about them.' He took the seat that Giselle offered him, opposite Xander and next to me, handing the files across the table as he did so.

'How was the one today?'

Cal blew out a sigh. 'Waste of petrol, mate. Nothing like the description really. For the time we'd have spent out on it, even a really good auction price would barely cover it. And an average one definitely wouldn't. Not worth the risk and effort.'

'These look promising though,' Xander said, scanning the paperwork. 'Here, Muppet, take a look at that.' Xander went to push the files towards me and then halted, glancing over at his boss. 'I mean, if that's all right? She knows a lot about cars.'

Cal grinned. 'Of course.'

I took the paperwork and studied the pictures and descriptions of the classic cars, both in a very sorry state of repair.

'Oh … this makes me so sad.'

I looked up to see Xander rolling his eyes. 'We shouldn't let you have wine.'

I slapped him with the papers. 'Oh shush. You know what I mean. Cal will know what I mean.' I scooched in my seat a bit more to face him. 'You know what I mean, don't you?' I said, pointing at the pictures.

'It's sad that such beautiful machines have been left to rot.'

'You see!' I threw Xander a slightly inebriated and very smug glance. 'Exactly. That's exactly what I meant. I knew you'd understand.'

Cal twitched an eyebrow and a broad grin showed briefly before the coffee cup hid it. He had a really nice smile. If I'd had another glass of wine, I'd have gone so far as to say it was a very sexy smile. But I hadn't, so I wasn't going to say or even think that at all. It really was no wonder half the mums wanted a play date with him. I didn't even have a child and I was a handful of squashed grapes away from setting one up myself.

'Oi, Muppet. What do you think then?'

'Are you really calling her Muppet?' Cal asked, his eyes shining with laughter.

Xander looked slightly confused. 'It's her name.'

'I thought it was Lexi.'

'Well, yeah. Officially.'

'Actually, officially it's Alexandra.' I did a sweeping sort of motion with my hand, like I was bowing but I couldn't be arsed to stand up.

'And you're really Alexander,' Cal said, nodding across the table.

'Yep. Born on the same day. Mums were in the beds next to each other, and they'd both decided on Alexander. Because Muppet here was supposed to be a boy.'

'I wasn't supposed to be a boy!'

'All right. You were expected to be a boy. But that sort of happened anyway.'

'Do you mind?'

'What? You're not exactly girly, are you?'

'Giselle does girly enough for the both of us.'

'She's plenty girly,' Cal interjected. 'Carry on.'

I wiggled my head at Xander in triumph and he ignored me.

'So, anyway, out pops this one and her poor parents hadn't even begun to consider girls' names because they'd asked not to find out and everyone was convinced in that mystical way people are, that it was another boy. Her parents had resigned themselves to it. And they'd spent so long choosing a name they just made it into a feminine version. Unlike the human being they produced.'

'You're such an arse,' I mumbled.

'But once we started recognising our names and especially at playgroup, it all got a bit confusing so they got adapted: hers into Lexi. Mine into Xander.'

'OK,' Cal said, breaking the leg of the gingerbread man that had now appeared in front of him and popping it in his mouth. 'That makes sense. But why "Muppet"?'

'Because she is one.' Xander looked at his boss as if this explanation was obvious.

Cal glanced at me and tilted his head. 'Ask a silly question …'

'It's fine. I don't mind it. It's all meant with love.'

'That's true. But you are a muppet. You have to admit that. Last year was the perfect example.'

'Xander,' Giselle said. Her voice was quiet but there was a definite hint of warning.

'What person, other than a total muppet, would travel halfway across the world, knowing that by doing so they were not only going to lose their job but their entire career as well, just to visit a friend.'

I let out a sigh. 'You know it was more than that.'

'I should never have called you.' Xander swirled the last of his wine around the glass.

'Oi.' I nudged him. 'If you hadn't, I'd have never forgiven you.'

'You'd never have known! And you'd still have a job.'

'Oh my God, Xander!' I sat back in the chair. 'This was not your fault. Or Giselle's or anyone else's but mine. You were in a state and Giselle was in emergency surgery for life-threatening peritonitis! You two mean more to me than any job, or any career! Don't you get that? If I had to do it again, I wouldn't change a thing. It was the right thing to do.'

'But she's fine!'

'Yes. Thank God. But we didn't know that, and I felt much better being here at the time and for Giselle's recovery than I would have done in a pit garage in some far-flung country. So can we just accept that and move on? I will sort out my life. You did the right thing in calling me that day and I did the right thing in coming home, whatever the fallout.'

Xander looked at me for a moment, half stood, and grabbed me in a gentle headlock before planting a kiss on my temple.

'See? Told you. Total muppet.'

I knew Xander felt guilty about having called me that day but it was true what I'd said. If he hadn't called me, whatever the outcome, I wouldn't have been able to forgive him, because in the back of my mind, there would always have been the 'what if' …

'He's been calling her that since I've known them both and we met when we were seven so …' Giselle said, turning to Cal as she did a little shrug and a very Gallic thing with her face and hands.

'It's all right. I call him much worse when he's not here.'

'That, I believe,' Xander shot back.

I smirked, downed the last of my wine, and pushed my chair out. 'I'd better start heading home.'

'Do you want me to give you a lift?' Giselle asked, already up and looking for her keys.

'No! You stay here in the warm. It's not like it's far.'

'It's sleeting out there now,' Cal volunteered and I shot him a look.

'Then I definitely don't want Giselle out in a car.'

'I'm pregnant, not an invalid!'

'Yes. You have precious cargo on board, which means you should avoid any and all possibly dangerous situations.'

Giselle rolled her eyes. 'Honestly, you and Xander are like mother hens on steroids.'

'Whatever works.'

'You'll freeze,' Giselle said, giving me a stern look.

'I can drop you off,' Cal offered.

'No really, it's fine. The walk will do me good. Sober me up.'

'It really is cold out there.'

'I have gloves and a coat and hat and most importantly, plenty of alcohol in my veins. Did you know there was a cook on the *Titanic* who downed a whole bottle of sherry, thinking if he was going to be plunged into an icy, watery grave he may as well be pissed too – but then he survived because his blood was thinned so much by the alcohol it didn't suffer the same effects as everyone else?'

'You're not planning to plunge yourself into the village pond, are you?' Xander squinted at me.

'No. Not intentionally anyway. Argh!' I threw my arms up. 'You're missing the whole point of the story!'

'I'll just take you.' Cal grinned. 'It's fine. It's on my way anyway and George would never forgive me if he found out I hadn't given his top Teddy Surgeon a lift home.'

I glanced over at Giselle who was nodding at me vigorously, the reasons for which were a little blurry. Kind of like my vision.

We exchanged goodbyes and hugs, and Cal led me to his Land Rover, catching my arm as I missed the footplate in the dark and nearly face-planted into the seat.

'Whoops.'

'Ups-a-daisy,' Cal said, as he boosted me in.

I turned my head and looked back at him, his face now in slightly soft focus. 'Ups-a-daisy?'

'I have a five-year-old. Sorry. Words tend to slip out in inappropriate moments.'

That delicious smile began to spread on his face and suddenly accepting a lift from him didn't seem like the best idea. Perhaps I was best off taking my chances with the frozen village pond. He shut the door and I lost the option.

'How do you know where I live? I mean, you said it was on your way, but it might not be.'

'I've dropped Dan home a couple of times after the pub and he pointed out your parents' place. You live above the garage, don't you?'

I nodded, trying to think back as to whether I'd told him this. I was pretty sure I hadn't.

'How do you know?'

'Xander mentioned it.'

'Oh.' I began to wonder what else my mate might have mentioned.

Cal started the car and we headed off, the wipers slapping

against the now heavy sleet almost in time to the classical piece that was playing quietly on the radio.

'Thanks for this.'

He glanced over briefly. 'You're welcome.' He cleared his throat. 'Hopefully it'll go some way to making up for coming across as so rude the other day when you offered to help me with George.'

'Honestly. There's nothing to make up for.'

He gave me another glance that indicated he didn't agree. His head turned away for a moment and then back towards me, his brow furrowed. It felt as if he was trying to decide whether to say something or not. 'I shouldn't have snapped at you. Sometimes my past has a way of invading the present,' he said eventually. Whatever it was that he'd been thinking of saying, I was pretty sure that wasn't all of it.

'You really don't have to keep apologising,' I said, as he pulled the car into the large driveway in front of the farmhouse and garage. 'It's already forgotten.' Looking up from where I'd been fiddling with the ribbon I'd attached to my mittens after losing one of a pair four times in a row, I met Cal's gaze. If I hadn't already met him, I'd have said it was the wine causing the slight hypnotic effect I was now feeling. But as I'd also had that feeling while perfectly sober, I knew it was pure Cal Martin.

'Whatever it was in your past, I'm really sorry you had to go through it.'

And me blabbing was pure wine.

'Thanks.' He smiled, not seeming to mind. 'Long time ago now.'

'That doesn't always make a difference.'

He drew a breath in and let it out slowly. 'No. True. But life's good now. I have George and my business, and moving to this village has definitely been good for me.'

'Really?'

'Oh yes.'

'I'm sorry if I kicked off some painful memories.'

'I told you. Forget it. It's all good now.'

I put my hand on the catch of the door, then hesitated, my brain telling me to leg it and my mouth, as usual, ignoring the sensible advice and doing its own thing.

'When you came in at Xander and Giselle's, you didn't happen to overhear …'

'Yep.'

I risked a look up. He was grinning. Damn.

'I didn't mean … it's just that what you heard …' Cal moved his head a smidgeon to the side, encouraging me to continue with my explanation, the smile still firmly in place. 'What you heard was out of context. It's not what it sounded like.'

'OK,' he replied, with a tone that implied he didn't believe a word of it.

'I should go. Thanks for the lift.'

'My pleasure. I'll see you around.'

'Ummhmm,' I said, noncommittally, waved, and took the few steps to where the metal stairs ran up to my little dwelling.

What I hadn't taken into consideration as I ran up the staircase was that the sleet, coming into contact with the cold metal, was freezing over. As I neared the top, one leg went one way and the other went in the opposite direction. I was so glad George wasn't there because the expletives were out and proud as I wrapped my arms around the banister and hung there for a moment, a foot dangling in midair either side of the steps.

'Lexi!' Cal's concerned call came as I heard the car door slam. 'Are you all right?'

'*Parfait*!' Oh God, now not only did I look an idiot, I sounded like one. What on Earth had possessed me to channel Giselle right at that moment, especially since I could guarantee this was not a situation my elegant friend would ever find herself in?

'Stay there. I'm coming up.'

'No! Don't! I'm not going to be responsible for you breaking your neck,' I said, flinging my feet around in midair, trying to

41

get a purchase on the step. Unfortunately, every time I tried, it slid straight back out.

'And I'm not going to be responsible for leaving you like that.' The metal reverberated through my arms as Cal's bulk stepped onto them.

'Jesus,' I heard him mutter.

'What's the matter?' I tried twisting around to see him.

'Nothing. It's just slippy. Don't look back at me. Just hold on.'

I flung my feet again and managed to get one on the step, at least lessening the strain on my arms momentarily before it slid and joined the other. On the plus side, I was no longer a starfish.

'Here. Hold on to me.' Cal's voice was now right behind me.

'Umm … that would mean I have to let go.' I glanced down at the bare branches of the bushes beneath me. 'So I think I'm going to go with a no. I'm fine. I'll just wait here until it thaws.'

Cal's laugh was deep and warm, and I could feel it in his chest as he wrapped an arm around me, the other gripping the metal banister.

'Let go. I promise I won't drop you. Xander and Giselle would never forgive me, not to mention my son.'

'Ummm …'

'Trust me.'

I turned my head as much as I could to try to see him. He leant forward and met my eyes.

'Let go.'

Squinching my eyes closed, I did. Cal pulled me back up and lifted me a couple of steps up so that we were both standing on the coir mat that lay outside my front door. Cal was big and the mat was small so it was kind of a squeeze. A little bit of my brain sent out an alarm that this should bother me. Another bit smacked the alarm with a hammer and the noise stopped.

'Thanks.'

'You're welcome. You need to get some salt or grit on these. That could have been nasty.'

'As opposed to just incredibly mortifying,' I mumbled as I fished around in my pocket for my key.

'I wouldn't go as far as "incredibly" …'

I tilted my head up to face him in the half-light of a waning moon. He was smiling and doing that thing that made the world disappear.

'I would,' I replied, plunging the key into the lock, and giving it a turn. Risking a look back up, I saw that the smile was still there.

'You sure you're OK?'

'Perfectly.'

'*Parfait*?'

'Oh crap. You heard that too.'

'I'm hearing a lot this evening.'

I rubbed a hand over my face. 'Like I said, that thing before was out of context.'

'I'd love to know what it was like in context then.'

'I don't remember.'

Cal laughed, deep, warm, and worryingly sexy. 'That's a cop-out answer.'

I shrugged.

He quirked a brow at me. 'And so's that.'

'It's my speciality.'

'Is it now? I shall have to remember that.'

'Actually, if you could just forget the whole evening, that'd work better for me.'

'But not me.'

I let out a sigh.

'Go on, get in before we both freeze.' Cal squinted against the shimmering moonlight peeking between clouds. 'It's actually turning to snow now. And for God's sake, be careful going down those steps tomorrow.'

I gave him a mock salute and he rolled his eyes at me. Even in the low light, I could see the humour in them.

'Night, Lexi.'

'Goodnight, Cal.'

I waited until he got back in the car and had turned over the engine, then gave a quick wave. He flashed the lights twice, swung the Landy in a circle and began pulling back onto the main road through the village.

I closed the door, peeled off my outer layers, and flopped backwards onto the bed.

Oh dear. As I had stated earlier, the very last thing I needed in my life was more complication. But I knew for certain now that there was a real possibility I was in danger of developing a quite mahoosive crush on Cal Martin.

Chapter 5

'But you look so adorable, darling!'

I gave my mum a look that showed her what I thought about that statement.

'Honestly, it might have been worth a night on a park bench in order to avoid this,' I grumped.

Mum straightened my elf hat, topped up my rosy cheeks with her lipstick, and told me not to be so ridiculous before welcoming a group of late-night shoppers and tempting them with the taster plate of Christmas Infused Chocolate Fudge she was brandishing.

'You know it's tradition.' Dan wandered up, his enormous feet encased in curly elf shoes.

'Just because something is traditional doesn't necessarily mean it's a good idea.' I waved my hand around him. 'Whoever saw a six-foot-three, seventeen-stone elf anyway?'

'It's called getting into the spirit. Use your imagination, Lex. Plus, we know for a fact that it helps attract customers. Proven statistics. Assuming said elves haven't got a face like a professional lemon-sucker.'

I gave him a very fake grin.

'Where's your beard anyway?'

'I may have donned the costume, hat, and shoes but I drew

a line at the beard. Last time I wore it I had a rash on my face for a week.'

Dan yanked his own nylon one down for a moment and took a big glug of mulled cider before letting it ping back in place.

'So … how's things?' he asked.

'Huh?'

Before he could answer, a group of late-night shoppers, already laden with bags, came upon us. Dan did a brilliant job of making them laugh and enticing them into the shop with the promise of mulled wine, cider, and nibbles. But not, of course, before they had insisted on taking a hundred and two selfies with us, immediately posting some to social media, and tagging the shop's website in the post. Excellent. Any hopes I'd had of keeping my humiliation confined to the village immediately disappeared. But on the bright side, it was always possible nobody would recognise me.

'So?' Dan prodded.

'What?' I asked

'I hear Cal Martin dropped you home the other night. Rumour is he had his arms around you.'

I turned to my brother. 'Really? You're believing gossip now? How would you even know that anyway?'

'So, it's not true.'

'Well, technically it is true—'

Dan opened his mouth and I cut him off.

'But! Only because I'd fallen through the bloody banisters and was having trouble getting upright.'

'According to my sources there's quite a few women around here who would like nothing better than to have trouble getting upright if Cal Martin is involved.'

I rolled my eyes. 'It's not like that.'

'What is it like then?'

A ping on my phone distracted me, which was just as well as I had no idea what it was like … or what I even wanted it to be like. I pulled the phone from the pocket of my elf shorts and yanked off a mitten.

'You can't shut everyone out for ever, you know, Lex.' Dan's voice was soft now and I shook my head, not looking at him.

'I'm not.'

'Are you sure?'

'Yes.'

Maybe.

I returned my concentration to my phone. 'Oh, you've got to be kidding me!' I was staring at the laughing face emoticon in the comments section under the elf picture on the shop's Insta page; it was from one of my ex-colleagues at the Formula One team.

Dan leant over. 'Ooh … shared. Good advertising. Well done, Lex.'

'Nooo, it's not! All it's done is advertised what an idiot I look. That's now popping up on the accounts of other teams, and drivers! I'm a bloody laughingstock!'

Dan wrapped an arm around me. 'No, you're not.'

'No one who sees that will ever take me seriously.'

'It's Christmas and you're helping out your family. You're dressed as an elf, Lex. It could certainly be worse.'

'How could it possibly be worse?'

'Oh, talk of the devil. Here comes Cal.'

Great. It just got worse.

'Hello.'

'Hi.'

'Hey, Dan, how are you?' Cal and my brother shook hands as I glanced back towards the shop front, wondering if I could make a run for it. My gaze drifted down to my oversized, curly-toed shoes. Running was most definitely out of the question.

'Lexi!' George appeared from a group of children and came charging towards me. Instinctively, I bent down and caught him, lifting him up and swinging him around for a moment before popping him back down. His cherubic little cheeks were rosy from the cold and excitement and his bobble hat kept slipping a little over his eyes. Cal bent and tugged the hat back a bit.

'You look like a real elf!'

'What makes you think I'm not a real one?'

George giggled. 'You're too big.'

'I'll have you know that Father Christmas likes all sorts of shapes and sizes when it comes to elves, just as he should.'

'But you don't have a beard.'

'That's because I'm a girl.'

He thought about that one for a minute, then shook his head, still giggling. 'I don't really think you're an elf but I like that you look like one.'

Dan crouched down to join us. 'I heard a rumour—'

I shot him a glance and beneath the fake facial hair I could see the lines around his eyes crinkle.

'—that the elves inside the shop have some free cake and biscuits. Do you want to come and see if that's true?'

George looked up at his dad. Cal nodded. 'I'll be in in a minute.'

Dan bent down. 'It's kind of busy in there so up you jump. We don't want someone stepping on you now, do we?'

'No! I definitely don't want to be stepped on,' George said, all serious. Cal smothered a smile.

With barely any effort, Dan hefted George onto his back and trudged into the shop, lifting his feet high with each step to accommodate the ridiculous shoes.

'How are you?' Cal asked, his eyes scanning my face.

'Fine, thanks.' I looked down at my shoes.

'Are you embarrassed about something?'

'What?' I looked back up.

'It's just that your cheeks are quite red …'

I gave him a rap with the large candy cane hanging from my belt. 'Very funny. Anyway, what are you doing here? Xander had assured me that you wouldn't be coming tonight. Some meeting or something?'

Cal took the cane off me and studied it for a moment before

beginning to twirl it between his fingers, absent-mindedly.

'Finished early, luckily for me,' he said.

'Unluckily for me.'

'Wow. I've made that good an impression?' Cal straightened and I suddenly realised how that sounded.

'Oh no! I mean … I sort of hoped you wouldn't be here tonight.'

'Right.' He gave a nod.

'Not because I didn't … It's just that … Oh for goodness sake, Cal. Look at me!'

'I am looking.'

'I look a complete idiot.'

'I think you look cute. In fact' – he leant towards me so that I could feel his warm breath on my ear, contrasting exquisitely with the crisp, cold air of the night – 'I think you might be the cutest elf I've ever seen.'

Never in my life would I have believed I'd ever think this but thank God my mum drew big rosy cheeks on me earlier, because right now, I was pretty sure my own would have been indistinguishable from them.

'You're making fun,' I croaked out, before clearing my throat.

Cal smiled and held out the candy cane. I kept my eyes focused on it for a moment before I closed my hand around it, my fingers brushing Cal's. Slowly my gaze began scanning up the broad chest, over the day-old dark stubble and finally arrested when it met those intense grey eyes.

'I'm really not,' he said softly, his voice almost a whisper, but roughened with the raw edge he always spoke with.

I swallowed, not sure how to respond. I was out of practice at all of this. Way out of practice.

'Oh,' I eventually squeaked out.

A fleeting expression of amusement mixed with confusion scudded across Cal's eyes. He held my gaze for a moment longer as he released his hold on the cane entirely.

'Thank you,' I mumbled, dropping my gaze as I felt the warmth burn again beneath my make-up.

'I should go and find George.'

I nodded.

Cal gave a half-smile accompanied by a tiny headshake and headed off into the shop behind me. As he left, I realised I'd been holding my breath. I let it out in one slow movement, waving at the passing shoppers as I tried to pretend I was feeling perfectly normal and parts of me weren't currently a lot more … alive … than they had been in a long while.

'Ooh la la!' Giselle exclaimed as she appeared beside me and gave me a big hug. She was followed by Xander who did the same.

I glanced down at my costume. 'Not the first expression that came to mind when I saw it again, I must admit.'

'I wasn't talking about the costume. I was talking about you and Cal!'

'I … What?'

'We were just on our way over when Dan went into the shop with George and left you two alone. Very tactful, by the way.'

'He wasn't doing it to leave us alone. He was …' I looked from Giselle to Xander. OK. So, apparently he was. I'd totally missed that.

'And from the looks of it, Cal was pretty pleased about it. All that whispering in your ear, and then the whole candy cane thing … Oh my!' Giselle flapped a cerise leather-gloved hand just under her chin.

I rolled my eyes. 'Did you two have popcorn while you enjoyed the show? Really, it was nothing. I'm sure he didn't mean anything by it. He's probably just had a mulled wine or two.'

'Cal doesn't drink.'

'Oh.'

'Well … maybe …'

'Maybe he likes you?' Giselle tilted her head at me. 'Ever think of that?'

I fiddled with the pompom on the end of my hat. 'Honestly?

No.'

Giselle gave Xander a glance.

'Maybe it's time you did think about it, Muppet. And you know I wouldn't be telling you that if I didn't think he was good enough for you.'

I nodded. 'I know. But honestly, that's the last thing I'm looking for right now. Plus, he has a little boy.'

'So? I would've thought you'd be the last person to be put off by that.' Xander frowned at me.

'I'm not put off. It's just … It's another consideration. I made a complete mess of my last relationship, and I'm not about to launch into something else feet first again, even if Cal was interested. Which, by the way, I don't think he is. Things get messy and painful and I'm certainly not going to involve a five-year-old in that!'

Xander gave me a quick squeeze around the shoulders. 'You can't think all relationships are going to end messily, you know.'

'I don't.'

'Good.'

'Just mine.'

Xander blew out a sigh and gave me a look. Giselle patted him on the arm.

'We shall see,' she said, enigmatically. 'Now, we're going to head off and do some pressie shopping. See you later.' Giselle kissed me on my bright red cheek, and they headed off towards to the warm glow of the village shops, all decorated for the season, their soft lights enticing shoppers in out of the cold.

Before I got a chance to think much more on the subject, another group of people surrounded me, and the inevitable elf-selfie session ensued. As they moved to swap places, over the top of them I caught a glance of Cal. George was boosted up onto his hip, resting his head on his father's shoulder with Bear cuddled into him. Opposite him was a tall, elegant woman. Her long, slim legs were encased in denim and finished off with boots that had a fur trim, as did the fitted jacket she wore. On her head she wore one of those big Russian-style fur hats. Her make-up was flawless and she looked – as did the young child whose hand she held – like she'd stepped from a magazine. Giselle was definitely right about Cal and his play date popularity status.

I smiled at the camera for the group still surrounding me before letting my eyes wander again. The woman laughed at something Cal said, her hand resting briefly – but a touch longer than was necessary – on his arm. He smiled and dipped his head as he hoisted George a little higher.

The group of shoppers thanked me and headed into the shop. Dan was right. The costumes definitely helped boost sales. I glanced at the woman and Cal and then down at my stripy legs, and the curly-toed shoes, which were now slowly wicking up dampness from the ground. I flicked the pompom on the end of my hat as it dangled in front of my nose. Sales it might boost, ego it most certainly did not.

Chapter 6

The newly installed bell tinkled on the back of the door, and from my position on a ladder restocking the top shelf, I saw Cal and George enter the shop. I called out a greeting and received a smile and wave from Cal and an unusually half-hearted response from the little boy.

'Be with you in a minute,' I said as I descended the metal steps and then folded them up, carrying them quickly to the back stock room and leaning them up against the wall. 'Hi!' I said, emerging again.

'Hello.' George's greeting was as lukewarm as his wave.

I glanced up at Cal.

'George isn't feeling too great and his friends are all playing snowballs. He's not really up to it so I thought we'd stop in here and see if we couldn't cheer him up a bit.'

'Oh no! Well, obviously I'm very happy to see you but I'm not happy you're feeling a bit under the weather.' George looked above his head briefly in response to my terminology, and Cal and I stifled a smile.

'What bit's feeling poorly then?' I asked.

George leant against his dad's leg. 'My tummy hurts.'

'Oh dear. That's not good, is it? I hope Bear's looking after you.'

George let out a sigh and nodded.

I ran a hand gently over the little boy's silky hair, being incredibly careful not to bump into his father's thigh. If that happened, even if George didn't have a temperature, I was pretty sure I might.

The doorbell tinkled and I glanced up, waving a hello to the Warner sisters, a couple of older ladies who had lived in the village for as long as I could remember. They were lovely, but it did pay to be careful what you mentioned to them as it soon had a way of becoming known by far more people than you'd originally intended.

'He doesn't feel warm but he does look a bit pale,' I said, resting the back of my hand against George's forehead.

'Yeah. I'm going to take him home in a minute and get him into bed. I think he just overindulged in Christmas treats earlier. He was keen on coming in to say hi and I thought it might take his mind off things for a minute.'

'I'm glad you did. Is there anything I can do?'

George had now relinquished his hold on his dad's leg and wandered across the shop. Cal glanced over to where his son was now talking to the ladies as they all looked at the individual crackers piled into a large, wide wicker basket threaded with red silk ribbon, their marbled paper making each one unique. His gaze moved from his son and landed squarely on me. The smile it brought with it made my insides go all flippy and warm.

Doing my best to ignore that and deciding instead that I needed an immediate distraction, I began unpacking a box of handmade lollipops, sticking their handles in a large piece of florist's eco foam I'd sprayed white earlier. One dome was for the gingerbread-flavoured ones, the other for peppermint.

'No, I don't think there's anything you can do,' Cal answered, 'but thank you anyway.'

I nodded without looking at him and finished displaying the lollies. Reaching behind me, I grabbed a gingerbread man from the shelf. 'Ginger's good for the tummy. And if George doesn't want it, you've already taste-tested them so I assume you approve and you can eat it as … support.'

Cal's mouth quirked. 'A support biscuit?'

I nodded at George. 'If he's anything like our lot when they don't feel well, believe me, you're going to need it.'

Cal brought out some change from his pocket but I pushed his hand away. 'It's on the house.'

'You need to stop giving me stuff for free. Don't you know anything about business?' The quirk grew into a wider smile.

'You'd be surprised what I know.'

George was now on his way back to us, the ladies completely enamoured with him, but not entirely missing the opportunity to give his dad a quick once-over with their eyes. One of them had clearly caught the end of our conversation. As I smiled at their approach, she gave me an eyebrow raise and winked. Cal noticed the exchange and chuckled, shaking his head. I blushed, grinned, and studied my shoes for a moment.

'I'm dreading what interpretation of that comment is going to be across the village by tomorrow,' I whispered.

Cal smiled. 'Don't worry. I'll reassure them it was all perfectly innocent if questioned.'

For some reason, this made me blush even more and I decided it was vitally urgent to get some gift bags ready for the next purchase and ducked my head under the desk, feeling my skin cool now I was no longer under Cal's direct gaze.

'Can I help you, ladies?' I asked, as I popped back up, smiling and hoping to affect an immediate diversion of their thoughts.

They smiled and nodded and handed over the basket they'd filled between them.

'We should be going,' Cal said.

I didn't want him to go yet. George seemed a little brighter and as silly and unexpected as it felt, I'd begun to realise that the more often he and George came into the shop, the more I looked forward to it. Cal glanced down at his son who was now peering at the lollipop porcupine.

'Do you want to help me with these, George?' I asked, nodding at the ladies' purchases.

George looked round at me, his little face still pale. He gave a watery smile and plodded over to the desk.

'I'm having trouble wrapping these up. Would you mind giving me a hand?'

'OK.'

I quickly bent down and hefted him up onto the desk so that his legs dangled over the edge.

'Right. So if I fold the paper here, would you be able to hold it while I put some sticky tape on it?'

George nodded and we did a couple of the ladies' parcels, passing idle chat with them about the weather, their upcoming plans for Christmas and the New Year, and anything else random I could think of in an attempt to distract them. I could already see the gossip forming in their brains from the partly overheard conversation, as well as the fact that the Prodigal Daughter was now back in the village and, with one broken engagement behind her, was now chatting with perhaps the most good-looking man in the entire county.

From the corner of my eye, I saw the odd surreptitious glance being sent Cal's way and could only hope he hadn't noticed. From the conversations we'd had, and from the snippets I'd heard from Giselle, Cal Martin was a private man and making himself the target of extra gossip, even if it was innocent, probably wasn't high on his to-do list. I was used to it all, but Cal hadn't grown up here and I didn't want it to be a reason for him to stop coming in.

I'd actually been telling the truth that first time when I told him their visit had brightened my day. Even though I wasn't about to get sucked into Giselle and Xander's imaginings about what Cal Martin's interest might be, I couldn't deny that I looked forward to seeing him.

I turned my attention back to George, who was now

participating but his pale and wan face looked a little fed up. I knew he loved the shop and all the toys and unusual items that he was allowed to explore and touch but, like any five-year-old boy, he would clearly much rather be out in the snow with his friends. I caught his eye and gave him a smile as I snapped some tape off the dispenser. He did his best to return it and my heart went all squishy. I got him to hold the edges of the wrapping paper and on the next fold, I stuck the tape right over the end of his fingers.

'Oh no! Oh dear! Look at that! You're all stuck to it too. It looks like these lovely ladies have got more than they planned with their Christmas shopping … although I'm not sure I've got a bag quite big enough to pop you in! Let me see here …'

George began to laugh as I pretended to look under the desk for a bag.

'Nooooo! Lexi! I'm not for sale!' He swung his legs a little as he giggled. Cal moved swiftly, a large hand providing a buffer between the toe of George's welly and my cheekbone.

I stood up, surprise on my face, exchanging the quickest of thank-you glances with Cal as I did so.

'You're not?' I said, shock in my voice.

'No!' George replied, his voice giggly. 'Of course, I'm not!'

'Oh dear. I'm so sorry, ladies. It looks like we'll have to keep him.'

'Oh no, what a shame!' They joined in the game and George giggled some more as I finished off wrapping the last purchase and processing the transaction. I handed them the gift bags containing their goodies, and we all waved them off out of the shop. Neither Cal nor I missed the slight glance they cast between us as they pulled the door closed behind them and headed out into the damp street.

'Come on, pest. Let's get you home and tucked up.' Cal effortlessly scooped his son up with one arm.

'Can I just look at the sleigh quickly, Daddy?'

Cal plopped George down on the floor. 'Two minutes.'

His son nodded, crossed the shop, and began investigating the sleigh Matt had built as another novel way of displaying stock. Within moments, he had climbed aboard and was busily amusing himself by having a long conversation with the oversized teddy driving it.

Cal leant back against the desk and grinned down at me.

'What?'

'You. This place. But mostly you.'

'Oh dear. What have I done now? If it's about earlier, when I said about surprising you with what I know, I didn't mean …'

Cal raised an eyebrow, waiting.

'Anything,' I finished, weakly.

'I know.' He grinned. 'Don't worry about it. I think you brightened up the Warner sisters' day anyway with whatever spin they were putting on it, from that wink she gave you.'

I laughed, feeling the anxiety lift from me. 'I was hoping you hadn't seen that.'

'I don't miss much.'

I made a mental note of that.

'Actually, I think it was George who brightened their day the most.'

Cal gave a wide smile and glanced to where George was now pressing his nose against the window, peering out into the dark and watching the snowflakes drift down.

'And I don't think you were too far behind in the stakes either.'

At my comment he turned back to face me. 'Sorry?'

I shrugged. 'Just saying.'

Cal laughed and shook his head. 'I should get him home. He'll keep fighting it otherwise and feel worse.'

'Dan and I were the same when we were his age, apparently.'

Cal raised a brow. 'From what I know of you now, I'd say not too much has changed.'

I gave a conciliatory shrug and smiled at George who was now drawing happy faces in the steam from his breath on the window.

'George,' Cal called, gently. 'Lexi's going to have to clean that.'

George looked round. 'Oops. Sorry, Lexi.'

'Don't worry about it, peanut.'

Cal mouthed the word 'sorry'.

'No, seriously. I have seven nieces and nephews. Believe me, if a window is the worst thing I have to clean up, I'm totally winning.'

Cal let out a laugh – deep and rumbling – and if I let it, I knew it would wrap itself around me like one of the cashmere blankets stacked up for sale, just as warm and just as soft. He cast his eye down at his son. 'They can definitely be a challenge in that department.' The love in his eyes showed he didn't mind a bit. I felt the familiar twist in my stomach and squished it down, pasting a smile on instead.

'Ready for home, then?' Cal asked.

George nodded.

'Say bye to Lexi then.'

I bent down and George flung his arms around my neck. 'I love coming here. It's like Christmas all the time.'

'It is at the moment – you're right. And you're welcome anytime you want, but you have to go to bed and get better first. OK?' I gave him a little squish. He released me and I stood.

'OK.' George took Cal's outstretched hand and waved as they headed to the door. Cal raised a hand and smiled as he turned, pulling the door closed behind him. The shop was quiet once more, except for the Christmas music playing subtly in the background. Reaching under the desk, I grabbed a duster and the bottle of window cleaner and headed over to where George had been drawing faces. I crouched and huffed over the same spot and the smiley face appeared again. I waited until it faded and then cleaned the glass.

Calmly, I walked back to the desk and tidied the cleaning items away, before stepping into the back room to flick on the kettle. It would be time to go home soon but I needed something to do, to occupy my mind. I went through the motions but it wasn't working. There were times when nothing worked. I only hoped that, one day, things might become a little easier.

Chapter 7

Weak winter sunlight filtered through the chink in my curtains where I hadn't quite pulled them enough, highlighting a strip of floor at the end of which lay the long, gangly legs of our family's Great Dane, Apollo. His big, square head rested on the rug beside my bed as he peacefully snored, the gentle rumbling causing the large pink tongue that lolloped out of the side of his mouth to reverberate with each exhalation.

I rolled over and watched him for a while, then dropped my hand down out of the warmth of the covers and stroked his golden coat gently with my fingertips. He snuffled a little, stretched out his back legs and pushed himself closer to the bed, then went back to snoring. We both lay there for a while until nature could no longer wait for either of us.

Getting up, I padded over to my door, unlocked and opened it. Apollo scooted down the steps, sniffed around for a suitable spot, did what he needed to, and then charged around the back of the house to find his breakfast. I did what I needed to, threw on some clothes and – after inspecting the bread I had in my little kitchenette – binned it and followed Apollo's example of heading to the main house in search of food.

Both suitably fed and watered and having given time for the

dog's breakfast to go down, I pootled back up to my room and tidied myself up a little more, slapping some protective BB cream on my face before wrapping a cosy scarf around my neck, shrugging into my down-filled jacket, and pulling up the fur-lined hood over my woolly hat. I grabbed my boots and sat on the doorstep lacing them up as Apollo wandered out, a lead attached to his collar and trailing behind him.

Mum tapped on the kitchen window, gave me a thumbs-up, and waved. I returned all the gestures and descended the steps, which, since hearing about my incident the other evening, my dad had been religiously gritting every day. When I got to the bottom, I picked up Apollo's lead.

'Come on then, boy.'

Apollo did the little excited dance he always did before going on a walk and we set off. Heading across the fields, I unclipped the clasp and let the dog run free. He charged about crazily for a while, braking suddenly every now and then when the possibility of an interesting sniff distracted him. Occasionally he would run back to me, assessing that I was indeed still there, before charging off again.

After a little while, he returned to my side and we made our way through the crunchy, frost-hardened grass and leftover stems of the autumn. Together we plodded along, Apollo stopping occasionally when he caught the scent of something else worth investigating, before trotting along to catch up and walk beside me again.

Cutting across the edge of another field, I clipped Apollo's lead and held it loosely over my wrist as we made our way back onto the pavement at the top of the village. In front of us stood the beautifully converted barn that was now home to Cal and George. I pushed open the gate, closed it behind me, and together we crunched over the gravelled circular driveway of the house.

I faltered a little as we approached the door, losing my nerve. But I was here now. What if Cal happened to see me and I just left? That wouldn't be awkward at all… I knocked on the door quickly before I had too much more time to overthink. There was no answer and I hesitated for a moment, shifting my weight from foot to foot as Apollo sat beside me patiently, his bottom out to the side in a slouchy puppy sit.

'What do you think, boy?' I asked him in a whisper. 'Do I knock again or shall we just go?'

Apollo looked up at me and tilted his head.

'Good idea. I totally agree. Come on then.'

As I made to turn away, I heard a bolt slide and the solid wood door was pulled open. Dressed in blue checked pyjama bottoms and a white T-shirt, Cal looked absolutely shattered, not to mention way too sexy in a rumpled, just-got-out-of-bed way, for this time on a Sunday morning.

'Lexi! Come in.'

I waved a hand. 'No, it's fine. I'm so sorry, Cal. I didn't mean to wake you. We were out for a walk and thought I'd just pop in and see how George was feeling.'

Cal rubbed a hand over his face and gave me a sleepy smile that I responded to in more ways than I'm sure he'd planned for – and certainly more than I'd planned for.

'Better, thanks. I'm sorry, maybe it wasn't just too much Christmas food. He went downhill after we left you and he's had a pretty rough night but seems to be over the worst now, thank goodness. He's got a little colour back and he's managed a bit of porridge so I think once he's caught up on his sleep, he'll be fine. I hope he didn't manage to pass it on to you or anyone else.' Cal looked sheepish.

I shook my head. 'I'm fine. And what about you?'

Cal looked confused for a moment. 'Me?'

I smiled. 'Yes. You.'

'I … OK. Thanks.' He gave me a half-smile that did little to disguise his apparent surprise at being asked after.

'Right. Because you look dreadful.' As soon as the words were out, I was aware how different they'd sounded in my head. Cal was just looking at me. And then he was laughing, really laughing in a way that couldn't fail to make a woman smile – even if she had just made an idiot of herself. Again.

'Thanks.'

'That sort of came out wrong.'

'Did it?'

'Yes.'

'So I don't look dreadful?' One eyebrow raised over still-sleepy eyes. Being auntie to a small hoard, I knew mischief when I saw it.

'No, you do, but … Oh crap. OK. I'm just going to stop talking now and let you get back to bed and rest.'

Cal threw me a half-smile. 'I wish. I've got a car to go and see. Martha should be here shortly to look after George and then I need to head off. It's a long drive.'

I took in the utter exhaustion on his face, and the way he was using the door to hold himself up.

'Are you sure that's a good idea? You look absolutely exhausted. Can you not put it off until tomorrow or something?'

He shook his head, stifling a yawn as he did so. 'Unfortunately, not. This guy already told me he's had offers from other people. If it's as good as it sounds, I'll be laughing at auction. But they won't wait. They're moving and are trying to clear stuff out as soon as possible. I can't afford to miss out on it.' The last word disappeared on a yawn and I shook my head.

'OK. Then let me drive you.'

'What?'

'If you really must go today, then let me come with you and drive. That way you can at least get some rest in the car.'

'You don't have to do that. I'll be fine.'

'Don't take this the wrong way – but you look far from fine. And if you won't do it for yourself, then think of George.'

Cal tilted his head down at me. 'Low blow.'

I screwed up my face. 'Did it work?'

'Yes. Are you sure?'

'Positive. It'll be nice for me to do something different too. Plus, it'll give me a chance to connect with cars in some small way again.'

'You miss it.' It was a statement rather than a question.

I nodded. 'I do.'

He gave one quick nod in response before his gaze dropped to the dog. 'Is Apollo coming for a ride?'

'No, I think he'd probably rather be sprawled out by the Aga for the afternoon.'

'Smart dog. Do you want me to pick you up or do you want to wait? I've just got to jump in the shower quickly.'

'I can wait, if you don't mind the dog coming in too? We can just stay by the door.'

'Don't be daft,' Cal said, ushering us both inside. 'I've got an old towel here somewhere …' He stuck his head in a cupboard in the hallway and pulled out a towel. 'Here.' He tossed it to me and I gave Apollo a quick rub over and then carefully dried his feet one by one as the dog gently laid each paw in my lap, ready for the familiar procedure.

'Wow. He's really good at that.'

'Practice,' I replied, glancing up at Cal as I stood. 'There. All dried.' I kicked off my own boots and wiggled my toes. 'But we'll stay here anyway.'

'No, you won't. I need coffee. Want one?'

That did sound good. 'OK. Yes, thanks.' We all shuffled off towards the kitchen and Cal made himself busy with the fancy coffee machine on his worktop. I could strip a car engine with my eyes closed pretty much but the coffee machine looked far more complicated than it needed to be for such a simple task. All I generally needed was a spoon.

'That looks fancy,' I said, eyeing the equipment.

'Yeah. I had a moment. Although it does make really good coffee. But then again, it should.' He pulled a face.

I shrugged. 'You should enjoy the indulgence. If you work hard, it's good to reward yourself sometimes. You shouldn't feel guilty about it.'

Cal gave me a maybe-yes, maybe-no face. 'I know you're right but …'

'You have trouble believing you're worthy of it?'

He shot me a look and I could see the faintest blush on his cheeks.

'Sorry. Mum tells me I can be a bit blunt sometimes. I didn't mean to—'

'No. It's fine. I like blunt. I know where I stand with blunt. And yes, I think you're right. No one has ever put it like that before. Or at least they haven't told me to my face.'

This time it was my turn to blush.

'I promise I'll just drive. I won't say anything else.' I made a zipping motion with my fingers across my mouth and mimed tossing away a key.

Cal gave that deep laugh. It was one of those that surrounded you and made you smile from somewhere deep inside. 'I really hope not. That would make what was shaping up to be an enjoyable day far more dull.'

I pulled my mouth to the side, unsure. Cal stepped closer to me and touched my fingertips with his own.

'I like your honesty, Lexi. Like I say, I know where I stand with you. It's … not always been the case.' His thumb brushed the back of my hand and I lifted my gaze, but his was on our hands. Sensing that he was being watched, his eyes shifted and met mine. I knew I should look away and that this was veering into dangerous territory. But I couldn't. I stayed exactly where I was, my gaze locked with Cal's.

His mouth remained serious for a moment and then, suddenly, he stepped back breaking the spell. The sensible part of me was relieved but the churn of emotions rushing through the rest of me said something else and I wasn't sure how I felt about that.

'Thanks for coming round. George was really upset about feeling poorly and missing out on playing in the snow yesterday.'

'There will be other times, I'm sure. I heard this morning they're forecasting snow for the next few weeks. The bookies have been cutting the odds of a white Christmas left, right, and centre.'

His mouth began to curve. 'Didn't take you to be the betting type.'

'No, not at all.' I laughed. 'I'm more the full-of-useless-information type.'

The half-smile grew and I did my best to remember that the last thing I needed was romantic complications in my life. Been there. Done that. Not prepared to go there again. I risked a glance back up at him. Bloody hell he was gorgeous. How did anyone look that good after being up all night up with a sick child? Was that even legal?

Cal took a breath in and the half-smile was back. 'Lexi, I—'

'Daddy!' George's voice, wobblier than it normally sounded, rang down the hall towards us.

Cal gave me a look and a little shake of his head, the smile turning from whatever it had been – I was still working on that – to resigned.

'Yeah, Georgie, I'm coming.' He turned to me. 'Do you two want to come and say hello? He was pretty miserable earlier. I'm sure seeing you both would cheer him up no end.'

'We'd love to.'

Cal smiled at me and I patted my leg for Apollo to come to heel and he plodded beside me, now a little weary from his explorations on our walk this morning. Cal pushed open the door wider and went in, holding up a hand to Apollo and me following just behind.

'Just let me check there's not been any more ...'

I nodded so that he didn't have to finish the statement.

'What is it, little mate?' Cal's voice was gentle and soothing, and I couldn't resist peeking around the corner of the doorjamb. I wasn't worried about seeing anything that might upset my delicate sensibilities – primarily because I didn't have any. I came from a large family that mostly consisted of men, and I had spent my college years mostly with blokes who, for reasons I still failed to fathom, felt that the best thing to do after downing a vat of beer was to top it off with a greasy kebab. I also had a small brood of nieces and nephews, from which not a single one stood out as not having weed, pooed, or thrown up on me at some point in time. In short, I didn't scare easily.

'I'm bored and my tummy hurts,' George said as he wriggled upright in the bed, his face pale and tired.

Cal was squatting next to him. 'Martha is going to be here soon and she can read you some more of your story. I know your tummy hurts but it's better than it was, isn't it?'

'Yes,' George replied, nodding sadly.

'Good. And it will get easier as the day goes on. It's just a bit worn out, like you and me, and needs some sleep. After your story and a little snooze, you'll be feeling much better. I promise.'

'OK. Do you have to go out?' George's little hand snuck into his father's large one.

From my hidden vantage point, I saw a wash of pain cross Cal's face and something twisted inside me.

'I'm sorry, Georgie. I do. If I could put it off, I would. But I want you to sleep as much as you can today to make up for last night, so you won't even notice too much that I'm not here.'

George nodded but he was clearly unconvinced, even though I could see by the state of him that Cal was right. The little boy was heading straight for zonkville. In an ideal world, his dad would be too but we both knew that wasn't going to happen.

'In the meantime, there are some people here to see you.' Cal leant back and saw me peeking. A smile slid onto his face at catching me. He indicated for us to come in and George's face beamed as he saw us. My smile got wider at his joy as Apollo loped towards him and laid his head on the duvet around George's lap and looked up at him with big heartbreaker eyes. George giggled and folded himself down to wrap his arms around Apollo's head and cuddled him.

'Do I get one of those?' I asked.

George sat up, still grinning as he threw his arms out for me. I wrapped mine around his little body and gave him a big cuddle as Apollo watched us, quirking first one brow and then the other. The dog let out a sigh and slid back into his puppy sit position, his hip resting against Cal's leg now that he had stood to make way for us next to the bed.

'I've had a poorly tummy,' George said as he released me.

'I know, sweetheart. But you're looking much brighter than you did yesterday so you just concentrate on getting better now.'

'OK.' George nodded, his hand gravitating to Apollo's head resting on the bed. He began stroking it and, within moments, both George's and the dog's eyes were beginning to droop.

Cal motioned to me and we moved quietly from the room. Once outside, he turned to me. 'Next time I have trouble getting him to sleep, can you pop over with the dog?'

I grinned. 'Sure. No problem.'

He returned my grin. 'OK, I'd better grab that shower. Martha has a key so she'll let herself in. Make yourself at home. I won't be long.'

'OK.' I watched as Cal walked off at a fast pace down the hallway and turned out of sight before pushing all random thoughts of him and showers firmly out of my mind. Wandering back into George's room, I saw the little boy had now snuggled down in his bed, one arm still around Apollo and the other around Bear. Someone was snoring softly. I ruled out Bear and after glancing at both the other sleeping forms, pinned the blame firmly on the dog and gave him a gentle stroke.

Apollo had soothed many a child – and adult – to sleep since he'd come to us as a gangly puppy three years ago. His gentle nature and mere presence had a way of calming even the busiest of minds. Which probably accounted for why he was currently sleeping at the side of, and occasionally on top of, my bed most nights now. Just knowing he was there made everything that tiny bit less overwhelming. And I was glad he had now worked his magic on little George.

I crossed the room quietly and headed back to the kitchen, listening out for movement on the gravel drive that would signal the approach of Martha. The kitchen was a bright, airy room, mostly white with flashes of lemon to add a bit of zing and take away any hint of sterility. There was plenty of workspace, plus a large island in the middle. An extension housed an eating area, and large bifold doors covered one entire wall, leading out onto a wide patio and the sprawling garden beyond.

Even on a grey and uninspiring day like today, light flooded into the room, making it cheery and bright. I wandered over to the fridge and smiled at the childish drawings held there by magnets from landmarks and cities around the world, as well as closer to home.

My stomach grumbled and I chewed on my lip for a moment, glancing around. I walked away from the fridge and sat down on one of the bar stools at the island. Another loud growl from my tummy broke the silence.

'Oh, for goodness sake!' I mumbled and headed back to fridge. Inside I found everything I needed for my plan bar one ingredient which was sitting on the worktop. I rummaged in one of the deep drawers of the island, pulled out what I needed, and set to work.

'That smells amazing!' Cal padded back into the kitchen, his socked feet making his approach more stealthy than I'd antici-pated. I jumped about three feet in the air. 'Hey! Only me.'

'Yes. Of course. I'm just used to noisier blokes. George and the dog are asleep. Here.' I handed him a plate with a warm bacon sandwich on it. 'I hope you didn't mind me taking over your kitchen but walking the dog always makes me hungry, and I didn't think you'd probably had much to eat looking after George. It seemed a good idea to have something before we set out.'

'Mind? A gorgeous woman shows up to check on us, soothes my sick child to sleep, and then hands me food that I didn't have to cook myself? That's definitely not a scenario I mind in the slightest.' He took a massive bite of the sandwich and made appreciative noises. 'So good!' He mumbled through it.

I smiled and began tucking into my own sarnie as I pondered over the fact that Cal Martin had just referred to me as gorgeous. Although that might have been the bacon talking.

'As much as I'd like to accept all that, in the interests of accuracy I feel I have to point out that it was technically Apollo who soothed George to sleep. I had very little to do with it. Nothing in fact.'

'You made the decision to pop round in the first place. That means you had everything to do with it in my eyes.'

Oh my God. Those eyes.

'Am I interrupting?' Martha's voice broke through. I glanced down at her shoeless feet, encased in thick, warm tights, perfect for silent movement – something that seemed to be the order of the day in this house.

'Not at all,' Cal replied, his tone easy and relaxed. 'Martha, do you know Lexi? Her family own The Four Seasons shop in the village. Lexi, this is Martha, George's childminder.'

I held out my hand and Martha shook it. 'Nice to meet you.'

'And you. I love that shop. It's always so interesting and full of such lovely things.'

'Thanks.'

'I must have missed you in there though.'

Aha, here we go.

I hadn't missed the look of curiosity that had passed over Martha's face when she'd found me standing in Cal's kitchen on a Sunday morning, sharing laughter and bacon sarnies. There had been more as well – a sense of protection. Yep. I was most definitely getting a hint of Mama Bear vibe. George was her charge but clearly it wasn't only little George under her wing. Cal was firmly nested there too, even if he didn't know it.

'No, I've been working away a lot for the last several years. I've only been home properly for a little while.'

'Oh. Will you be leaving again soon or are you here on a more permanent basis?' Her tone was light and interested but there was no doubt I was under scrutiny.

Cal, busy loading the dishwasher, completely missed it. But then he was a man and, in my experience, men weren't always good at subtle so that wasn't exactly a big shock.

'I'm not really sure to be honest. But I'm enjoying getting to spend time with my family and friends.' I smiled, hoping that was enough to satisfy her for now.

I saw her mouth begin to open.

Obviously not.

'So!' Cal stood back up from the dishwasher, closing the door as he did so.

Perfect timing.

'I'm just going to go and check on George. He was bit fretful earlier, but Lexi and Apollo have the magic touch and managed to get him to sleep while I was in the shower.'

'Apollo?'

'My dog.'

'Oh!'

'We popped in after our walk this morning to see how George was feeling.' Perhaps if I let her know I hadn't spent a passionate night with her employer, it might make her worry less that I was about to break his heart. Or whatever it was that she was worried about me doing.

'Oh, that was nice of you.'

Did I detect a little softening there?

George was still out like a light to the soft accompaniment of doggy snoring. I hated to wake Apollo but I had no idea how Martha felt about dogs or what time I'd be home. I didn't want him missing his dinner later if we got held up. I glanced at Martha, catching her expression. OK, so she might be a dog person after all. I gently nudged Apollo from his slumber. George's hand slid softly down his fur until it landed on the duvet and Cal snuggled his son into the bed further. Martha and I walked out, the dog close by my side.

'He's beautiful,' she said when we got to the hallway.

'Thank you.'

'The name suits him. Very regal.'

I laughed. 'You might not think that when he's on his back, legs in the air, snoring like a freight train.' She laughed at the image of a not infrequent sight at our place.

Cal joined us. 'He's still zonked. Thanks so much for this. I would have put it off if I could have.'

Martha waved his protestations away. 'It's my pleasure. Derek's decided that having now read one of the books, a *Game of Thrones* marathon was his calling this weekend and after a day of it yesterday, honestly, it's a pleasure to be here even more than usual. There's only so much tits, arse, blood, and gore I can take.'

My mouth had dropped open but Cal was laughing. Martha had that whole prim, respectable look going on and certainly didn't seem the kind of woman who said "tits and arse"!

'What did I say?' she asked, genuinely confused.

I snapped my mouth shut, and Cal just shook his head and gave her a squeeze around the shoulders. 'Nothing. Thanks again and just message or call me if you need anything at all. OK?'

'Of course. Now go if you must. But for goodness sake, have a window open or something. You look shattered, boy!'

'Don't worry. Lexi's driving. She very flatteringly told me I looked hideous and then used George as emotional blackmail to make me relinquish my keys.'

'Did she now?' Martha turned to me. 'Well done, you.' She winked and weirdly I felt like I'd passed some sort of test. Or at least one stage of it.

'In my defence, the word "hideous" was never used. He's exaggerating.'

Martha shrugged. 'He's a man ...' She left the rest of the sentence open to speak for itself as I laughed.

Cal raised an eyebrow. 'I'm feeling distinctly ganged up on here so I definitely think it's time we left.' The shower had revived him somewhat but his face was still drawn from tiredness and the worry of last night. But right now, his eyes sparkled with the fun of the tease.

'Come on, boy.' He looked down at Apollo. 'We know when we're beaten.' Apollo looked up and tilted his head.

I pulled on my boots and grabbed the hat I'd stuffed in my pocket. It wasn't the most flattering thing I'd ever worn but it was cosy and until the car warmed up, I valued my ears too much to give vanity the upper hand.

'Cute hat.' Cal grinned.

Being the mature adult that I was, I stuck my tongue out at him. 'I don't care. It's warm.'

Cal leant briefly towards me. 'I was actually being serious.'

I looked up, surprised. 'Oh!'

He gave a dip to the side with his head, considering. 'It suits you.'

'Thanks. I think,' I replied, laughter bubbling through my words. Even after a night of no sleep Cal Martin still had a smile capable of knocking me right out of my fur-lined boots. To prevent that happening, I bent and fiddled with Apollo's lead for a moment, giving myself time to reset and a mental shake.

I had a whole day ahead of me with this man. Yes, he was hot. And yes, I liked him. And even though I was usually really obtuse in such circumstances – I blame growing up surrounded by men – I was getting the idea that he might like me too. But I had no clue what I was going to do with my life right now. And as I'd said at Giselle's, at the most inopportune time possible, getting involved with anyone right now was probably not a great idea. Absolutely. Right! Good. That was sorted then.

'Are you anywhere nice?'

A deep voice with a definite hint of a smile broke into my thoughts.

'Huh?' I straightened up and came face to chest with Cal. He bent his knees a little and looked at me straight on.

'You were miles away …'

'Oh … that. Yes. No.'

Cal quirked an eyebrow and hit me with that smile again. Oh crikey. This was going to be an interesting day.

Pull it together, Lexi!

'Come on, boy. Up you get.' Apollo leapt into the back of the Defender and Cal shut the door. We both walked around to the driver's side.

'Umm, you're not driving, remember?'

'I'll be fine.'

'OK. Then you don't need me to come with you.'

Cal took a deep breath. 'You can talk to me and keep me awake.'

'The idea was for you to get some sleep. Which you need.'

'Yeah, but—'

'No buts. Keys please!'

He gave me a look. 'Considering you're best friends, you and Giselle are very different, aren't you?'

'That we are. She'd get you to give over the keys without you even realising you were doing it. I, on the other hand, don't have her beauty or persuasive skills so I tend to find that a more direct approach has to be employed.'

Cal smiled. 'Direct can be good too.'

'I'm glad you think so.' I held out my hand for the keys.

Cal laid the small bunch in it, but as I closed my hand around it, he didn't quite relinquish his own hold.

'I'd take issue with the beauty thing too. You shouldn't do yourself down.'

'Huh. Oh. Right. Good. Thanks. Thank you. Good to know.' I

nodded a little too vigorously and did a mental eyeroll at myself. It was quite impressive how inordinately bad I was at this kind of stuff. From the corner of my eye, I saw Cal run a hand across his chin, and I was pretty sure it was disguising a smirk.

Keeping my eyes averted, I pulled my hand a little to gain full control of the keys and opened the door of the Land Rover, putting myself into territory I was far more relaxed in. As I settled myself behind the wheel, I risked a glance up at Cal as he walked around the bonnet to the passenger side. He was grinning. Well, I definitely wasn't going to win any prizes for my feminine wiles but at least I provided amusement for those around me.

Cal pulled open the door and hefted himself in. Leaning forward he switched on the satnav and pulled his phone from a pocket in his jacket as he waited for it to boot up. I glanced back at the dog while I waited. Apollo had his head resting on the back seat, watching and waiting patiently.

'He's a great dog,' Cal commented without looking at me as he tapped a postcode into the machine.

I smiled at Apollo and stretched back an arm to give him a quick head rub. 'He is.'

'George has been going on about getting a dog for ages. I don't think this morning is going to have helped.'

I looked round at him. 'Oh! Sorry. I didn't mean to cause any awkwardness. We were just passing and—'

Cal held up his hands. 'That came out wrong. It wasn't meant as a criticism. Maybe you're right in that I need a rest.'

I studied the satnav for a moment. 'I don't think there's any maybe about it.'

He laughed and pressed 'Go' on the device.

'Fair enough. What I meant is if I can find such a great dog as this one, it might not be a bad thing. I'm aware that George is an only child – it could be good for him to have some company at home. Someone to bond with. Nothing I said could bring a smile to his face or get him to settle this morning and then you and Apollo walk in and he's happy and asleep within minutes.'

'It's my scintillating personality. It often sends people to sleep.'

'Now that I know is a big fat lie.'

I gave him a shrug. 'OK. So if I can just drop the dog off at home and let my parents know that I'm out with you and not in a ditch somewhere, then we can head off.'

'Is it likely they think you're in a ditch?'

'You'd be surprised.' I turned over the engine as Cal plugged in his seatbelt. 'It's my mum's catchphrase. Whenever one of us was late, even just a few minutes, we'd be greeted with her telling us off, saying that she had been convinced we were lying in a ditch somewhere.'

'On the plus side, it's nice that someone cared if you were or not.' Cal's mouth was smiling but as I gave a quick glance to check the road was clear, I saw that the smile didn't reach his eyes.

My stomach twisted. 'I'm sorry. That was insensitive. I didn't think—'

Cal laid his hand over mine on the wheel for the briefest of moments, before resting it back on his lap. 'It's fine. I don't want you second-guessing everything you say to me. But I can understand how your mum feels now. Every minute your child isn't where they should be feels like hours.'

I nodded.

'You seem very close to your nieces and nephews so I'm sure you've already got a good idea.'

'True.'

'And then, if you have your own….' He blew out a sigh. 'It seems like every day is a worry sometimes.'

I swallowed, and looked away from him up the road, checking for traffic.

'Is it clear your way?'

'Yep.'

I pulled out and headed back towards my parents' place, doing my best to push Cal's innocently made comment out of my mind.

Chapter 8

We'd dropped off the dog, put Mum's mind at rest, and had now been on the road nearly half an hour. Cal had finally given in about ten minutes ago and was sleeping soundly in the passenger seat. A couple of dips in the road had him bumping his head against the window on which he rested but he didn't wake. Each time I heard it, I winced.

As the next lay-by came into sight, I pulled off, keeping the engine running. Unwinding my scarf, I rolled it into a small bundle and leant over Cal. Wrapping one arm around his side, I hefted his not insubstantial weight away from the window momentarily and with the other, rested my scarf there. Gently I released him and made sure his head was now against the soft material, rather than the hard glass. I didn't fancy having to explain to little George that I'd been kind enough to drive his father so that he could sleep, but in doing so, had also managed to brain him.

I pulled to a gentle halt and checked the address again. It seemed this was the place. Cal was still sleeping and I hated to wake him. Being up all night with his son had clearly taken it out of him, plus I knew from Xander that Cal had recently been working at night after George had gone to sleep, trying to get on top of things after a recommendation by a celebrity had increased demand for his services even more.

As I sat for a moment, the engine ticking and cooling in reaction to the bitter air surrounding it, my phone rang. Diving my hand into my pocket, I fumbled for a moment and pulled out the mobile, almost juggling it in my haste to shut it up.

'Hi,' I whispered.

'Why are you whispering?' Giselle asked.

'Cal's asleep.'

There was a pause. 'Oh, really?' she asked, the biggest of smiles in her voice. 'Well, at bloody last. Honestly, I can't remember the last time he went out with a woman on her own and I know for certain it's been far too long for you.'

'Actually, I've never dated a woman on her own, or otherwise,' I countered, my smart-arse gene coming to the fore.

'You know what I mean. So? How was it?'

'How was what?' I asked, confused.

I could practically hear her rolling her eyes.

'The sex of course!'

'Giselle. We're in the car.'

'Wow! Really? I guess once the fire's finally lit, there's no stopping you two! OK, so same question.'

'Gis, it's definitely not what you think.' I was still whispering but I had a feeling I could have played a short concerto on the car horn and Cal wouldn't have stirred. He'd barely moved since he'd closed his eyes, even when I'd manhandled him earlier.

'It isn't?'

'No.'

'Are you sure?'

'I know it's been a while, but yes. I'm pretty sure I would know if something like you're suggesting had happened.'

'Shame.'

'Not really. Too complicated.'

'Life is complicated.'

'This is true. Which only illustrates my point better. Why add more to the mix?'

Giselle let out a sigh as she was prone to do whenever we veered onto the topic of me dating. Or more specifically, not dating. 'So, what is happening then? Where are you and why is Cal with you but asleep?'

I gave her a quick catch-up and then got to the crux of it.

'So, how do I wake him up?'

'What?'

'What's the proper form for waking him up?'

Giselle's tinkly laugh, unlike my own head-back belly laugh, drifted down the phone.

'What's the problem? You have a male best friend, three brothers, and worked with a tonne of blokes. I've seen them dozing in the garage on the television. Surely you must have had to wake one of them up before.'

'Of course. All of the above, I just give a shove and tell them to wake up.'

'So?'

'That doesn't seem appropriate here.'

'Why not?'

'I ... don't know.' And that was the truth. I had no idea why this was such an issue. Cal was like any other bloke. Except I already knew that wasn't entirely true. Which was exactly the problem.

'Oh, for goodness sake, this is ridiculous, I should just—'

'Kiss him,' Giselle offered.

'What?' I squeaked. This was something I very rarely did. Especially not in a whisper.

'Kiss him. I can categorically say he won't mind.'

'I might!'

'Liar.'

I didn't have an answer for that.

'It's not appropriate.'

'Says who? Honestly, hon. I'm telling you he really wouldn't mind. And I don't think you would either. Maybe it's time to—'

'OK. I think he's waking up anyway. Talk to you later. Bye!' I hung up and glanced over to Cal who was still completely sparko. It wasn't an outright fib to Giselle. Cal had actually moved slightly, but his breathing stayed deep and steady and rhythmic and whatever I'd hoped, he wasn't about to wake up. Damn.

'Cal?' I called, quietly.

Nothing.

'Cal?' I tried again.

Nope. Bugger. I wrapped my hand around a bicep that even under his squidgy jacket still felt pretty prominent. This time I gave him a gentle shake as I called. There was movement but no definite result. I shifted position, leant over a little more, and tried again. Cal's head moved and his thick-lashed, heavy-lidded eyes opened sleepily and looked directly into mine.

Oh crap. That's so not a helpful image to have in my mind right now! I sat back quickly and gave the rogue thoughts of Cal's "just woken up" look starring in other possible situations a good hard shove out of my brain.

'Hi.' He smiled. His voice had that sleep-roughened edge. The thoughts I'd dismissed previously sniggered and crept back in. I did my best to ignore them.

'Hello!' I said brightly. 'Nice sleep?'

Cal shoved himself up a little, noticing the scarf under his head. He caught it as it slid down.

'I'm pretty sure that wasn't there when we started out. In fact' – he looked at it and then me – 'I'm almost convinced it was around your neck.'

'It was. But your head was making some rather unsettling bumping sounds against the window.'

He was looking at me in that world-disappearing way again. 'Thank you.'

'No problem,' I replied, trying to keep my voice sounding

casual as I took the scarf back from him.

'I didn't mean to sleep the whole way and leave you to it. I'm sorry.'

'Really not a problem. You needed the rest and it's nice to get out for the day anyway.'

Both of us peered out at the blackening sky and the odd large raindrop that had now started bouncing intermittently off the windscreen.

Cal laughed. 'You sure about that?'

I shrugged and chuckled. 'I am. I've not actually been outside the village since I got home. It's good to get a change of scenery.'

Cal nodded and rubbed his hands over his face, trying to wake himself up. 'OK. Let's go and check out the car before this scenery – and us – start getting distinctly soggy.'

'Oh. I was just going to wait here.'

'Don't you want to come? I thought you might be interested?'

'I am but I didn't want to overstep or get in the way.'

Cal shook his head. 'Get your arse out of the car and come help me decide whether this is a good buy or not.'

I pulled a face. 'That I can do.'

Cal shot me a grin through the glass as he closed the door and before I knew it, I'd returned it, full wattage. Jumping out and walking around to the front of the car, I looked up at him.

'Cute hat,' I echoed unthinkingly as I took in the fleecy beanie he'd now rammed down to try and protect his ears from the vicious wind that was swirling around and nipping away at us.

I couldn't see them thanks to the hat, but from the expression on his face, I was pretty sure his eyebrows just shot up. The laugh that followed confirmed it. He wrapped an arm around my shoulders, gave a squeeze, and hustled me towards the porch of the house.

Cal had been right not to delay seeing the unloved classic car. It was apparent that with some skilled TLC, he'd more than recoup his money on it at auction and should make a very healthy profit. The bulk of the rain had held off as we'd loaded it onto the empty trailer I'd been towing behind us. We then made sure it was well covered with a tarpaulin.

But now, as we sat in the cosy window nook of a pub, the nearby fire warming us through, the temperature had fallen and the earlier threat of rain had turned into very real snow. Large flakes tumbled in the wind, bumping against the wibbly, leaded glass of the window and settling into a pile in the corners of each small pane. We'd ordered food and were now sitting with our drinks at the table, stomachs growling. It was hard not to notice Cal's eyes regularly flicking to the car outside. He'd let me choose where we wanted to sit but had seemed pleased – and perhaps relieved – when I'd chosen this table.

'It's all right. It's still there,' I said, as his eyes drifted again.

He gave a half-smile, as if he were a little embarrassed at being caught. 'I'm sorry. It's incredibly rude of me to keep looking out of the window when you're sitting in front of me, especially as you've given up your free time to help me!' My arm was resting on the table and Cal covered my wrist with a large, warm hand. 'I am grateful. I hope you know that.'

I flapped my other hand. 'Don't even worry about it. I totally understand. There's a lot of money sitting under that tarp. I'd be the same. And besides, you don't have to apologise to me. It's not like we're on a date or anything!'

His fingers contracted with just the slightest pressure on my wrist and I felt a tingle in places I'd known to be tingle-free for quite some time. I took a sip of my drink and gave my own glance out of the window, glad for the warmth of the fire to excuse any flush in my face. His hand moved from my wrist to his drink.

'No. But that's not the point. I'm enjoying your company and yet I'm blowing it by staring off out the window. I'm sorry.'

I shrugged. 'You're still paying more attention than some actual dates I've been on, so don't be too hard on yourself.'

'Then they were idiots.'

I smiled. 'No, not really. I just don't think I was exactly what they were expecting.'

'What were they expecting then?'

I stirred my drink and stabbed the lemon slice with the straw a few times. 'Not a tomboy.'

'You don't always dress like a tomboy.'

'I know. Sometimes I dress up as an elf.' I grimaced. 'But … well, they were dates set up via Giselle, and I think these blokes thought that as I was her friend, I'd be similar.'

'It'd be boring if everyone were the same.'

'That is true.'

'And I still think they were idiots.'

I chuckled and took a pull on my straw. Cal smiled and took a sip of his drink. Placing his glass on the table, his long fingers then stretched out to snag a spare cardboard coaster. Turning it around on its edge, he let it slide between his fingers before turning it onto the next edge and repeating the motion.

'I meant what I said. I really do appreciate you coming today. It was very kind of you.'

I nodded, confused at the expression in his eyes. If I didn't know better, I'd have said it was surprise. Also, if I had known better, I'd have kept quiet at this point.

'You seem surprised.' Clearly, I really didn't know better.

Cal kept his focus on the beer mat. 'Not entirely. I …' He flicked a glance up and then went back to the beer mat. 'Like I said at the shop the first time I met you, it's different here. It's taken some getting used to.'

'People in the village just want to help. We don't mean to be nosy or butt in. And most people will back off if you refuse nicely.'

I'd had my own experience of this when I'd returned home for a few weeks after my last relationship had ended badly, painfully, and very publicly. It wasn't always easy and although they were being nosy, for the most part people did actually care. In today's world, that wasn't always an easy concept for people to grasp. Especially outsiders, so I could see how Cal might struggle with this aspect of village life.

'It's nice that people want to help, and although I really made the move down here for George, I think it's been good for both of us.'

'All that fresh air!'

He laughed. 'Something like that. So, you were born in the village, Xander said, right?'

I met his gaze and held it for a moment. He'd deftly moved the subject away from himself and he knew I'd caught it. I smiled and let it go. It was up to Cal what he shared with me. And like I'd said, it wasn't a date. We weren't there to discover how much we did or didn't have in common. It didn't matter. So, why did the fact that he'd just shut me out bother me so much?

I pushed away the feeling and kept the smile. 'Born and bred.'

'A lot of people seem to have stayed, from what I see, even if they work in London. It's nice that it's kept a community feel. Very few of the places I looked at had that.'

'So what made you choose our little village?'

Cal spread his hands on the table. Large and strong, the right one had a scar running across the back of it, silvery and faded as though it had been there a long time.

'It just felt right,' he replied eventually. Looking up from his hands, Cal pulled his mouth to the side – an action I'd seen George doing when he was thinking. When George did it, it was so cute it made me want to squeeze him. When Cal did it, I wanted to do a whole lot more than squeeze him. I rubbed a hand over my face and cleared my throat unnecessarily.

'You think that's daft?' he asked.

'No. No, I don't,' I replied, meeting his eyes in reassurance. 'I think sometimes the universe has a way of telling us what we need to do.'

The corner of that delicious mouth quirked. 'The universe told me to do it? Is that what you're saying?'

'Maybe. Or whoever, or whatever, you believe in.'

'OK.' Cal was nodding.

'If I even begin to think that you're mocking me, I'm leaving you here. You know that, don't you?'

He laughed. 'I'm fully recovered now. I can drive myself.'

I dangled the keys to the side of me, making sure they were just out of reach. 'Not without these.'

Cal rubbed a hand across the darkening stubble on his jaw. 'So the rumours about you being smart as well as pretty weren't unfounded then?' He laughed.

'I think that depends on the lighting but yeah, we can go with that.'

Cal fixed me with a look and I was prevented from having to deal with any comeback by the arrival of the waitress.

'Two lasagnes?' the waitress asked us.

'Yep, that's us. Thanks.'

'Be careful. The plates are hot.'

'Thanks.'

The food smelled delicious and my stomach let out a growl in anticipation.

'Ooh, sounds like you need to get that down you!' The waitress chuckled.

I gave a half-embarrassed smile and busied myself unfolding my napkin and laying it on my lap.

'Sorry it's taken so long to get some food. We probably should have stopped for lunch before we saw the car,' Cal said.

'Don't be silly,' I replied, digging into the lasagne, my mouth watering as I loaded up my fork. 'If we had, it would have put us behind and we'd have been loading the car up in this now.' I nodded sideways to the window. Outside, the snow was falling steadily. The roads still looked clear and the traffic moving, but in places that didn't have cars, or hadn't been gritted, the snow was settling quite nicely.

'That's true.'

'It just means I appreciate this even more now.'

'So you know, I'm paying.'

I waved my now empty fork at him, unable to argue with a mouthful of delicious, and very hot, lasagne.

He waved his own back at me. 'No arguments. You've done more than enough today. It's the least I can do.'

I swallowed. 'I was happy to!'

'And I'm happy to pay so it's all good.' He took a big forkful and grinned, before his eyes widened and he put his hand over his mouth. 'Oh shit … hot!'

Chapter 9

Having demolished the lasagne and two rocky road sundaes, Cal ordered us coffees. I could see him keeping an eye on the state of the nearby road and he'd checked his phone for traffic and weather reports. He wasn't in a hurry to rush off so I trusted him in the knowledge that he wouldn't put himself or me, or – come to think of it – his new purchase, in danger.

We sat over our coffee, the accompanying mints having disappeared within seconds of their arrival. I'd had a large glass of wine and was now feeling a little more brave, and possibly less inhibited than usual.

'The comment you made earlier … about having someone care whether you were lying in a ditch or not …'

Cal kept his eyes on his coffee cup, long lashes shading his expression. 'Hmm?'

'Was it really that bad? Your childhood, I mean?'

He took another sip before replacing the cup in the saucer, and still without looking at me, stretched his fingers out to reach for the balled-up foil wrappers from our after-dinner mints.

'I'm assuming you've heard from somewhere that I had a bit of a rough childhood. My best guess would be Xander and Giselle?'

'Yes. They mentioned something but that was all they said.

All they seemed to know, actually,' I said, honestly. A thought suddenly flew into my mind. 'They weren't gossiping about you! It's only because they care.'

This was true and the last thing I wanted to do was drop my best friends in something, especially as one of them worked for him.

'I know. Don't worry, I'm not about to fire anyone if that's what the sudden look of panic on your face is about.' His own expression was one of amusement.

I relaxed a little at his reassurance.

'Admittedly, that's taken some getting used to though, I can tell you.'

'What? People caring about you?'

He set the foil ball aside. 'Yes. And, I suppose, letting them.'

'Sometimes there's no stopping them. Especially not in our little corner of the world.'

A smile lit his face and he laughed. 'That's true.' He ran his hand through his hair and glanced out of the window again.

'I'm pretty sure there's far more interesting things to talk about than me. Like you, for instance.'

He flashed a grin, and I knew that most women would have been flattered, which was clearly what he was intending. Cal Martin obviously had a few moves up his sleeve when he required them. The compliment, combined with that heart-stopping smile, was a sure-fire ego boost for any woman. But me being me instead homed in on the fact that he'd just shut down my attempt to delve into his history. Again.

'How are you finding being back in the village?'

I nodded. 'It's good. Nice. I hadn't realised quite how much I missed it actually.'

'So does that mean you're thinking of staying?'

I shrugged. 'I don't know. It depends how things go really. I thought I'd totally burned my bridges but I actually got a reply back from one of the teams yesterday. They've offered me a position. I have a meeting with them just after Christmas but basically if I want it, the position is mine.'

'Right. Wow. That's great!' Cal looked at me. 'It is great, isn't it?'

'Of course. Yes. I mean, it's what I want. What I've been trying for since I lost my last job.'

'So, you've accepted?'

'Not quite.'

He said nothing but raised a dark brow.

'I will. I mean, obviously.'

'Forgive me for saying, but you don't seem as thrilled as I thought you would be about it all.'

I let out a sigh and blew my fringe out of my eyes. 'I know. I am. I will be. It's just that …'

'Go on.' Cal's voice was soft as he touched my hand, prompting me.

I gave him a half-embarrassed smile. 'I hardly know you and I'm blabbering away.'

'Surely that's how people get to know each other better, isn't it? By blabbering away?'

I looked back at him and met a grin that I imagined had got a lot of women to say a lot of things.

'If you have the knack of scintillating conversation and the ability to flutter your eyelashes.'

He laughed. 'You're plenty scintillating, and fluttering eyelashes has always been vastly overrated, in my opinion.'

I couldn't help the smile. 'You really are a charmer, aren't you?'

'Only when it's worth the effort.'

'What a line!'

He joined me in my laughter. 'It really wasn't, but I have to admit, it did sound like one.'

'Just a bit.'

'So?'

'So?'

'Why are you having doubts about taking the job?'

'I'm not. I mean, not really.'

Cal gave me that look again.

'OK. I guess over the past year I've just got used to being able to come home for things. I really did love my job but the downside was being away a lot, which meant missing out on stuff. Family stuff, you know?'

He gave a sad nod and I immediately felt bad. He saw it and covered my hands with one of his, shaking his head, the softest of smiles on that dangerously tempting mouth.

'Anyway. I will take it. Of course I will. Obviously it's not ideal as it's a couple of rungs down the ladder from where I was, but it'd get me back into the industry and it's what I do. What I'm good at.'

'That doesn't mean you wouldn't be, or aren't already, good at something else.'

'No. I know.' I picked up the coaster he'd been fiddling with earlier and twiddled it in my fingers. 'I'll be fine. Once I'm back in among it all, I'll know it's where I'm supposed to be. It's just because I've been away from it for a while.'

He nodded. 'Maybe.'

'What does that mean?'

Cal didn't elaborate, his gaze sliding to the weather outside the window momentarily. 'But you're enjoying being back in the village?' he asked, looking back at me.

My smile gave him the answer.

'It's quite a special place, isn't it?'

'It is. And I can't wait for the Christmas Festival! Were you there for it last year?' I put the coaster down.

'We were but poor old George had caught a stinking cold and by the time the festival came around, we were both in bed, dosed up to the eyeballs with medicine.'

'Oh no! What a shame! You have to go this year. George will absolutely love it. The whole village turns out, and there are stalls and fairground rides and a parade with Father Christmas. There was a choir last year and I think Mum said they're coming again this time. They don't just do carols either. They did some pretty amazing covers last year. Actually,' I said, my coffee cup halfway to my mouth and one finger pointing at Cal from it, 'they did a take on "All the Single Ladies" at one point and got all the single women and men to come out in front of them. There was definitely a bit of chemistry in the air that night! You missed out.'

'Actually, that sounds terrifying. I'm almost glad I was in bed now I've heard that bit.'

'To be fair, I think a few of those involved ended up there too.' I gave a giggle, stopped abruptly, and put my cup down, shaking my head. 'I really shouldn't have had that wine on an empty stomach.'

Cal was grinning. 'It's fine. It's ... entertaining.'

'I don't want to be entertaining!'

He shrugged. 'Too bad. So were you one of the single ladies shaking their booty in this magical scene?'

I gave an eyebrow raise. 'No. I mean, yes. But no.'

Cal did a slow blink. 'OK. I'll admit to not understanding that answer even vaguely.'

I rubbed my eyes and took another swallow of coffee. 'Yes, I was technically a single lady but no, I wasn't up there dancing. I have no desire to shake my booty, or anything else, in front of the general public. At least definitely not while sober.'

He pulled a face. 'Well, that gives us some leeway.'

I rolled my eyes. 'Don't hold your breath.'

'No mulled wine for you that night then?'

'No. It was a flying visit. I couldn't take the whole weekend off so I set off back that night after everything was finished. Or at least most of it.'

'Must have been a late night.'

'More like an early morning, but it was worth it to get to spend the evening with my family and friends.'

'I'm sure they loved having you there too.'

I nodded. 'They know I love what I do ... did ... do ... I don't know. They know I loved what I was doing but spending over half the year out of the country and the rest of it several hours' drive away hasn't always been easy on any of us. I know my mum hates it when there's a celebration or something and I can't make it. Which was quite often to be fair. Made me feel kind of bad.'

'She does?' Cal was frowning.

'No!' I looked up, horrified. 'God, no! They've been nothing but supportive ever since I started. They put on a brave face.'

He nodded, agreeing. 'You know, I'd heard Dan talk about his little sister, but I didn't put two and two together until I met you and realised you and Xander's best friend and my mate's little sister are the same person.'

'Yeah. Dan tends to do that when he's talking about me. He's kind of protective.'

'And not saying your name helps that? Are you an international spy on the side?' Cal flashed his eyes at me but the humour in them died as he caught my expression. 'What have I said?'

I shook my head. 'Nothing.'

'OK. I know I'm a bloke but when you grew up like I did, you get pretty good at reading expressions. If I'm not mistaken, you're the one putting on a brave face now.'

'I'm not. This is the only face I have.' I smiled, and even to me it didn't feel like it fit quite right.

Cal's expression told me it hadn't fooled him either. The ocean-grey eyes held mine, concern showing in the crease of his brow. 'I'm sorry if I've said something I shouldn't have. But if you give me a clue, it will at least stop me from cocking up again.'

'I … just had a bit of a tough time with my last relationship. Dan's always been protective but all that kind of enhanced it.'

'Somebody hurt you?' He'd pushed his jumper sleeves back earlier as the warmth of the pub's fire thawed us out, and as he asked the question, I saw the tension in the corded muscles of his forearms. I laid my hand on his arm, feeling the tautness release under it.

'Not like you're imagining.'

Cal laid his own hand over mine momentarily. 'And here I was thinking I was good at hiding my emotions.'

I gave a laugh. 'Well, you're good at deflecting conversation that involves talking about yourself, that's for sure.'

'Says the woman who's just done the same thing.'

I opened my mouth, then closed it again. He was right. I had.

'OK. So I tell you one thing and you tell me …' I tapped my finger against my chin, thinking what it was I wanted to know the most.

'Ugh. I'm beginning to wish I hadn't asked now.' Cal pulled a face but there was a tease in his eyes. I tugged my top lip in with my teeth, thinking. I had a feeling that getting Cal Martin to open up was still going to be like cracking one of those walnuts that sit in the bowl all through Christmas, refusing to be beaten – or eaten – and his comment, although teasing, confirmed it so I went with an easier starter.

'Right. You tell me why you moved to the village and how you feel about it now you've been here awhile and have got over the initial shock.' I grinned.

'OK. Deal.'

We sat in silence for a moment.

'But you go first,' he said.

I moved the coffee cup a little and then raised my gaze, bumping into Cal's. He was studying me. His fingertips brushed mine, just for a moment. 'If you don't want to though,' he said softly, 'you don't have to.'

'No,' I said, putting on that brave face again, 'we made a deal.'

'Screw the deal. We're friends. I want you to be comfortable with me, and right now you don't look it.'

I shook my head. 'It's not you. I mean, it's not that I don't want to tell you anything.'

And the weird thing was, I did. I was used to spilling everything to my family, which by extension, meant Xander and Giselle, mostly because I didn't have a choice. Trying to hide something from any of them was impossible. They knew me too well. But outside of that precious, protective circle, my business was my own and that was how I liked it, which made what had happened all the more difficult to handle.

But there was something about Cal Martin – nothing to do with how good he looked, how great he smelled when he'd come into the kitchen this morning after his shower, or how he had a smile that could scramble your brain at ten paces. It was more than that and it was kind of exciting. Also, it scared the pants off me.

'I'm kind of surprised you don't know really. Or maybe you do.' I was stalling.

When he spoke, his voice was soft. 'Until you tell me, it's a little bit tricky to answer that.'

'It's nothing really,' I said, flapping a hand in dismissal at the same time as I felt the heavy knot in my stomach form at the memory.

'Clearly it's not nothing. You've gone almost as pale as George was in the night.'

'I used to go out with one of the racing drivers for a while. Actually I was engaged to him. It … kind of all got a bit messy towards the end, and the paparazzi were used to following Marco anyway, so when everything hit the fan, it not only spread around the paddock but got splashed across the papers too. My poor family had the media on the phone and some even turned up at our home trying to get soundbites and gossip. Since then, Dan switched to referring to me as his sister rather than using my name, just in case.'

Cal said nothing for a moment. 'Surely he didn't think I was a media informant?'

I shook my head. 'Of course not. But I guess you were new to the village, and to be honest, I think it's just a habit for him now. And if it makes him worry about me less, then I'm good with that.'

'So when you say Marco, you mean Marco Benoit?'

'Yeah. I know. Unlikely, huh?' I laughed, trying to relax the tension from my shoulders.

Marco was well known for his penchant for leggy models and actresses. Being none of the above, no one was more surprised than me when he'd asked me to dinner, and it had taken him several attempts to convince me that I wasn't actually being pranked.

'No, that's not what I meant. I was just checking we were talking about the same person.'

'Right.'

'I follow Formula One but I must admit the gossip side of it all – what's going on in the drivers' lives – tends to pass me by. It's all about the cars and the racing for me.'

'It's a shame not everyone feels that way.' I smiled, rolling my shoulders. 'Unfortunately the world's insane obsession with celebrity tends to mean blanket coverage these days.'

'And you got caught in the middle of that?'

'Yeah. Kind of,' I answered, not looking at him, my fingers worrying the paper napkin I'd replaced on the table from my lap.

Cal caught my hand. 'I'm sorry you weren't given the privacy you deserved at what was obviously a difficult time.' I nodded, keeping my head down, concentrating on keeping my breathing even. 'From the look on your face, I'm feeling kind of shitty about asking you anything now.'

My head snapped up. 'No! Really, don't. I did, do, want to talk to you.'

He smiled, the warmth of it doing as much for me as the fire crackling just across the room. 'Thank you.'

'And really you don't have to tell me anything about you. I promise not to ask again. Actually that's a lie because like I said, I can be accidentally blunt and I may ask questions that might cross your boundaries, but I will at least try not to delve into your personal life again.'

Cal gave my fingertips a quick squeeze as he gave another

glance at the weather. 'No. We had a deal and I dug up painful memories for you, albeit unintentionally,' he added as he saw my mouth open to protest, 'so the least I can do is tell you why I moved. It's not exactly personal.'

'Have you told anyone else?'

He waggled his head a little. 'Vaguely.'

'Then it's obviously personal to some extent.'

'Do you want to hear this or not?'

I returned his smile and felt the last knots unfurl as Cal's eyes caught the firelight, the laughter in them not entirely masking his earlier concern. Somewhere inside me I felt a swirling but this time it wasn't tension or stress. This time it was a far more intoxicating feeling, and one I knew I should ignore. The last time I'd felt something similar it had been wonderful, then awful. And I knew from the way it was filling every part of me that if I let it, this time the pain would be so much worse. But I wanted to enjoy it, enjoy Cal, for just a few minutes while I listened to that deep, smooth voice. Surely a few minutes wouldn't hurt?

'You're miles away.'

'No. Right here.' And I was, savouring every moment because I knew I was on a slippery slope and I couldn't afford to lose my grip.

Cal gave me an unconvinced look but began anyway.

'OK, so I moved from the city for George really. I'm a city kid – at least I thought I was – but there's no doubt that having a garden he can get outside and play in, spaces to run about in, clean air to breathe … it's all so much better for him. He's made great friends here and really come out of his shell. And I think the fact that I'm happier has had a really good impact on both of us.'

'You think you're happier?'

He smiled, softly. 'I know I am.'

'But you must have wanted to move too, surely?'

'I guess I thought it would be OK, but I grew up in the city. Really, it's all I've known but I wanted George to have more.'

'I get the feeling you don't think about yourself all that much.' I raised an eyebrow, daring him to challenge my statement.

Cal smiled. 'Not so much. There's not a lot of time between my son and the business. George is my world, and I have to keep the business doing well so that I can make sure he always has everything he needs.'

'What he needs the most is you.'

He frowned and sat back from me. 'I spend every moment I can spare with him. I always read him a story at night and—'

I held up my hands. 'Cal, that wasn't what I meant! I know you're a brilliant dad. All I meant is that you need to look after yourself too. For George's sake and yours.'

Cal studied me for a moment, the furrows in his brow smoothing. 'Oh. Yes. Sorry. And, of course you're right.'

'It's difficult. I know.'

'Admittedly, Martha has made things a lot easier. George loves her to bits, and everyone in the village has been really helpful and kind from the start. When I took George to nursery the first day, I felt like I was the new boy, not him. I'm pretty sure I was the more nervous!' His laugh was deep and smooth and brought to mind dark, melting chocolate.

'It was mostly mums there but they were really kind and supportive. George had already whizzed off and was busy making friends, and I was just stood there feeling a bit bereft! I must have seemed quite a pathetic specimen. A few of them were heading off for coffee and asked me along.'

I bet they did …

'At the nursery in London the parents were all in little cliques and sectioned themselves off. I think there was one other dad I kind of nodded hello to but that was about it. It was a completely different experience here from day one.'

'But in a good way?'

'In a great way. To be honest, it took me a bit by surprise – the kindness and generosity. The way that people here are happy to help each other out, even an interloper like me!'

I laughed. 'You're not an interloper!'

'No, you're right. I've never felt like that here. I did worry that we might though. You know some little places, you go in a shop or pub and they all stop talking and look at you?'

'Yeah, we're not like that.'

'Definitely not. Thank goodness.'

'We happy to let any old Tom, Dick, or Cal rock up and be welcome.'

He gave me a grin that immediately thawed out my still-cold toes and still had a bit of warmth left over for other areas.

'So, does that mean you plan on staying then? Xander had said you weren't sure initially.'

'No, I wasn't to start with. I needed to see how George and I settled in but as that seems to have gone pretty well, I think we could be here for some time to come. George has really blossomed since we've been here and I don't want to be someone who keeps moving around. I want George to have stability growing up.'

'Because you didn't and you know what that feels like?'

Cal's expression turned wary for a moment.

'Sorry. I told you I miss the Edge-Of-Boundary signs sometimes. Especially when I've had a large wine on an empty stomach. And as you bought that for me technically it's your fault, so you only have yourself to blame.'

The wariness dissipated. 'Of course it is.'

'So, is that true?' I prompted.

'Man, you don't give up, do you?'

'My brother Joe says I must have had the word "tenacious" stamped on my bum at birth.'

Cal burst out laughing and any last strands of resistance were broken. 'Maybe next time we can get you two glasses of wine and we can check the accuracy of that statement.'

I balled up my napkin and threw it at him. 'You definitely have to answer the question now for that cheeky comment.'

'I'm kind of distracted at the moment. I've actually forgotten what the question was!' His eyes were dancing with mischief.

'Focus, Martin.'

'I am.' He wiggled his eyebrows and this time his own napkin bounced off the side of his head.

'OK, OK.' He held up his hands. 'You win. Yes, I know what it's like to be shifted from pillar to post. I want George to have as stable a home life as I can give him, in the circumstances.'

'And?'

Cal held my gaze. 'I think Joe might actually be right! OK. Yes. I suppose, deep down, there's something in what you say. Stability can be good at any stage of life. I'd honestly never thought about it before.' He laughed. 'There. Are you happy now?'

'I think the more pertinent question is, are you?'

Cal held up his hands. 'Oh no. The deal was one question. His eyes slid to the weather outside the window and, still smiling, he picked up his phone and pressed the screen a couple of times. 'Besides, I think we need to make a move. There's some heavier weather coming in across the country and although they're saying the roads are clear at the moment, I don't want to risk leaving it too long.'

He reached back into his coat hanging on the chair behind him and pulled out his wallet.

'I'm paying half of that,' I said, pointing at the bill with one hand as I dug into my pocket with the other.

'No, you're not. I already told you, I'm paying as a thank you to you for giving up your day off to help me out.'

'But I enjoyed it so it was hardly a chore.'

Cal ignored me, tucked his card inside the little wallet the bill had arrived in, and shut it again. My gaze drifted to it.

'Don't even think about it.' Cal grinned at me.

I looked up.

'And don't give me that innocent look either. I know you were thinking of swapping my card for yours.'

I emphasised the innocent look, widening my eyes, and he laughed.

'Yeah right. Like I'm buying that.'

'You know, you have quite the suspicious streak.'

'It helps keep me on my toes.'

'I see.' I chewed my lip.

'Lexi, don't overthink it. I'm grateful to you for helping me out today. I was shattered this morning and driving wouldn't have been the most sensible or safest thing I could have done. But I couldn't afford to miss out on this car. Whether you enjoyed it or not—'

'I did!'

He grinned. 'Good. But either way, you put yourself out to help me. Please just let me pay this to go some way to showing you how appreciative I am of your kindness.'

'Fine. Then thank you.'

The waitress returned with the payment machine, Cal tapped his card on it and tucked the receipt in his wallet.

Cal pulled his coat from the chair but his warm, grey gaze remained fixed on me. 'Why are you so uncomfortable about this?'

'I'm not,' I said, trying to pretend I was telling the truth.

Cal's eyes remained on me as I fussed about with my scarf and wiggled my coat off the back of the chair.

'You know I don't believe a word of that, right?'

I zipped up my jacket and having composed myself, looked up at him and shrugged. 'Your prerogative. Ready?'

Cal threw a glance out of the window, the faintest of furrows showed on his forehead as he watched the snow still falling.

'Yep. Let's go.'

Chapter 10

Back in the car it wasn't long before the day began catching up on me, so I was glad Cal was refreshed enough to drive back. He'd stuck the heater on and I'd pushed off my boots and now sat curled up on the seat. He fished a blanket from the back and draped it over me.

'You OK?'

I nodded.

'Get some rest.'

I shook my head. 'I'm OK.'

Cal leant towards me, his fingers gently tucking a loose strand of hair back behind my ear. The rough plait I'd stuck my hair in this morning was finally giving in.

'Are you always this stubborn about everything?' he asked, his voice low.

I didn't answer and instead kept my eyes focused on the dashboard, trying to keep my breathing even as his hand brushed against my skin, the warmth of it contrasting with the coolness of the snowflakes that had been stinging against it just a few moments ago.

His eyes were on me, I knew, but I didn't dare look into them. I knew if I did I'd be lost. Cal Martin was gorgeous, intelligent, funny, and loved many of the same things I did. And I was pretty sure now that he liked me too. Which all meant one thing. Trouble. And right now, that was the last thing I needed.

Cal sat back and, glancing around to check it was clear, began pulling out of the pub's large car park, carefully manoeuvring the trailer with its precious cargo onto the main road and back in the direction of the village. We still had a long drive ahead of us and the snow was heavier now. Luckily it was mostly main roads we had to use to get home and, as we saw another gritter lorry on the opposite carriageway, it was reassuring to know that these were being kept as clear as possible.

I was doing my best not to fall asleep but it was a struggle. I wasn't sure exactly why I didn't feel comfortable giving in to the tiredness now seeping through my body and mind. It wasn't that I didn't trust Cal or his driving. In fact, I had a nagging suspicion it was quite the opposite. Today had been one of the best days I'd had in a long time and I knew it would soon be over. Childishly, I was forcing myself to stay awake so that I didn't miss any of it. Well, that and the very real worry of sleep drooling. Nobody needed to see that. Especially not Cal Martin.

He glanced across at me and seeing that I was indeed stubborn enough to fight sleep, gave me a quick roll of his eyes. My body was also protesting at my choices and had apparently decided that if all of me wasn't going to sleep, as least some of me was. I wiggled a bit in the seat.

'Numb bum?'

'Ummhmm.'

'Want some help?'

I cut my eyes to him and he gave me the briefest of glances, a wickedly tempting smile on his face, before he focused back on the road. Honestly, he really wasn't helping my resolve to be sensible and stick to the plan. Not that I had that much of a plan but I did know getting involved with Cal Martin wasn't part of it.

'No. But thank you for the offer.'

'Any time.'

The worrying thing about that reply was that I wasn't entirely sure it was a joke.

'So,' Cal said, seeing that I was determined to fight closing my eyes. 'You said you thought you missed out on a lot of stuff before, being away with the job?'

I wiggled a bit more. 'I did,' I said a little sadly, thinking of the celebrations I'd only been part of vicariously through seeing photographs and videos on email and social media. 'This past year has been a bit of an eye-opener. I've been able to attend birthday parties, weddings, even just regular dinners with my family and friends. All things I'd missed out on for the past several years. It had become normal to not be able to attend. When someone asked me if I could make an event, I almost said no automatically because that was usually what the answer ended up being.'

'It can't have been easy to miss out on stuff when you have such a close family and great friends, which you clearly do.'

'No. And I think I'd just got used to it, which isn't right, really.' I shuffled around in my seat a little to face him more. 'I think what really brought it home to me was the first time I said I could attend something. It was one of my brother's birthdays and we were going to have a meal at my parents', like we always do. Anyway, when he asked and I just casually said yes, I'd be there, I happened to see my mum's face. She actually had tears in her eyes. I never really realised – or at least I suppose I'd forgotten – how much it means to her and Dad to have everyone around them on occasions like that. Any time really, but especially for special occasions.'

'That must have made you happy then? That you could make your mum happy like that?'

'Actually, I felt like the most enormous shit for making her unhappy on all the previous occasions when I'd had to say no.'

Cal kept his eyes on the road, but he reached out his hand and took mine for a moment. 'You were doing what you loved. She

104

understood.' He gave my fingers the briefest of squeezes before resting his hand back on the wheel.

'I guess.'

'Are you missing it all? Not the being away a lot part, obviously. But the work? Your colleagues?'

'Sometimes. It's what I know. What I'm good at. Although I have been enjoying getting involved in the shop much more than I thought I would, really. Growing up, I spent so much time there. I know it's just a shop but I missed it. It's been hard work for my parents and brothers, making it the success it is, but we all love it. It's part of the family. And while we're really busy at the moment, it's a nice busy. There isn't the same pressure that there was with the team. I thought I needed that pressure but apparently, it turns out I quite like it when it's not there.'

He nodded and flexed his fingers on the wheel before letting them curl gently back around it. 'I can see why you're a little undecided about going back to it. It seems you have entries in both the for and against columns.'

I stared out at the falling snow as we drove on through the darkness, flakes glinting as they crossed the beams of the headlights. Glancing back at Cal in reply, I wondered if I should start making a for and against chart with him as the topic. But no. I didn't need that. I already knew the sensible answer to that question.

I slid a look sideways and studied my companion's profile for a few moments. I'd had such a lovely day … I knew what the sensible decision was but I was fairly sure that, if he wanted, Cal Martin would be more than capable of helping me forget what the word 'sensible' even meant. But that wouldn't do. As much as I liked him, relationships and me just didn't get along. They were complicated. They weren't like a car engine where you knew what went where and what you had to do to make it work.

Although Cal had backed off from telling me too much, there was clearly more to his story. He'd had a rotten childhood, and he deserved everything in his adulthood that the world, and the woman he chose, could give him. I already knew that as much as I was interested in him, I wasn't the one for him. I couldn't be. Cal slowed behind other traffic as the lights ahead turned red, the shades above each bulb holding a small pile of snow. He pulled on the handbrake and looked over at me.

'We've still got a bit of a way to go yet. You look exhausted and I assume you have work tomorrow?'

'Yes, but I'm not tired.' The fact that I said the last word through a yawn didn't really help my case all that much.

'No, I can see that.' He laughed. 'Honestly it's even harder to get you to admit you're tired than it is a five-year-old. I promise I'll drive carefully. Apart from anything else, I'm pretty sure Dan would hammer me to a pulp if I let anything happen to you. I mean, I can take care of myself, but I'd rather not risk it.'

My eyes, heavy-lidded until now, widened. 'You think I don't trust you.'

He checked the lights before returning his gaze to me. 'I think you're used to being in control. Or at least wanting to be.'

'No, not always.'

I saw the quirk of his lips and the sparkle in his eyes, and I rolled mine in response.

'Typical man.'

'I'd say sorry but I'd hate to lie to you.' He was still grinning.

'Anyway!' I said, pointedly. 'It's not that I don't trust you. I do. Totally. I know you wouldn't do anything reckless or stupid. Not least because you have a very precious cargo back there.'

'I'm pretty sure the one in here is more precious.'

I met his eyes, surprised. His mouth smiled but it was hard to tell his true expression in the low light.

'I don't know whether you're teasing me or not sometimes.'

From the corner of my eye, I saw the lights ahead finally begin to change. Cal quickly hooked an arm around me, pulled me closer for a moment, and dropped the briefest of butterfly kisses on the top of my head.

106

'Close your eyes for a little while,' he whispered before pulling away.

I'm assuming that my body overruled my brain because the next thing I knew, I was blearily blinking awake as the car's interior lit up. Cal passed in front of the car, lit by the sidelights he'd switched on while dropping me off, and then he was at the passenger door as I tried to shove my brain into gear.

'Hello.' He smiled as I began wrestling a foot into one of my boots. Cal peered around me. 'Try the other one.'

'Huh?'

'The other boot. You're trying to put your left foot into the right boot.'

I sat up and stared down. He was absolutely correct. Excellent. I wasn't trying to impress Cal but neither did I have any desperate inclination to make myself look an idiot either. One out of two wasn't bad. I quickly swapped the boots round and rammed my feet into them before jumping out of the car, his hand at my elbow as I did so.

'I hope the car works out well. Thanks for dinner.'

Cal stood in front of me, causing me to tilt my head back some way in order to meet his eyes.

'You're welcome,' he replied, his voice soft. The main house was some distance away from the garage and had excellent double glazing these days, but I still crept around once it started getting late.

For a moment, I thought he was going to say something else. And for a moment I really wanted him to, despite knowing it would be a bad idea. Despite the fact that I still wasn't sure what I was doing with my own life, let alone with someone else who was responsible for a child. Despite the fact that there was a possibility he might want more from me than it was possible for me to give. For that moment, none of it mattered. All I wanted was for Cal Martin to wrap his arms around me and—

'Lexi?'

'Huh?'

'I said are you OK?

'Oh. No. Yes. I'm fine. Just tired. Long day.' I walked to the now gritted steps that led up to the little flat. As I turned back to say goodbye to Cal, I caught the concern in his look.

'But good. It was a good day too. I did honestly have a great time. Thanks for letting me come and get involved. I really enjoyed it.'

'You know your stuff. I value your input. It was purely a selfish move on my part, taking advantage of your knowledge. It's good to get a second opinion on things sometimes. And' – he took a step nearer – 'if I'm honest, I wanted to spend every moment I could with you.'

'Cal …'

'Lexi, I know you're wary. I'm not sure why exactly at the moment, but I want to find out. I want to find out everything about you. It's been such a long time since I met someone I've felt like that about.'

I felt myself blush and looked down at my feet, unsure of what to say. I could banter with the best of them and swear like a sailor on shore leave if I needed to, but this? This was definitely out of my comfort zone.

Cal hooked a finger under my chin and gently lifted it back so that I was once more looking into those maddeningly hypnotic eyes.

'Are you blushing?'

I pulled a face. 'Of course not,' I said, as my hands went up to my cheeks. 'It's the cold.'

'Fibber.'

Looking at him, he knew he'd caught me out. I lowered my gaze.

'I'm sorry. I'm just not very good at this.'

'And you think I am?'

I looked back up at him. 'You seem to be. Yeah.'

'I'm pretty out of practise.'

'I think you're doing fine.'

'Says the woman whose last boyfriend could whizz her to Monte Carlo for lunch in a jet if it took his fancy?' He was teasing but the comment hit a nerve.

'I wasn't with Marco for his money,' I replied, turning away and taking a step towards the garage. It was by no means the first time I'd had that accusation levelled at me but somehow, coming from Cal, it hurt more. I gave a quick head shake of frustration, the action sending miniature snow flurries from my hat onto my shoulders. 'It's late and it's snowing and I'm cold. You should get home to—'

Cal's hands were gently cupping my face, and suddenly I didn't feel quite so cold any more.

'I'm sorry. I never meant to imply that you were. I haven't known you for very long but I know you're not made that way.' He dipped his head, making me catch his eye. 'Like I said, I'm way out of practise at this.'

'What is this?' I asked, the confusion I felt telling in my voice.

'Honestly? I don't know yet. I really like you. I mean …' He ran a hand across the back of his neck and gave the briefest of smiles. 'I *really* like you. That's something new for me, and right now, I'm not quite sure what to do with it. I don't know how you feel, and I don't think asking you would help as I don't think you're sure of the answer to that question yet either. You may be leaving again, and I have a five-year-old son to consider in anything I do these days. George is already nuts about you, and the last thing I want is for him to get hurt.'

I felt tears sting my eyes unexpectedly. 'You think I would hurt him?'

'No! Not intentionally.' Cal reached over and ran his fingers across the end of my plait, the snowflakes that had settled on it dissipating under his fingers. 'I just meant that if we …' He stopped, scratched his forehead, and looked away. 'George understands as much as he can at his age about why he doesn't have a

109

mum who lives with us, or that he even sees. The last time I went to dinner with someone, George's first question was whether she was going to be his new mummy.'

'Oh. Wow.'

'Yeah. And that was a business dinner so you can imagine how complicated something that wasn't might be.'

I nodded and lifted my head, meeting his eyes. 'Cal, I'm not looking for anything from you. From anyone. I don't do well with relationships, and I'm certainly not going to get involved with someone whose child could get the wrong idea and be upset. So let's just leave it at that, shall we?'

'Are you saying you don't want to see me at all?' Cal frowned at me.

I'd only known him for the shortest of times and yet the thought of not seeing him caused my insides to twist. I'd got used to seeing him. Looked forward to it. The thought of not doing so …

'No! Not at all. I just meant that I think we're better as friends. We know where we are and no one gets hurt. I think it's a good plan.'

'That's not what I meant.'

'Well, it should have been. It's right. For both of us.'

Cal studied me for a moment until I could take the scrutiny no longer.

'You should go before you turn into a full-blown snowman.'

'You're probably right.'

'I'm definitely right. Goodnight, Cal.'

'Night, Lexi.' He leant forward and his warm lips lightly brushed my cheek. 'You're freezing,' he whispered.

I wanted to make some smart-arse comment about that being because I'd been standing out in the snow talking to him but I couldn't. My cheek tingled from his touch and his warm breath close to my ear was sending a whole lot more tingles throughout the rest of me.

'Thanks for today, Lexi.'

'You're welcome.'

Neither of us moved.

'I should go.'

'Yes.'

No!

I raised my gaze and fell into the grey storm of his eyes. For a moment we just stood there. And then he smiled briefly and turned away. As he crunched back to the car, I let out the breath I didn't even realise I'd been holding and made my way up to my room, fumbling in my pocket for the front door key as I did so. The wind whistled through the banisters and I yanked my hat further down as the cold bit into my ears.

'I'll call you tomorrow,' he said as he reached the door to the car. 'Now get inside and get warm. I've kept you out here long enough.'

'I have three brothers who all played rugby. Believe me, I've stood in the cold for worse reasons.'

He grinned and shook his head.

'Drive carefully. And I hope George is fully recovered now.'

'I will, and thanks.' Martha had texted Cal a couple of times in the day saying that George had slept well and it sounded like he was well on the way back to being his perky self. The relief on Cal's face had been obvious but I knew he'd feel better once he'd seen the evidence for himself.

I scooted up the last few stairs and let myself into the flat, tucking myself against the door and waiting as Cal turned over the engine, returned the lights to their main setting, and began to pull out of the drive. He held up a hand in goodbye as he left and I waited until he was out of the farm's drive completely before closing the door.

Chapter 11

I'd just filled Giselle in on the day out with Cal, listening to her disappointment at the fact that there was nothing steamy to report. When I told her about the conversation Cal and I had had as he'd dropped me off, she gave a dramatic sigh.

'Honestly. You two.'

'What? It's the sensible thing to do.'

'Are you going to go through life being sensible now?'

'Yes.'

'Well, that sounds incredibly dull.'

'Maybe. But there's a lot less chance of anyone being hurt.'

'Lexi, everyone gets hurt at times. You heal.'

'I'm not talking about me.'

The sigh came again. 'There were two of you in that relationship, and Marco's a big boy. He can take care of himself. It wasn't just down to you.'

'Part of it was.'

'Even he knew not being able to conceive wasn't your fault. It's not like you chose not to.'

'Sometimes I wonder if he did know that.'

'Of course he did. Why? Did he ever say that?'

'No. I don't know why I even said that. I just ... ugh, it was such a mess, Gis. And the thought of going through all that again with someone else? And someone who also has a young child to think about. I can't even begin to think about how awful that would be.'

'You sound like you're expecting any relationship you have to break down.'

'I do.'

'Wow. Good positive attitude there.'

'It's not that. I'm just not good at them. And relationships do break down, all the time!'

'You know what, if you decide not to take that job you could always go into relationship therapy. Clearly you're a natural.'

'Smart arse.'

'You can't go into something looking at it like that. All you'll do is possibly miss out on something wonderful.'

'I didn't go into things with Marco expecting it to break down but it did anyway, and I very nearly lost one of my closest friends for ever. I did for a while, anyway.'

'But things are good between you now.'

'Yes. But I've been lucky there. I like Cal. I really do. But it's not worth the risk of losing a friendship I already value.'

'Sometimes friends turn into lovers and it works out just perfect.'

'Yes, well, you and Xander are special.'

'So are you. Much more so than you think.'

'Hmm.'

'Don't *hmm* me. Think about it.'

'What?'

'Cal likes you. You like Cal.'

'Which is exactly why I'm not going to mess it up.'

The bell above the shop door tinkled and a group of pensioners began trailing in. The village – with its chocolate-box cottages, pale-stone-walled houses, and tall-spired church along with the assortment of individual shops – made it a prime stop on several tourist routes.

'I've got to go. A coach just dropped off.'

'That's convenient.'

'Convenient but true.'

'Fine.' Giselle laughed. 'But don't think this conversation is over.'

'I can live in hope though, right?'

'You're really quite impossible sometimes.'

'I know, it's why you love me. I'm a challenge. Talk to you later. Love you! Bye.'

'Love you too, and the bump is waving.'

'Bye, bump!' I called before hanging up.

Tucking the phone back into the pocket of my jeans, I sat back and smiled at the customers filing in. A gust of the cold wind they were sheltering from blew across me as the last one closed the door behind them, but the shop was cosy and snug and as I listened to the festive music playing softly, I suddenly realised that I was happier than I'd been in a very long time. It wasn't that I'd been unhappy at work. I'd loved my job. But I hadn't realised how much other things truly meant to me until I was back immersed in them, finally able to appreciate and enjoy them properly.

And now there was something else to appreciate. The addition of Cal Martin and the gorgeous George in my life. If I let myself drift off into la-la land then yes, maybe I did want more from Cal. There was no doubt that just being near the man set off feelings that had been happily lying dormant for quite some time. And I wasn't a nun, for goodness sake. But it was better this way, for everyone.

Cal was lovely. Really lovely. It would have been so easy to take that chance like Giselle said, but I knew from experience getting swept along by things might be romantic but it wasn't always the best option. And letting myself get swept along by Cal Martin was only going to end badly. It was too quick. Too complicated. Too … perfect. And when something's too perfect, it usually has a way of turning around and showing itself to be quite the opposite.

The coach party had cleared out and we'd made some substantial sales. I'd seen various members of my family as they dipped in and out with deliveries, collections, information, and just to say hi and check up on me. Whatever my age, I don't think I was ever going to be thought of as anything but the baby of the family. I had my suspicions that the extra attention was partly because it was such a novelty for me to be home for this length of time.

Everyone knew about the job offer I'd received – and because they were my family, they also knew I wasn't as excited as I might have been. Taking a step down the ladder and a pay cut wasn't ideal but it had taken me months to even get that, so I knew I should be grateful. And I was. So, if I was grateful, why wasn't I excited?

My phone rang, distracting me from my ponderings. Cal's name and a cute picture of him and George lit up on my screen. I smiled without thinking.

'Hi!'

'Hey. Just checking you'd recovered from your long day yesterday and not facedown in the mistletoe.'

'No. That was earlier.'

He laughed and my smile widened.

It felt so right, just chatting with him. Natural. And I knew that if I let it, anything else that followed would feel just the same – so, so right. But it wasn't. Cal was settled here and had a child to consider. I couldn't go mucking about with that, especially if I was going to be leaving again after Christmas. Assuming I took the job. Which I would. Obviously. Most probably.

In the background, I heard George call his dad, and he told him he'd be there in a moment.

'Sorry.'

'Don't worry about it.'

'I had a great day with you yesterday.'

'So you said.'

'I know. I wanted to say it again.' I could hear the smile in his voice.

George called again.

'I have to go. But can you come round tonight? I'll cook.'

I hesitated.

'Just friends. I promise.'

'Look, only my family are supposed to be able to do the whole mind-reading thing. It's in the rules.'

He let out that delicious laugh again. 'The rules?'

'Yes. I'm not going to be able to keep any thoughts to myself if every Tom, Dick, or Harry has access to them.'

'OK. Well, just amend it to add my name. We'll make sure Tom, Dick, and Harry are still excluded.'

'Yeah … I'm not sure adding your name is such a good idea.'

'It's going to happen whether it's in the rules or not.'

I made an "ugh" sort of noise. Cal laughed.

'Just head over whenever you're ready. Although ideally, the sooner the better.'

I could hear that sexy smile in his voice and my insides felt soft and warm. My brain, however, was doing its best to overrule my body but I was really going to have to fight to listen to it.

'I've told George you're coming and he's bouncing with excitement.'

'Oh.' Somewhere in the back of my mind, a balloon deflated sadly.

'But don't worry. I've already explained that it's just like when he has friends over to tea.'

'Oh. Right. Good.' I forced brightness into my voice and the metaphorical balloon made a last ffttt noise and lay limp.

We hung up and I sat for a moment just looking at the phone, but not really seeing it. This was good. Cal was respecting my wishes about just being friends. That should make me happy. So why didn't it?

I blew out a long sigh, grabbed the box of new stock Joe had dropped off earlier, and ripped off the seal. Diving into the new goodies, I forced myself to concentrate on them and the best place to display them, pushing all thoughts of Cal Martin and all the goodies he had to offer, firmly to the back of my mind.

'I'm sorry it's nothing fancy,' Cal said as he placed the plate in front of me.

'If I didn't have to cook it, I'm happy. Thanks so much for this. It smells delicious.' I kind of hoped it didn't taste quite as good as it smelled because then I was not only avoiding getting together with a man who was gorgeous, funny, intelligent, and kind, but also a man who could cook. Honestly. It just wouldn't be fair. Once Cal had sat opposite me, I took a forkful of the parmigiana. And it wasn't as good as it had smelled. It was better. Of course it was. I gave a little groan.

'Is everything all right?' Concern creased the handsome features.

Oh crikey. That was out loud.

'Umm, no. I mean, yes. I … er, just remembered I forgot to do something today at the shop but it's not important. I'll do it tomorrow.' I'd been nervous of the mood lighting originally, but right now I was glad of its help in hiding the flush I could feel on my chest and cheeks at my fib.

We finished the food and having placed the crockery in the dishwasher, Cal set about fiddling with the complicated coffee maker. Taking the drinks, he led the way through to the snug.

'I thought it might be nice to sit in here. But we can go into the living room if you'd prefer?'

I didn't prefer. The room was beautifully cosy with an open fire prepared and ready to be lit, and lined on one entire wall with bookshelves. A squishy sofa was opposite the fire and heavy, padded silk curtains draped at the window, puddling on the floor.

'Silk? With a small child? You're a brave man, Mr Martin.' I smiled, sinking into the softness of the sofa.

His back was to me as he lit the fire, but he threw a look over his shoulder and gave a laugh that did more to warm me than the fire was ever going to do.

'I know. But they looked so good in here, I asked the sellers if they would consider leaving them as I liked them so much. It turned out the owner had made them herself so she was quite flattered apparently. George knows that his fingers and those curtains are not to meet.' He stood up from where the fire had now caught and stretched his back before taking the seat next to me, filling the space. 'He's pretty good, actually.'

'You've obviously taught him well.'

He smiled into his mug. 'Thanks.' His eyes lifted to mine. 'Don't tell anyone, but I'm totally winging this whole parenting thing.'

'No one would ever know.'

He transferred the smile to me, and my traitorous mouth returned it. I took a sip of the rich, dark coffee and listened as the fire crackled and popped. Heavy rain was beating against the silk-covered windows. Cal frowned, his head turning towards the sound.

'It sounds really foul out there.'

'Yes. Not the most pleasant of evenings.' I caught a glance. 'I mean out there. Obviously.'

A small smile curved his mouth. 'You need to relax. I didn't think anything.'

'Oh. Right. Well. Just checking.'

He raised a dark brow.

'So, anyway.'

'That was a smooth change of subject.'

I gave him an eye roll and stuck out my tongue for good measure. 'You said you were winging it, you know, the parenting thing. Xander said something about you doing this on your own since George was born. Is that right?'

Cal took a deep breath.

'I'm sorry. I didn't mean to pry. I forget that you're not originally from here and not used to our nosy ways.'

'No. You're not prying. It's fine. And yes, you're right. George's mother wasn't interested in having anything to do with him.'

I thought about the little boy in his bedroom across the house, and what she was missing out on. Staying silent, I let the decision as to whether to tell me more fall to Cal.

'When Annabel found out she was pregnant, her first thought was to get rid of it. She'd never had a particularly regular cycle so when she didn't come on for a few months, she didn't think anything of it. It wasn't unusual for her. She wasn't sick and she'd been entertaining clients a lot, so the small amount of weight she did put on, she just put down to rich, late meals. By the time she realised she was actually pregnant she'd missed the window to do anything …' he paused '… like she wanted to.'

'But you were obviously happy about the baby?'

The smile that came onto his face as his thoughts returned to that moment would have melted the iciest of hearts. Mine, therefore, was total mush.

'Thrilled to bits!' He slid a half-smile to me. 'Much to my surprise. I'd never considered having kids. It wasn't like I'd had an idyllic childhood, and so I guess I had kind of a skewed vision of what bringing a child into the world meant. I wasn't interested in anything like that. The most in-depth relationship I ever had was with the cars I worked on. I definitely never had any intention of taking on responsibility for a being who relied on me for every single thing.'

I smiled. 'I sense there's a but coming.'

He flashed me a grin. 'But. The moment she told me? All of that went away. Completely. I felt something change, somewhere deep inside me. Like a switch or … I don't know. Maybe a barrier lifting. I'd grown up feeling that the only person I could trust was myself, and that children were so often just pawns, or weapons, in a relationship when it goes wrong. But from that second, I knew that this was really what I wanted. What I'd maybe always wanted but had never accepted and just shut out because I didn't think I had anything to offer a child.'

Without thinking, I laid my hand on his. 'Cal, never say that. You have so very much to offer.'

He moved his hand and mine slipped within it, as his strong, warm fingers closed around it, squeezing mine gently.

'It was a revelation to me. From the moment she told me, I had so much love for this little being who I hadn't even met yet. I never realised I was even capable of feeling that much.'

My throat was too thick to say anything so I returned the hand squeeze and hoped that said everything I couldn't form into words right now.

'Annabel was definitely less than thrilled though,' Cal said, pulling a face. 'She lives a very high-flying lifestyle and she was on the fast track to a huge promotion and partnership. A baby was the last thing on her mind then, or ever.'

'You had no plans for a family together then?'

'No. Not at all. We didn't really have any plans full stop. We met at a function. I'm not big on attending that sort of thing but I had to go to this particular one and she was there, and clearly in her element, unlike me. I think she took pity on me and came over to talk to me.'

Glancing at Cal, I doubted pity had been the main reason for her move but kept quiet and let him continue.

'Annabel's incredibly career driven. She works hard and she likes to enjoy herself too, but her enjoyment was a little more sophisticated in taste than mine. Absolutely loved a dinner party, and admittedly there were always interesting people to talk to, and I did get a certain amount of business from them, which I think was part of her plan. Nothing was ever purely for fun with her, but in a way, I admired that. She'd worked hard to get where she was. Neither one of us was looking for anything deep and meaningful at that point. We were having fun. I found her interesting and intelligent and she liked the fact that I forced her to relax a little sometimes and showed her that not everything had to be about business. That sometimes it was OK just to do something for fun.'

'So finding out she was expecting didn't go down well with her then?'

Cal raised his brows and took a deep breath in, letting it out slowly. 'That,' he said, 'is a bit of an understatement. I understood that it was a shock. It was for both of us, but I thought that once that passed, we'd be able to talk about things. But in the end, I actually started to get a little worried.'

'About what?'

'She made a couple of remarks. They were kind of in passing but something in her tone got me thinking that she might actually do something a bit dodgy. Money can pretty much buy you everything and she had plenty of that.'

'You thought she might go for an illegal abortion?' My stomach twisted at the thought.

'I'm not sure. But I know the thought went through her head because I asked her outright. She'd developed a pretty good poker face over the years, doing negotiations and so on. But I grew up watching expressions and trying to suss out what people were thinking, so I had the edge on her, just through experience. A pregnancy risked putting a dent in her career as far as she was concerned, and right then, her career was the most important thing in Annabel's life.'

'But you managed to convince her to go through with it, obviously.'

'Yes, thank goodness. To be honest, I don't think she really wanted to get rid of it so late. She was just panicking. This baby was ruining everything she had ever worked for, and nothing I said could convince her otherwise. So we came to an agreement that if she went through with it, looked after herself during the pregnancy in order to give the baby its best chance, then once it was born, I'd take full responsibility and she wouldn't have to see either of us again, if she didn't want to. Apparently, she definitely didn't want to and was more than happy to sign on the dotted line. Quite literally. She actually drew up a contract.' He gave a sad smile. 'Because that's what Annabel does. Everything was a transaction. It's just the way she is.' He turned to me. 'You have a strange look on your face.'

I pushed my hand back over my hair, my fringe flopping back into place. 'I'm just trying to get my head around it all. I mean … she wasn't just signing her baby away. She was signing you away too.'

Cal stood and crossed to the fire. He picked up the poker and prodded at the flames, adding another log to them and waiting to make sure it caught before giving another final prod and returning to the sofa.

'You don't have to say any more, Cal,' I said, laying my hand on his as he sat. 'I keep forgetting I'm not at home where we all just blurt and blab all the time.'

He turned his hand and laced his fingers through mine and I did my best to ignore the sparks his touch sent flaming throughout my body.

'I think it's lovely that you all blurt and blab. Feel free to do that as much as you like.' His fingers gently squeezed mine before he released them and returned them to his lap. I felt the withdrawal keenly, and not just in my hand.

'Annabel and I had never been serious. We weren't in love but I cared for her. And I thought she cared for me. I think she did, in her own way. But once the baby arrived in the picture, it was different. She was different. It … and I … were a problem to be solved. A deal to be negotiated.'

'But she knew about your childhood?'

'Vaguely.'

'And she didn't see that what she was doing might be a little insensitive to someone who'd spent their early years the way you had?'

'Are you asking if I felt rejected?'

'Did you?'

He ran his finger along the scar on his hand. 'I'm not going to lie and say it didn't hurt. I know we weren't in love but I did think we'd meant more to each other than a signature on a dotted line and a cease and desist letter. But to be honest, I didn't have too much time to dwell on it. I had the prospect of a new baby to think about – something I literally knew nothing about – and a successful business to run, something that was even more important now that I'd have a child to support. And then I had George. Right there in my arms.'

I kept silent, not knowing what to say. Or even if there was anything I could say. My throat felt raw from the pain this man had suffered in his life, and the way he just boxed it away, almost accepted that that was how things were. That was how people got treated. The knowledge that I'd never once had to feel like that – never been left alone, or made to feel like I had no one, that no one cared – nearly broke me.

'Thankfully, everything went to plan with the delivery. But when it was all over, she wasn't interested in seeing the baby or holding him at all. He had a little cry and then he was just there. Helpless. This tiny little boy. But as far as she was concerned, her side of the deal was complete. Before long she was back on the phone arranging meetings.'

'Wow.'

'Yeah. I know. I, meanwhile, had lost every last shred of machismo and was standing there, holding this tiny little baby and blubbing more than he was!'

My eyes filled as emotion pushed itself up. 'I think that's lovely.'

'I couldn't believe she didn't want anything to do with him.

He was so perfect.' In the low light Cal's eyes were shining with remembered emotion.

'Do you think she'll ever change her mind?'

'She signed a legal document that she wouldn't.'

'But?'

Cal let out a sigh and glanced down at his hands, resting loosely in his lap. 'I'd consider it. She's his mother. But I really don't have any expectations. I sent her a picture of him on his first birthday, you know, in case she was regretting anything. She sent it back saying that she hadn't, and wouldn't, change her mind about anything. She told me that, in reality, she had been nothing more than a surrogate and would appreciate it if I "would desist with contact".' He pulled a face.

I didn't know what to say.

'Does George ever ask where his mum is?'

'He has a couple of times.'

My heart broke at Cal having to have a conversation like that with his son.

'I tried to explain to him that there are all sorts of different families …' He shrugged. 'I had no idea what to say really. I'm not about to tell him at this age flat out that his mother wasn't interested in him. I know all too well what that's like, and what that can do to you. As he gets older, I know he'll have more questions and we can talk about it more then. That's why it's been so good coming here. Everyone just mucks in, and he's treated like one of their own, especially with your family. It's gone a long way to helping him not feel like he's different. And there are a couple of other single parents in the village too. Sasha was really helpful when I first got here. It's sometimes good to know you're not the only one, in any situation.'

'Sasha?'

'Yeah. Quite tall, blonde?'

My mind cast back to the uber-stylish woman with whom Cal been talking at the late-night opening.

'Oh. That's good,' I said brightly, desperately trying to muster more enthusiasm than I actually felt at this knowledge. I really was glad that Cal had support in the village, but it was pretty obvious to anyone that Sasha wasn't just offering this out of the kindness of her heart. Even my brothers had made the odd comment in this respect, and they were normally the last ones to notice anything in that sort of vein. I hadn't realised exactly who'd they been referring to at the time, but putting two and two together now, my maths was perfect.

'Yes. Obviously I'd have loved for George to have a loving mother too – even if we weren't together. He's such a good kid.'

'He's lovely. He kind of stole my heart the moment I looked up from stabbing my thumb with that holly.'

Cal smiled. 'Yeah, he has a knack for that kind of thing. And obviously we come as a package.'

'I don't think anyone could fail to fall in love with him.'

Cal stretched, shadows under his eyes telling tales of late nights catching up with paperwork. 'I agree, but I'm biased. But yeah, I'm not ruling out the possibility of him having a loving mother figure in his life, one day. And believe me, a year ago, I'd have never thought I'd consider that a possibility either. This village definitely has some sort of magical power, I think.'

I shuffled myself on the sofa in my quest to sit up a little from where I'd comfortably slunk down in the cosy warmth of the room. 'It's certainly special, that's for sure.' I smothered a yawn. 'I should get going. I have to be in the shop early to get some orders packed. Claire's been under the weather so I said I'd do it.'

Cal nodded. 'Will you be OK? Driving in this, I mean?' he asked as we headed back to the hallway.

'Yes, fine. It's just a bit of rain,' I said, aware that this was an understatement as the gale outside lashed the downpour against Cal's front door. 'My little car is more than up to this.'

He smiled. 'Text me when you're back.'

'Yes, Mum.'

He shook his head at me and took the woolly hat I had in my hand, pulling it on and down over my eyes.

'That's a good look, I think. Although probably not practical for driving,' I said, laughing as I pushed the brim back up a little.

He grinned. 'See? Smart as well as pretty.'

I felt myself blush, and this time had no chance of using the fire as an excuse.

'It's cute when you blush.'

I felt myself get redder. 'You're not helping.'

'I know. It's actually quite fun.'

'You're meaner than you look.'

He grinned and the full wattage of his smile warmed up places other than my face.

'Thanks for this evening.'

'You're welcome. I enjoyed it.' His eyes locked on to mine, darkening as they held my gaze. 'Very much so,' he added, his voice soft.

For a moment I thought he was going to kiss me. And right then, despite all my reasonings and the knowledge that it would be a Very Bad Thing, I wanted nothing more than for him to do exactly that. The truth was I had the feeling being kissed by Cal Martin would actually be a Very Good Thing.

And then he pulled back. Just a fraction. But the moment was gone.

'You'd better go before that gets any worse.'

I nodded, unable to speak as emotions tossed around me. I adjusted my hat and yanked on the leather gloves dangling from the ends of my sleeves.

'Thanks again,' I forced out eventually, my hand on the catch. 'Hey?'

Glancing back over my shoulder, I saw that Cal had spread his hands. 'We share a meal. You unwittingly initiate me into the blurt and blab club, and I don't even get a goodbye hug?'

I turned more, leaning against the door. 'Initiate you into the blurt and blab club?' I asked, laughing.

'Seriously! What you got tonight is the equivalent of a full confessional in my world.'

'Wow.'

'I know. Believe me, you aren't the only one who's surprised.'

I dropped my gaze, focusing on my boots for a moment as I turned a thought around in my mind.

'Are you sorry you told me?'

'Not for a moment.'

I smiled, happy that he felt relaxed enough to share something with me.

'Don't get used to it though.'

I laughed. 'I don't think there's any danger of me doing that.'

Cal put a hand on the catch, above my shoulder, and his gaze settled on me but I couldn't work out the expression behind it.

'No. I don't suppose there is.'

'Cal—'

A heft of wind slammed into the door I was leaning against, and the hall lit up as lightning split the sky. In the distance, thunder rumbled low and ominous.

'Go on. Get yourself home before that gets any closer. And don't forget to let me know when you're back.'

'It's just down the road!'

Saying nothing, he fixed me with a look.

'OK, OK.'

'Thank you,' he said, pulling me into a hug. I wrapped my arms around him and, just for a moment, enjoyed the feeling of being close to him, his arms holding me tight against his chest. And then it was over.

'Drive carefully,' he said, dropping a swift kiss on my cheek before pulling open the door.

I nodded and called that I would as I ran to the car, unaware if my answer ever got to him or was cast away by the wind.

Pulling open the door, I slid quickly into the seat. I yanked hard on the door to shut it against the wind. In front of me, broken twigs flew up in the air, and soaked leaves whipped up into tiny little whirlwinds on the spot. I watched them for a moment as the headlights shone out and knew that, if I could see them, that was exactly what my emotions would look like right now.

Chapter 12

A few days later, Cal and I were both up to our ears in work and helping out with the arrangements for the Christmas Festival. My family had always been involved in a big way but Cal was kind of new to it all and had got roped in by Sasha to help out with a few chores. We'd chatted a little on WhatsApp and had grabbed a quick conversation or two in the village hall during some preparation time.

I'd found myself looking forward to every meeting, every conversation. And from the look he'd given me the last time he'd seen me enter the hall, I had an idea I wasn't the only one.

As we lay together underneath the big old convertible Mercedes that had served as the basis for Santa's sleigh for longer than I could remember, freezing our respective behinds off, Cal rolled his head towards me.

'I'm out of practice at lying on cold, draughty floors tinkering with cars. I've gone soft. I like a nice warm, clean workshop.'

'Why do you think I've still not got around to doing up Dad's old Jag since he gave it to me?'

'I thought that was because you were never here long enough.'

I swallowed at the accuracy of his statement and tried to ignore it. If I took this job, I'd be away again and the beautiful car that

Dad and I had spent many happy hours together tinkering about with, and driving down country roads on, would sit and continue to rot quietly.

'I'm used to a lot more high-tech than this too. This past year doing bits and bobs back in normal garages was a shock to the system!'

'Then what are we doing lying down here?'

My mouth formed an 'o' of mock shock. 'This is for Santa!'

I saw the smile and then the laugh burst from him as he shook his head. 'You're bloody nuts.'

'Thanks. That might be the nicest thing you've ever said to me.'

Cal laughed even more until a plummy voice cut through our giggles. 'How are you getting on?'

We both looked back up towards the front of the car where a pair of slim legs topped off with five-inch heels stood. From this angle, I could see the red sole.

'Yep. Not too bad, Sasha,' Cal called out.

I widened my eyes. The truth was we hadn't actually done very much at all apart from moan about the cold, and giggle.

Cal held up his finger to his lips, which only made me want to laugh even more. His eyes glittered with humour as he waggled his eyebrows. I snorted as I tried to stifle a giggle and quickly turned it into a cough.

'I think we've isolated what the problem is now,' Cal said, giving a bit more flannel and seeing I was about to lose it, stuck one large hand over my mouth.

'Do you want anything, Cal?' Sasha asked.

I gave my own eyebrow waggle and got a warning glance. I had the full-on giggles now and pulled at his hand but it wasn't moving.

'Ummm, no, I don't think so. But thanks.'

We stayed still momentarily, and then Cal picked up a spanner and knocked on the chassis a couple of times with it. Tears streamed down the side of my face. The red-soled shoes turned and began click-clacking across the concrete that separated the barn where the Merc lived from the village hall where all the other prep was taking place. I managed to peel a couple of fingers off my face.

'If you don't move your hand, it's in dire risk of getting something other than grease on it!'

Cal burst out laughing again but removed his hand.

I fished around in the pocket of my overalls and found a tissue to blow my nose on. 'Why does laughing make your nose run?'

Cal grinned and shook his head.

'Well, I guess we'd better fix this now you've just told Sasha we've isolated the problem.'

His grin turned into a chuckle.

'Oh wait. I think I know what the problem is.'

Cal turned to me as I made my declaration. Taking the spanner he'd used earlier, I tapped the same spot on the chassis. 'Yep, that's definitely it.'

'Give me that.' He laughed, reaching over to grab it back as I tried to hold it out of reach. But Cal was bigger than me and his fingers caught it easily. However, in doing so, his body was now rammed up against mine in the close confines under the car, our faces almost touching.

'Have dinner with me tomorrow.'

'What?' I croaked, my mouth feeling dry as the sandpaper I'd been using earlier to deal with some rust.

'Dinner. Tomorrow. You and me.'

'Why?'

One side of that tempting mouth curved up. 'Because we both need to eat. Because I want you to. And because I think you want to as well.'

Was I really that obvious?

'But you said …'

'I know. I know what I said but … it's just dinner.'

Was it?

'OK.'

Uh-oh.

'Good. Now come on. Let's get this bloody thing sorted before bits freeze and drop off.'

'Off the car or you?'

'Both.'

I reached for the lamp to focus on the area we were working on. 'Well, if that happens, frankly Sasha's welcome to you.'

The thought of dinner with this man scared and excited me. In fact, it scared me just how much it excited me but right now – freezing my backside off but warmed by his laughter – I knew there was no place I'd rather be.

'What about this one?' Giselle was holding up a red dress for me to consider. I'd called an Emergency Wardrobe Meeting following Cal's invitation, deciding I needed professional help in finding the right outfit for tonight's dinner.

'That's nice,' Xander offered through a mouthful of biscuit from his slumped position on an oversized beanbag.

'You said that about the last three,' I said.

He shrugged. Well, as much as you can shrug ensconced in such a chair. 'They were.'

'I don't want "nice".'

'What do you want?' He frowned at me.

Giselle was hanging the dress back up. 'She'll know it when she sees it,' she said confidently.

I flopped onto the floor beside Xander and took a biscuit from the packet. 'Don't bet on it.'

Giselle turned and folded her arms at us. 'Stuffing biscuits before your dinner isn't something I'd advise.'

I took another one and bit off a chunk. 'She's going to make such a great mum. She already has all the catchphrases perfect.'

Xander and I were grinning like we were five years old again, and Giselle was doing her utmost not to join us.

'Honestly,' she said, flicking through my wardrobe, 'I don't know why I bother.'

'Oop! See, there's another one!'

'Oh, be quiet, you. Now what about this?'

'God, no!'

'Why? It's lovely.'

'It is. On the right occasion. Definitely not this occasion.'

'Why not?'

'Way too much boobage.'

Xander snorted. 'You wish.'

I hit him with the biscuits.

'Ohh!' Giselle held the dress out in front of her a little more. 'Oh yes. You're right. I didn't realise it was the same one. Looks different on the hanger.'

'Probably not that much different. That hanger's got about as much cleavage as Lexi has.'

Like having three brothers wasn't enough. I had to have an honorary one too.

'Don't be so rude!' Giselle actually wagged her finger at him, pulling off the gesture without looking ridiculous. 'She's got just the right amount for her frame and in this dress with the right bra … well! Let's just say Cal wouldn't be able to concentrate.'

'Isn't that what you want? For him to fall down with his tongue lolling out?'

'What an attractive picture you paint. And no. That isn't what I want. I want him to be able to sit and talk to me. Properly.'

Xander blew out a dramatic sigh. 'Why do girls always want to talk so much?'

'Here,' I said, handing him the remote, 'put some cartoons on and amuse yourself.'

He pulled a face, stuck out his tongue, and began channel surfing.

'This!' Giselle exclaimed from the depths of my wardrobe. 'Now, this is perfect!' I studied the midnight-blue boat-neck dress

133

with its full circle skirt. It was pretty but classic. Elegant but not dramatic.

'I think you might be right.'

A mumbled 'Hallelujah!' drifted over from Xander's direction.

Cal had wanted to pick me up but I'd decided it might feel like less of a date if I just met him at the pub. I wasn't actually sure if this was a date and had sort of forgotten to ask. Hence the hoo-ha with the wardrobe choices. He'd booked a table for us in the adjoining restaurant for half seven and I was now there ten minutes early, trying to ignore the interested glances I could feel being thrown my way.

Maybe dinner out of town would have been better. I'd dealt with this, and a whole lot more, but Cal was still relatively new here and from what I heard, he wasn't big on dinners for two with anyone other than George. This was fresh fodder for the gossip machine and I worried how Cal might feel about that.

Straightening my back, and smoothing down my dress, I walked to the bar. I'd done the same thing plenty of times before over the years but rarely in a dress. It felt different. I felt different. The dress was beautiful and I really did love it but I'd spent most of my life either in jeans or overalls and that was what I was used to. When I put my team overalls or shirt on, I knew what I was doing. Who I was. This was a whole new experience and I was way out of my comfort zone.

But there was a part of me that felt excited by that. By all of this. I was still doing my best not to totally fall for Cal Martin but when he looked at me and the rest of the world went into soft focus, it felt right. Even if it was wrong. And OK, so that feeling never lasted long. I was, after all, much better at reality than fantasy. But a little bit now and then couldn't hurt, could it? And choosing this dress for tonight, saying yes to dinner, even as friends, gave me that feeling again.

I'd actually loved putting on this dress and may even have done a twirl or two in the privacy of my own room. Afterwards, I'd popped into the house to see Mum and check I looked OK and she'd burst into tears. Not helpful to my whirling, contradictory thoughts but kind of lovely.

'Wow!'

I hadn't seen Cal when I'd arrived and so had ordered an orange juice while I waited. I looked up and saw an expression of appreciation on his face.

'You look amazing.' He bent and placed the lightest of kisses on my cheek as a small smile began to tug at one corner of his mouth. 'I don't think I've ever seen you in a dress before.'

'It's not really my thing.' My hands went to smooth the skirt again.

Cal caught my hand, stopping the nervous motion. 'It really should be. You look stunning!'

I fiddled with my bag for a moment, keeping my eyes lowered. However much I wanted to be like Giselle and laugh prettily, accepting the compliment with the grace it deserved, I had no idea how to do that.

'It really is so cute when you blush.' Cal's voice was low and close to me.

I twiddled the chain of my bag. 'It'd be easier on both of us if you'd stop saying things like that.'

'I know.'

Even without looking I could hear the teasing smile in his voice.

'OK. I apologise for making you blush but I don't apologise for the compliment. Expect more.'

I risked a glance up to find him smiling down at me, warmth – and possibly something else I wasn't going to even think about right now – dancing in those storm-grey eyes.

'Let me get you a drink.'

'I have one, thank you.'

'You do?'

'Yes. I got here a little early. I didn't know what you might want so I didn't get yours I'm afraid … and now I feel really rude. Oh God, I'm bad at this. I'm used to getting rounds in.'

Cal chuckled. 'I love your femininity.'

I clonked him on the arm with my feminine bag.

'Anyway, you're not supposed to get mine. I'm supposed to get them.'

'You do know what year it is, don't you? A woman can buy a man a drink.'

'I know, I know. I didn't mean it like that.' He rubbed a hand over his freshly shaven jaw.

'Besides, this isn't a date anyway.' I fiddled with the straw in my drink for a moment. 'Is it?'

Cal didn't answer.

'I'd rather you just be yourself,' I said, feeling the need to fill the silence between us.

Cal gave me a long look. 'Good advice.' He lifted the non-alcoholic beer he'd ordered from the bar and raised a quizzical brow. 'I'm not sure why, but you seem nervous tonight. More so than you did the other night.' He bent close to me. 'Don't worry. I promise I'm not going to do anything you don't want me to.' The uninvited thoughts of where that statement took me caused another rush of heat to my chest and face. 'I said friends, and I meant it. So perhaps we should both just be ourselves?' he finished.

I took a sip. 'In that case, I need to nip home and put my jeans on.'

Cal grinned. 'Don't you dare! I love this look. I'm making the most of it.'

'That might be a good idea because it's unlikely you'll see it again for a while.'

He slanted his eyes towards me. 'You decided to take the job.'

'What? No … I … I mean. Yes, I probably will but I meant about the dress. I don't tend to wear them very often.'

'Maybe you should.' Cal held me in that gaze again and the hint of a smile teased the corners of his mouth. 'Maybe you should try something different. You might find it suits you.'

With some effort, I broke the gaze. 'The last time I tried something different it didn't end well, so I think probably I'm best at sticking with what I know.'

'Then how you do ever discover new things?'

'New things can be overrated in my opinion.'

He shook his head, the smile still in place as he steered me carefully away from a bar that was beginning to get busier and louder, his arm protectively blocking me from any bumps or shuffles.

'I think you like wearing that dress.'

'Oh pfftt.'

His smile broke into a grin. 'Now I definitely know I'm right.'

'Cal, your table's ready.' With perfect timing, the owner appeared through the restaurant door, easily spotting Cal thanks to his height and size among the crowd.

'Ready?' Cal asked.

I nodded and he indicated for me to go first, his hand resting ever so gently on the small of my back as we were shown to the table.

'Carly will be with you in just a moment.' The owner smiled at us both and headed off into the kitchen.

'Can I say – as a friend – you really do look beautiful,' Cal said, his eyes on me as he took his seat.

I couldn't help the smile that formed, both at the tease and at the compliment. It was a long time since I'd felt, or been told, I looked beautiful.

'Thanks. You look … good too.' I gave myself a mental kick at the lameness of my repartee. The truth was, Cal always looked good. Not in a spend hours in front of the mirror way, just in a natural, effortless way. I, on the other hand, had indeed spent hours in front of the mirror and had extra help in the form of Giselle.

'I mean, not that you don't always look lovely, but—'

'It's fine, Cal. I know I don't do the whole hair and make-up thing a lot.'

'You look lovely, with or without.'

Flicking him a slightly awkward smile, I turned my attention to faffing with my napkin.

'Have you decided what you'd like?' The waitress was keen, young, pretty, and smiling full wattage at Cal. I got the distinct feeling she wished she were on his menu.

'To be honest, we haven't had a chance to look yet.' He smiled disarmingly, charming her. 'Could you give us a few more minutes?'

'Of course, sir.' She flashed him a big smile, turned, and walked off, her hips swaying a little more than they had on the way over.

'Perhaps we should choose,' I said.

Cal looked at me for a moment. I could see he'd figured out that there was something else going on here, something unsaid. But we both knew the waitress would be back shortly, interrupting the conversation flow again.

'Yes. Of course. You're right. Do you know what you're having?'

I scanned the menu and made my choice. Indecision when it came to food wasn't a problem I ever experienced.

'Yep.'

'Please tell me it's not salad.'

'OK. It's not salad.'

'But is it actually salad?'

'No. Of course not. It's bloody freezing out there. Why would I be ordering salad with only a few weeks until Christmas?'

'It's not exactly unknown for a lot of women to order salad, even when they don't need to.' He pulled a face that indicated he wished he'd never started this conversation.

'Oh. I see. Yes. Well, each to their own I guess. Personally, in this weather I want good old rib-sticking, stodgy, warming goodness. Not a couple of lettuce leaves and a pretty radish, however good it might be for me.'

Cal grinned. 'I'm glad to hear it.'

'You might not be, when you have to try and get me to move later.'

'I'm sure we can come up with a solution.'

The waitress was soon back, taking our orders on an electronic tablet and checking that we were OK for drinks, suggesting a wine we might like. I was definitely not going to drink anything. I needed a clear head so that I could avoid doing something stupid, like say, kissing Cal Martin because for once I felt pretty and he'd told me I looked beautiful. And kissing Cal Martin was, as I had already told myself, a bad idea. As would be alcohol.

'I'll have a large white wine, please.'

Oh well. It's the thought that counts, right?

'And for you, sir?'

'Mineral water, please. Still. Thanks.'

'Great. I'll be back in just a moment with those.'

Silence settled over the table momentarily.

'George was really excited about going over to Dan and Claire's tonight. It was kind of them to invite him.'

I gave a wave of my hand. 'They love it. All the kids love going to their place, especially in the summer with that fantastic tree house he built.'

Cal fiddled with the butter knife for a second. 'I heard about the miscarriage. It's heartbreaking the problems they've had. They're so great with the children.'

I looked off to where the waitress was setting up our drinks on a tray, my stomach twisting a little at Cal's comment.

My face obviously twisted a little too.

'Should I have not said anything?' He let out a breath. 'I'm sorry. I shouldn't have ...'

'It's OK.' I turned back to him and gave a practised smile as the waitress arrived with our drinks order. 'You're right. It is heartbreaking.'

I took a sip of the cool, crisp wine, its fruity notes zinging around my taste buds, before replacing the glass on the table. For some reason, my nerves had me wanting to down the whole glass and order another before the waitress had even turned on her heel. Cal was still looking uncomfortable at the thought of having put his foot in something. He lifted his gaze and held me in it.

'I can hold a meeting with anyone and not be fazed. Make deals for cars worth hundreds of thousands but I don't feel like I'm getting things right with you this evening. Which is kind of weird because normally I feel completely relaxed with you, and I thought you did with me too. So, I'm guessing between the other night and this evening, something's changed. Any chance you want to share what that is with me?' His hand left the fork he'd been worrying and he sat up a little straighter.

'It's nothing. Really.' I could see that he didn't believe me. I wasn't a good liar and normally I didn't care. It wasn't a skill I was interested in honing, but right now it would have been easier if Cal Martin couldn't see straight through me.

'If it's nothing, then why do you look so sad?'

What I really wanted to say was that none of this was fair. Not on him or me. It wasn't fair that I'd finally met a man I felt so comfortable with, could be myself with, had a tonne in common with, and who actually liked me – and I still couldn't have him.

'Dan told me himself about everything, you know. I'm not gossiping. Believe me. That's definitely not my style.'

My eyes widened. 'Oh goodness, no. I didn't think you were. Although you must have got used to the idea it's hard to keep anything a secret here. I assume you know the fact that we're friends – and more than, according to some – is already a favourite topic of conversation in the village. By tomorrow, they'll know exactly what we ate tonight.'

'Is that true?' Cal looked a little unsure.

I gave a little head wobble. 'For the most part, yes. It's a great village. But it's shit at keeping secrets and great at gossip, even though that gossip generally isn't unkind.'

'Right.'

'You're putting the house on the market tomorrow, aren't you?'

Cal let out a laugh, and his beautiful smile lifted the concern from his face. 'Not a chance.'

'OK. Don't say I didn't warn you.'

'So, hypothetically, if I were to lean across right now and kiss you, you're saying that might be headline news tomorrow?'

I tried not to smile. 'I'm pretty sure that might even make the late edition.'

Hypothetically, I didn't give a monkey's and right now I wanted nothing more than for him to follow through. I stole a look at him through my lashes as he glanced at the screen on his phone. He'd already apologised for having it out but he had a small child at home and I understood. Running a hand around the back of his collar, he then stretched his neck, tension showing on his face.

I shouldn't have said yes to dinner. We were too close. This was too close to what each of us wanted it to be, and what both of us knew couldn't be.

Chapter 13

I craned my neck around Cal. Where the heck was our food? I desperately needed a distraction from those eyes and that body. I could see him looking at me as I kept my eyes on my wine glass. He knew I wasn't as calm as I looked. Which in truth probably wasn't very. He knew something was up, and somehow he also knew that trying to force it out of me was probably the worst thing he could do. I'd dated Marco for almost two years and he never did figure that out.

'So, this car of yours we were talking about? Have you had a chance to do much work on it since you've been home?'

I shook my head, the relief of being back on a topic I was comfortable with showing on my face, if the twitch of Cal's dark brow was anything to go by.

'No, unfortunately. Between helping out with the festival stuff, plus the upsurge in orders we've had since the shop got featured in that glossy mag and then several influencers picking up on it, there just hasn't been the time. It's kind of crazy how much sway these things can have, isn't it?'

He nodded as he took a sip from his mineral water.

'When I have had the chance to do a bit, it's been so damn cold in the barn. Like you said the other night, I've gone soft too.'

'I don't think anyone could accuse you of being soft, Lexi.'

I accepted that. It was, after all, the face I'd been putting out to the world for most of my life. Acting like nothing bothered me. Only my family and close friends knew the truth.

'Although, I'm pretty sure that's all a front. I don't think anyone who's as tough as you make out you are goes around mending teddy bears and taking care of people the way you do.'

'That's just being a nice person.'

'No, I think it's being a softie.'

My mouth made an 'o' shape. 'Don't you dare go spreading rumours like that about me!'

He laughed and I felt it wrap itself around me, warm and comforting, just like the scarf I'd tied on George's Bear the first time I'd met them.

'What rumour? That you're a marshmallow inside?' His mouth was serious but there was humour in the eyes. That and a shadow of wariness.

'Anyway, I'm not sure I'm going to be able to finish getting it ready to take Dad out in as a surprise at Christmas like I planned. I might have to think of something else and make that a birthday present.' Although I knew that once I took this job, being home would be more infrequent. It was easier to rent a flat nearer the factory, so living at home, or even somewhere in the village, was going to involve a killer of a commute. And once the season kicked in, I'd be abroad a lot. 'To be honest, I might have to look into paying someone to do it. At least then Dad could take it out for me occasionally, get some use out of it instead of it sitting there looking sad and unloved.'

'We could take it over to my workshop. I've just shipped out an order so I've got some space at the moment. It's warm and dry and you can come and do stuff on it as and when you get the time. But if you're OK with it, I can get the guys to do a bit of work on it too so that you meet your Christmas deadline.'

'Oh, Cal, that's really lovely of you. But I couldn't ask—'

'You didn't ask,' he pointed out. 'I offered.'

'Yes, but …' It was a brilliant offer and really would help. But I didn't feel right accepting it. I'd already got to know Cal's generous nature firsthand, and from what my family and friends had told me. I knew he'd end up doing a lot more than just provide a warm space to work. But Dad would be so thrilled to see his car restored back to glory again …

'Whatever it is you're thinking, don't. There's no caveat. I'm not expecting anything. It's just a favour, and frankly, it hurts me to see the poor old thing sat there when it could be a real beauty.'

'I know. It's sad.'

'Good. That's decided then. I can send the truck over tomorrow. Do you want your dad to not know it's happening? If so, just let me know when's a good time.'

Oh God. He was so nice. What was I doing? I nodded, trying to keep the smile on my face but having the distinct feeling it was slipping. Cal's eyes registered it all and I could see my own confusion reflected back at me.

'Cal, I—'

With perfect timing, our food arrived, looking delicious, and the needs of my stomach overtook everything else. Some people couldn't eat when they were nervous but not me. It could have been a hangover of my mum being the greatest at providing comforting, delicious food at such times. We'd all come home at various times, having fallen out with friends, broken up with girlfriends or boyfriends. Mum had always been there with a warming stew and hunks of homemade bread, the smells encompassing us and the whole experience as much of a comforting hug as the ones Mum and Dad both gave us.

The food this evening was great – the local chef had been the recipient of several awards – but Mum's comforting kitchen was hard to beat. Although, I had a feeling I might be taking advantage of that in the coming days.

Over dinner, the conversation turned to lighter subjects, and

I went between feeling relieved that I was getting to spend more time with Cal to just wanting to get the conversation I knew I needed to have with him over and done with. It had been a long time since I'd felt so comfortable with a man like this, a man who actually remembered I was a woman, and certainly made me feel like one in a whole bunch of different ways.

And of course, there was little George. Family had always been important to me. Coming home had reminded me just how much, and now here was this big, gorgeous man apparently willing to consider letting me be a part of his ready-made one. But the problem was that, from what he'd said the other night, there was every chance he might want more than that. More than I might ever be able to give him.

We'd had our desserts and now sat savouring the rich, dark coffee.

'You know I'd never want do anything to hurt you or George, don't you?'

Cal sat back, his stormy grey eyes fixing on me with an expression I couldn't read. 'That sounds ominous.'

'I just …' I cleared my throat a little and tried again. 'I just don't think us … seeing each other quite so often is such a good idea.'

The competent explanation of the situation I'd been forming completely disappeared from my head the moment Cal had looked at me.

'What's going on, Lexi?' Cal's voice was soft and enquiring, and against my better judgement – but unable to stop myself – I raised my gaze to meet his.

'I can't do this,' I said simply, swallowing hard to try and hold back the tears I could feel threatening.

'Do what, exactly?'

'You. Me. Us.'

'I thought we'd agreed that there was no "us" in that sense of the word.'

'There isn't.'

'OK. Then I'm confused.'

'I can't do this. I can't be this close a friend with you.'

'Did I do something?' He looked genuinely concerned.

'No.' I let out a sad laugh. 'God. No. Not at all. In fact, you're very lovely.'

He spread his hands. 'Still confused.'

I rubbed my hands over my face, remembering too late that I was wearing make-up and hoping that I didn't now resemble Coco the Clown.

'Is this anything to do with the gossip you mentioned earlier?'

'Sort of. But not in the way you think.'

'I'm not sure what I think right now. OK, but you have plenty of male friends, right?'

'I do.'

'But suddenly I'm an exception.'

He definitely was, but not in the way he was thinking.

'In this case, yes.'

'Right,' he said simply, and took a sip of his water, unlocking his gaze for a moment.

A muscle flickered in his jaw, giving away the fact that he wasn't quite as collected as he seemed. I took the opportunity to take a few deep, calming breaths and tried to remember the cool, sensible reasoning I'd been planning throughout dessert to lay out to him by way of an explanation.

'Is that it, or do I get some enlightenment as to this sudden change of heart?'

'Cal, please don't be upset.'

He gave me a look that told me I was on a losing track with that particular hope.

'It's for the best, really.'

'That's still not an explanation.'

'No … I know. I'm … I think it's better this way.'

'That's a repeat of what you just said, but in different words.'

146

His tone was tense and I could feel my neck aching as I reacted to the stress now flooding my body.

I let out a sigh. 'I really like you, and I'm already head over heels for your son.'

Cal remained silent, but his expression showed the confusion my apparently contradictory statement caused.

'The things you were talking about the other night. What you're looking for in the future for you and George …'

Cal reached across and gently took hold of my hands, which at this point were busy screwing and unscrewing a napkin into a state of oblivion. 'Oh, Lexi. That's just a someday scenario.' He gave me one of those devastatingly dangerous and incredibly sexy half-smiles. 'This is clearly the downside of feeling able to tell you anything. There are obviously things I should keep to myself for a little longer.'

'No. It's not that. I think it is lovely that you felt you could say those things to me. In fact, it's good to know that sort of stuff now. It's good to know things now before we're both more … invested in the friendship.'

Cal sat up a little more and removed his hands. He didn't snatch them but there was a definite drawing away, and I could hardly blame him. 'I'm already invested and, stupidly, I thought you were too.'

'I am, Cal. Please don't be upset. I …' Panic built inside me as I felt my chest tighten and tears begin to blur my vision. 'I'm doing what I need to do for both of us. I'm not good at any of this stuff and I've tried to handle it like a normal person and it's too hard, OK? I can't do it. So I have to do it in my own way before anyone gets hurt.'

He flashed me a look and I knew I was already too late on that front. I could only hope that he didn't feel anywhere near as awful as I did.

'I think I deserve to know what I did, Lexi.'

'I already told you – you didn't do anything. It's me.'

'"It's not you, it's me"? Really? Surely we both deserve better than that.'

I gave him a glance under my lashes, feeling uncomfortable and miserable. It didn't look like anyone was eavesdropping. Luckily, the tables weren't crammed together so that you couldn't help but overhear conversations. But I still knew I needed to get out of here as soon as possible.

'Please, Cal,' I said, steeling myself. There was no way I was going to cry in the restaurant. We were still under the radar at the moment but that would put us firmly in the crosshairs. 'As a friend, can you just accept that I can't do this right now? It's not right for me, and it's definitely not right for you and George.'

'Oh. So, we are still friends?' His voice was low but his tone had more than a hint of sarcasm streaking through it.

'Of course. If you can do that. It'd make things easier over Christmas at least. It's hard not to bump into people in this village, especially at this time of the year and with the children being such good friends. I just can't spend time with you. Like this.' I knew it was a lame explanation and Cal's expression showed he was of the same opinion. 'I really would like to be friends still, but I can see it's a big ask so I'll leave that decision up to you. Thanks for dinner.' I began pulling my purse from my bag.

'What are you doing?' Cal asked.

'Leaving some money for the bill.'

'Don't. I asked you to dinner and have no intention of using that money even if you leave it.'

'Yes. But—'

'I said I've got it, Lexi.' His tone was definite.

I gave a brief nod and then left the table in as understated a manner as possible. I was in no doubt the news that our what-ever-people-had-labelled-it was already on the rocks would soon be round the village, but I was still prepared to do what I could in the meantime to avoid drawing any more attention.

I was pretty sure most people in the village already thought

I was kind of rubbish when it came to relationships. I'd had a couple of longer term relationships that had fizzled into nothing and more recently I'd been on the verge of a much sought after 'celebrity lifestyle' and I'd chosen to hand it back.

There were still those in the village who couldn't understand my choice. I knew that. There'd been sympathetic looks and whispers that perhaps Marco had let his eye wander, and photographs of him hanging out with beautiful women at the races didn't do anything but fan the flames. He'd thought it was amusing. It was one of many points we'd differed on by then.

I'd desperately wanted to dispel the rumours. Marco and I might not have been talking at that point, but I still hated that people might unjustifiably be thinking badly of him. The paparazzi had intruded into our relationship from the beginning, and it had been overwhelming and a little scary. But the one thing Marco had taught me was to just ignore them. Never respond. They'd only twist what you said to make better copy anyway, he said, so I'd kept quiet and hated it.

All in all, my history left people wondering what it was about me that meant I couldn't seem to make things work when it came to relationships. My parents were still as happy as ever, and all my brothers had now married and settled. It was just me who couldn't seem to get it all figured out. And now, once again, from the outside, all people would see was me stepping away from someone who seemed perfect. The trouble this time was that he seemed pretty damn perfect to me too. Almost.

Cal remained at the table, his expression unreadable as I pushed my chair back. I turned and walked through the restaurant, stopping at the coat rack and lifting my long bottle-green wool coat off a peg. I missed the armhole on the first go, snagging it on the second attempt before starting on the second one.

'Here, let me.' Cal's deep voice was behind me, and I felt him close by as he held my coat and guided my arm into it. His hands went to the belt that hung loose and then settled on my hips, turning me slowly to face him. He didn't meet my eyes, instead focusing on the belt, ensuring the coat was wrapped around me before he tied and knotted the belt.

'Too tight?'

I shook my head. Why did he have to follow me? I'd had the strength to walk away from the first man who had made me happy in the way I now knew I should feel. And now here he was. Way too close.

'I have to—'

He wrapped his arms around me and moved, so that he could see my face. 'Lexi, you've never seemed the complicated type.'

I shook my head. I really wasn't. But I did have a past that I couldn't help but let affect my future. It was all intertwined and always would be. Did that make me complicated?

'I'm not. Really. I promise.'

'I don't know what's going on with you, but I want to, Lexi,' Cal whispered, his eyes meeting mine and holding me as firmly as the hands that now rested on my waist. 'I think we both know I want so much more than that.'

'I can't give you everything you want.' My voice was supposed to come out controlled and calm. Instead, there was a hint of wobble and it finally cracked on the last word.

Cal looked down at me, studying me almost, it seemed. 'I don't want to do this with an audience.' He took my hand and led me out of the pub, giving the landlord a raised hand in acknowledgement as we left. The car park had been gritted but I kept my head down, concentrating on my steps in the heels that I wore. Cal unlocked the car and let me in before striding round the other side and turning over the engine. As he got in, he began pressing the buttons for the heated seats before reaching for my hands, which were folded on my lap.

'Lexi. Even as a friend you've already given me more than I ever thought I'd find. Or ever allow myself to find. You're beautiful and intelligent and have the best comebacks I've ever heard. Plus, you share my interests, not to mention having the complete adoration of my son. All that is so much more than I ever thought I'd find, and it's more than enough. Whatever it is you think you're lacking, you're not. I care about you. Very much.'

'I care about you too.'

'So … that's good then. And I definitely don't think giving up is the answer. We have the beginnings of something great here. I know that. And I think you do too.'

I nodded and a sad, heartbroken tear released itself down my cheek. Cal's hand, warm and gentle, brushed it away.

'Don't cry, Lexi. Please. We'll work it out.'

I carefully wrapped my fingers around his hand and lowered it from my cheek.

'It's not something that can be worked out, Cal. I'm sorry.'

He watched me for a moment, before sitting back in his seat.

'There are few things that can't be worked out. If people really want them.'

'And what if the fact that you really want something is the actual problem?'

He caught my chin with the side of his finger. 'That's not a problem, so far as I can see.'

'But that's it. You don't see. But you would in time.'

'Lexi, I—'

'I'll be taking this job next year and I'd hardly see you. I'd hardly see George. How's that going to go down?'

'Then we'll come up to you on holidays and spend the evenings together. You'll get some holidays. We'll work it out. So far I'm not seeing anything insurmountable. And certainly nothing worth throwing a connection like this away over.'

'Cal, I couldn't make a relationship work when the man was right there beside me! How much more difficult is it going to be when I'm thousands of miles away half the time?'

'It would be different. I'm not Marco Benoit, if that's who you're talking about.'

'It's not just him. I'm just not good relationships.'

'Maybe because you never give them a chance? You're running away before I've even got to ask you out properly this time!'

'I have given it a chance. For God's sake, I was going to marry Marco! Don't you think that's giving something a chance? I don't want to go through that again! And I'm not prepared to put you or your son through something that's avoidable.'

'Like I said, I'm not Marco. And let me worry about what is and isn't good for George.' His jaw was set. I knew what I needed to do but I hadn't expected Cal to fight for me.

'You told Dan you'd like a family.' I unloaded my biggest weapon.

'I have George. And yes, in the future, I think it would be nice for him to have some siblings.'

'I can't give you that.'

'Lexi' – he shook his head – 'I didn't mean tomorrow. It was an "in the future possibly" scenario. We were just talking.'

'There is no "possibly" for me. Well, very little chance anyway.'

Cal's face was serious in the low light of the cloud-filtered moonlight through the car windows. 'What do you mean?'

There was something about Cal that would have made it easy to tell him everything. That in itself was pretty unusual for me, and my subconscious prodded me, rolling its eyes at me, knowing exactly what was going to happen, despite all the above.

'I … nothing exactly. I just meant that … I kind of live a very peripatetic lifestyle and it doesn't leave a lot of space for … other things.' I turned away from those searching eyes and drew some beads of window condensation together with my finger, hiding my face as Cal considered my vague answer. Glancing back, I could tell he knew I was holding back, but I prayed that, for now at least, he'd do an Elsa and just let it go.

But this was Cal Martin. The man who'd been kicked out on to the streets at eighteen, and built up a multimillion-pound business. The man who'd taken on a newborn baby and raised him into a wonderful, kind, funny child with very little help. Of course he wasn't going to let it go. But I was exhausted and I didn't want to do this any more.

'I'd like to go home now. I can just call a taxi if—'

'No. I'll take you.'

I risked a look up at him as he reached over and turned the key. His neck muscles were corded with tension and his mouth was set in a line. I'd hurt him and I couldn't even give him the whole explanation as to why. I was surprised he wasn't just tossing me out into the cold, sleeting night.

We drove home in an atmosphere so thick you'd have needed a chainsaw to get through it, and I'd never been happier to see my little flat, the lamp I'd left on shining in the window, white fairy lights twinkling a pretty welcome.

'Thank you,' I said, my hand already pulling the catch.

'Wait. I'll get that,' he said, reaching for his own, but I was already half out of the car.

'I …' I looked back up. His hands were on the wheel, the muscles in them as tight as the rest of him. What did I say? What was there to say?

'Thanks for the lift,' I repeated, just for something to fill the silence.

He nodded briefly, keeping his eyes front. I deserved that. I'd broken a friendship and rejected the possibility of having something more, all without giving the man in question any sort of decent explanation.

Tiny flakes of snow were just starting to drift lazily down as I ran up the stairs to my flat faster than I ever though I could move in heels. I didn't turn as I got to the top. I didn't want to see him drive off. Leaving. Instead, I just ran inside, pushed the door closed, and leant on it. The low rumble of the engine idled for a few moments before taking the strain, and driving off. Waiting until I was safely back inside, he'd left, just as I'd wanted him to. The sound quickly got fainter and I felt like a piece of me had gone with it.

Sliding down the door, I wrapped my coat tighter around me, as though trying to warm away the misery I now felt in my very bones, as I thought about the wonderful man and child I'd just successfully pushed away. It was what I wanted, wasn't it? No more complications? Avoid the heartache – that had been the plan. So if it was such a great plan, why did I feel worse now than I ever had before?

I kicked off my shoes and slowly made my way over to my bed. Lying down, I felt tears tickle my ears as they ran horizontally down my temples. I sprawled out on my back and gave in to the knowledge that the fledgling life I'd started building here – with my family, friends, and with Cal and George – wasn't meant to be. I should have learned by now.

The whole settling down thing wasn't for me. I'd tried once before and it had ended painfully, not to mention publicly. What made me think this time would be any different? It wasn't meant for me. It was meant for people like Giselle and Xander, Mum and Dad, and Dan and Claire. But the universe had other ideas for me apparently. Stick to what you're best at, Lexi, it said. PS: this isn't it.

I swallowed a hiccup and laid a hand on my aching ribs as the sobs subsided and I became aware of a scratching noise at the door. Rolling my legs over the side of the bed, I pulled myself up like a marionette that needed restringing and padded over to the door, being careful to avoid even the minutest glance in the antique framed leaner mirror as I passed. I had a pretty good idea of just how awful I looked right now without adding definitive confirmation.

After unlocking the door, I peered out. Apollo was sat under the little porch roof staring up at me as fine snow fell silently around.

'Hello, boy. In you come then.' I opened the door enough for him to trot in and then closed it again, throwing the lock. Tiny flakes of snow glistened on the dog's coat, and I grabbed a towel to give him a little rub down. He made appreciative groans as I did his chin and his ears and, despite everything, I felt the faintest of smiles on my face. Resting my head against his, I sat on the floor inelegantly – one leg either side of Apollo's warm, solid body – and cuddled him. With that innately possessed sense of knowing, the dog moved his head, resting it on my shoulder, and let out a sigh.

'Yeah, me too, boy,' I mumbled through the tears that were falling again. Tears for what I'd had and lost and for what I'd never have. For someone who'd spent much of her life determined not to cry in front of others, pretending everything was fine when actually all I wanted to do was bawl, I was most definitely making up for it tonight. I could get knocked flying by a Formula One car and have a bruise from ankle to hip and laugh it off, albeit somewhat painfully. But Cal Martin had left a wound I knew would take me a long time, if ever, to recover from.

Chapter 14

I woke the next morning unable to move. Finally managing a wriggle, I lifted my head and looked down. Apollo was sprawled out on top of the bed, and me, with a serene look on his face, snoring gently. Dogs were definitely family in our house but they weren't allowed on the beds, not least because with a habit of always finding the biggest pooch in the rescue centre, it left little room for the humans to whom the bed belonged. As expertly demonstrated by Apollo right now.

'Apollo. Come on, boy, wake up.'

The dog continued to snore. I made an attempt at wiggling. He groaned, shuffled, and snored.

'Apollo! Get off! I need a wee!' At this, he opened his eyes, looking as bleary as I felt. 'Seriously, boy, if that happens we're both going to be in trouble with Mum. You're not even supposed to be on here.'

He gave a little whine.

'I know. My fault. I won't tell if you don't, so long as you get down now.'

Apollo gave a little sigh and stood up. I let out an 'oof' as he stretched, putting one front paw on my stomach and arched his back down. I gritted my teeth. 'That's really not helping matters, dog.'

Wrapping myself in the new, oversized, thick fleecy dressing gown I'd found hanging in my wardrobe when I'd got home, I opened the door ready to mooch over to the house for breakfast before work. Luckily, I wasn't starting early today. I'd finally risked a look in the mirror when brushing my teeth and what greeted me hadn't been good. Hopefully some of Mum's cooking would help.

The fine snow that had given Apollo a dusting last night had built itself up into a heavier effort overnight and a covering of white now draped itself over everything, softening edges and muffling sounds. Yanking on my wellies, I let Apollo out and he raced down the steps, leaving paw prints in the pristine snow and then another less adorable sign of his presence. Pulling a bag out of my pocket – like any good dog owner, it was a rare piece of clothing that didn't have a poo bag stashed in it somewhere – I tidied up and dropped the bag in the bin on my way into the house. Crossing to the sink, I washed my hands and then flopped down at the long kitchen table, its pine faded and worn from many years of use and scrubbing. Mum came in from the living room and wrapped her arms around my shoulders, dropping a kiss on my cheek.

'Morning, darling.'

'Hi, Mum.'

She bustled about and moments later, a steaming cup of tea was placed in front of me. Mum took the chair next to me.

'What would you like for breakfast?'

I took a sip of the tea and savoured its soothing heat as it warmed its way down. 'It's all right. I'll get something in a minute if I feel like it.'

'I don't mind doing it.'

'I know.'

'Actually, I'd quite like to make the most of fussing over you if you're thinking of taking that job with the new team. You know there's always a job here for you, if you want it. The boys say you've been such a help with the shop since you came home. I know it's different but I'm just saying, the option is there if you ever fancy a change.'

'I know. And thank you. I have actually enjoyed getting stuck in and working with them more than I thought I would. But … being a race engineer is what I know. What I'm good at.'

'You're allowed to be good at more than one thing, Lexi, darling. And clearly you are. I know the boys don't say much but honestly, take it from me. You've made their lives a lot easier.'

'Is that emotional blackmail?'

Mum gave a laugh. 'No. It's not. I just want you to know that you're valued here. It's not just nepotism. You're already proving yourself a real asset to the business, so don't jump into anything you're not absolutely sure of.'

I took Mum's hand and fiddled with her engagement ring, twirling it round first one way and then the other.

'Would you be upset if I started with another team? You know, being away a lot again?'

'Not as upset as you are about whatever happened between you and Cal last night I'm thinking.'

I kept my head down, focused on catching the light with her diamond.

'Do you want to talk about it?' she asked.

I'd learned a long time ago not to play innocent with Mum.

'I don't really know.' I leant my head on her hand and closed my eyes. 'I know it's the right thing to do, so why does it feel so wrong?'

'Maybe you're trying too hard, my love. Emotions rarely fit into boxes. You have a very logical mind. You know what goes where, and why things work on machines. But that logic can't be applied to some decisions. Sometimes you just have to follow your heart.'

'I am. Sort of.'

Mum gave me a look I'd seen on more than one occasion. Generally, when she thought I was telling porkies.

'From the look on your face, I'd definitely say this was your logical brain sticking its nose in. Your father and I have never told you what you and your brothers should or shouldn't do. We always thought that the best way for you to learn was to make your own mistakes. So, assuming that wasn't going to result in anything terrible, we've left you to it, offering advice but never dictating. I'm your mother, and it's hard to see you so sad like this. You've had enough pain and seeing you happy and relaxed again these last few weeks has been wonderful. Having bumped into Cal at the newsagent early this morning, I know for certain that you're not the only one hurting this morning.'

'He'll get over it.'

'Alexandra.'

Oh crap. Now I was in trouble. My full name only ever came out when she was serious. I sat up.

'What?'

'I know you're nowhere near as callous about people's feelings as that comment just made you sound.'

'I'm not being callous. I didn't mean it like that. I meant … it's better for him that he does.'

I wrapped my hands around the mug and let its warmth filter through me.

'So, that's it?'

I pulled my blank stare away from the middle distance and focused back on Mum.

'About what?'

'About Cal. About the fact that when you're with him you look the happiest any of us have seen you in a long time. Are you really going to just let that go because there might be bumps in the road? We both know that's not like you, Lexi. Even when the odds are against you, you've never given up. If anything, it's just made you want it even more.'

I rested my head on her shoulder. 'Oh, Mum. I'm not afraid of bumps. I'm afraid of a bloody great roadblock.'

159

She wrapped her arms around me and cuddled me in, resting her head on the top of mine.

I sighed. 'And sometimes even fighting for something doesn't mean you can get it.'

'That's true. But it's unlike you to give up on something this early. Especially something as important to you as Cal and little George clearly are.'

'It's better this way.'

She sat me up. 'And how do you figure that one out?'

'Because … it just is.'

'I do so enjoy a well thought-out argument.' I gave Mum a look and she winked at me. Sarcasm was definitely a family trait.

'Taking this job will be good for me, and him. I don't want to mess up the friendships he's finally built since moving to the village, so it's easier that way. And then I'll be gone a lot of the time. The longer I'm out of sight, the further I'm out of his mind, and him out of mine, and he can maybe meet someone who can offer him more. Racing is what I'm supposed to be doing with my life. It's what I'm good at. I'm not good at relationships. So I should just stick with what I know I can do. And not least because it's a whole lot less complicated.'

I was trying to sound convincing, but I had a pretty good idea that it didn't matter how far away I was from Cal Martin, he'd still be right there in my head.

'A bit of complication is nothing when someone's worth it. And I know that you think Cal is worth it.'

I shook my head. 'I know you don't really want me to take the job because it means I'll be away a lot again, but I think it's for the best.'

'Oh, Lexi.' Mum rested her hands on my shoulders, gently squaring me towards her. 'I want you to do whatever fulfils you and makes you happy. Of course I love it when you're back, and having you here has been wonderful! But if the mechanic's job is what you want more than anything, then you should take it.

But that doesn't mean you can't work things out with Cal as well.' She dropped her hands to mine.

'I wish it were that simple.'

'Lexi, tell me what it is. There are few things that can't be fixed if you really want them to be.'

I opened the dishwasher door and put my cup in. Closing it, I leant on the sink and looked out over the softly curving fields of white in front of me. Sheep dotted about made tiny little blips in the perfect covering as they plodded through the snow.

'I'd thought Cal was happy with just having George. I mean, that's the impression I'd got. Or maybe the one I'd interpreted for myself. But I've found out that he isn't. He wants what we have here – what you have. And we both know that can't be fixed however much I wish it.'

'We don't know that for sure, Lexi. The doctors have never said it's impossible.'

'Mum,' I sighed, 'Marco and I tried. Nothing ever happened.'

I saw the surprise in her face. 'For how long?'

'About a year, on and off. We were getting married anyway and we knew we both wanted children. After the accident, Marco was keen to celebrate life in every way possible. I didn't tell you we were trying because you were already dealing with Dan and Claire, and being supportive of them. I could see how difficult it was for you two watching them struggle and I didn't want to give you and Dad something else to worry about, especially with Dad's heart.'

Mum swooped me into her arms, her voice thick with emotion. 'Oh, my darling! You should have told us. There's enough love and support in our hearts for every one of our children. I can't bear to think of you going through all that alone.'

'It's OK, Mum. I'm sorry. I never meant to upset you. And I wasn't exactly alone. Marco was there.'

'You should have told me,' she whispered, placing a kiss on my head. 'Promise me you'll never think you can't come to us again.

It doesn't matter what else is going on. We will always be here for you. Me, your dad, and every one of your brothers.'

I nodded against her tight squeeze.

'Promise me,' she said again.

'I promise.'

We stayed there for a few moments, watching the landscape outside the kitchen window. 'I hate that I've upset Cal. But getting involved with someone who definitely wants more children wouldn't be fair to them. I know that now. Relationships are hard work and adding in extra pressure just makes it harder. Honestly, Mum. It's better this way.'

Perhaps the more I repeated it, the more I'd believe it. Like some twisted kind of mantra.

'Have you talked to Cal about it?'

I shook my head. 'He doesn't know the whole story, no.'

'No wonder he's upset. You know you're the first woman he's shown an interest in since he moved here?'

I blew out a sigh. 'Aren't you supposed to be on my side?'

'I'm not on anybody's side, darling. I don't think there is a side in this case. You both look as miserable as one another.'

Pushing my hand back over my hair, I looked back out of the window. 'There's no point going through it all with him. Especially not now.'

'Why not?'

I turned and leant on the sink. 'Well, for one, he probably doesn't even want to talk to me.'

'No. I don't suppose so,' Mum said, inspecting her nails for a moment. 'That's probably why the first thing he did when he saw me this morning was to ask how you were.'

I tried to process that, putting it to the corner of my mind when it proved too hard.

'Mum, you know what he's like. He and Marco are quite alike in a lot of ways. Definite alpha male type.' I sighed. 'He'll say what Marco did. That we'll get through it all, et cetera. But I've been there before. I'm not prepared to be the one to take away his dream. The one who causes him to have to explain to George why he won't be getting the brothers and sisters he wants. It will be the same thing all over again but even worse. They're hopeful at the beginning. Typical alpha males who think they can fix anything. But then things don't get fixed, and things don't go their way, and watching that hopefulness fade in someone's eyes is just awful, especially knowing you're the reason.'

'Lexi, that's not true. It's not like you wished this on yourself.'

'No, I know. But the result is the same.'

'There are other options, if it doesn't happen. You know that, and Cal is a sensible, down-to-earth boy. I'm sure he does too.'

I nodded.

'There are always options in life, Lexi.'

'In the end, it's always going to be the same. I'm sorry, Mum. I know you'd prefer I stayed here and built a life like you and Dad have, but I can't. It's better for everyone if I go back to what I was doing. I enjoyed it for the most part, so I think it's best.'

Mum looked at me. 'I'd be happy for you if I thought it was what you really wanted.'

I blew out a sigh and squared my shoulders. 'It is, Mum,' I said. She caught my gaze and we both knew I was lying.

Later that day I got a message from Cal. My tummy gave a little twisted lurch as his name popped up on the alert and I wondered how long it would be before that stopped happening. Truthfully, I knew it wasn't going to be for a long while yet.

Your Jag is currently being loaded to come to workshop. Saw your mum this morning and she promised to get your dad out of the way for an hour. Will get what we can done on it and you are free to come and work on it any time if you get a moment.

After I'd basically dumped him last night, the last thing I thought he would be doing was sticking to an agreement that I knew, even if he wouldn't admit it, would cost him money. I glanced up and pasted on a smile as the doorbell tinkled and a family got swept in through the door, along with a light dusting of snow. Looking back at my phone, I began composing a reply. Before I could send it, another message bounced in. Cal again.

PS: hope you're OK.

I couldn't decide whether Marco's reaction of not talking to me for the best part of the year was easier to deal with than Cal's calm, mature one. The emotional side of me was screaming at me that no, I definitely wasn't OK. I'd finally found a man who was damn near perfect for me but I couldn't have him. I was actually nowhere near OK. And I had a feeling that "OK" wasn't something I'd be feeling again for a while.

Yep, thanks.

My brain told me that was a big fat fib. I ignored it and carried on typing my reply.

And thanks so much for the help with the car. Really appreciated. Make sure you bill me for everything.

I pondered whether to add a kiss to the end of the message as we both had been doing up until now, but I'd noticed his didn't have one and so that probably meant I shouldn't either, right? Bloody hell. Why was everything so complicated? Were there books with all the rules and etiquette in them about all this stuff? If not, there damn well should be!

The family that had come in a little earlier, having now chosen several items, were approaching the desk so I quickly just pressed send and began putting through their purchases. Their arrival was the first in a steady stream that continued until closing time, thankfully keeping me and my overactive mind occupied for the rest of the day.

The rest of the week followed in much the same manner. When I wasn't in the shop serving, I was in the stockroom boxing up orders and getting them sent off or liaising with suppliers and discovering new ones. This latter aspect had been something my family had been trying to build on, keen to find other cottage industries and small businesses to support.

I found I enjoyed looking out for new and exciting products and making contact with their producers. I'd even tentatively lined up a couple of trips abroad in the new year to go and see a few of the ones I'd been talking to. Obviously one of my brothers would have to take these as I'd have moved away again by then with the new job.

It was difficult to ignore the niggling feeling I had about how much that bothered me. Part of me was desperate to follow my discovery through, and I did love to travel. My brothers were already running close to maximum, and Mum and Dad had stepped back from travelling for business a few years ago, when Dad had his heart attack.

As we sat at the long dining table one night, talking about the potential new suppliers and their products, I could see the conflict in their eyes. Everyone was keen on growing the business more, but it was clear that it was getting to a point where they'd either have to keep it at a certain level or start looking into hiring people.

The Four Seasons shop had always been a family concern when it came to staffing, which made things easier. Discussions could be held over dinner, arguments never went too far, and most of all there was utter trust. They'd seen other companies eaten alive from within once they began to grow, and the wrong hire would make a pleasant working day into a stressful one full of people walking on eggshells. That was never a situation my family wanted to get into but I could see them having to now consider the real possibility of employing someone outside the family.

'I could always take some holiday and do those trips before the season really got going,' I suggested as mention was made of a wonderful new supplier I'd discovered in southern Italy.

Mum patted my hand then went back to daintily loading her fork. 'I'm not sure you'll be able to fit it all in, darling, but thank you so much for offering. We do appreciate it.'

'I could. I'm sure,' I persisted.

'Lex, it's not just that trip. There's that one to Australia, and another in the Highlands that we need to plan for,' Dan added.

'No, I know,' I said, pushing my food around my plate a bit. 'I just thought I could help … a bit.'

Dad gave me a smile and a wink.

'You could help out a lot if you actually committed to the business full-time.' My youngest brother, Joe, had always been the most blunt.

Feeling a little bit raw on the emotional front, I had no hesitation in reading far more into his comment than he probably meant.

'What's that supposed to mean?' I snapped.

Joe looked at me, having just emptied a forkful of dinner into his mouth. 'What I said,' he mumbled through it.

'Don't speak with your mouth full, please, Joseph.' Mum admonished.

'I'm no good at committing to anything. Is that what you're getting at?' I snapped.

Joe screwed up his face as he swallowed. 'No. It wasn't.'

'Lexi. You're reading too much into it. Now finish your dinner before it gets cold,' Dad added from his end of the table.

'Although, as you brought it up …' Joe raised an eyebrow at me.

Dan nudged him with his elbow and I gritted my teeth, willing myself not to burst into tears. I didn't know what had happened to me since I got back. It was like the squishy side of me had finally rebelled and now decided to make up for all the times I'd stopped myself from crying, determined not to be "girly" or show any hint of what I had somehow twisted into a perception of weakness.

'Don't go blabbing about stuff you don't understand, Joe.'

He snorted. 'It's not exactly rocket science, Lexi. You somehow manage to get a billionaire to go out with you—'

'Joseph.' Mum gave him a warning look.

'What? I'm just saying. First a billionaire wants to marry you

166

and you say no—'

'Actually, I said yes,' I pointed out, pedantically.

'Yeah, but then you said no.'

'It was complicated.'

'Whatever. And then Cal asks you out – a bloke who, by the way, half the women in this village would trample your body to get to – and you dump him after one date!'

'We didn't have any dates, which technically means I did not "dump him".'

Joe cocked an eyebrow. 'Are you still seeing him?'

'No.'

'So you dumped him.'

'No! It was a mutual decision,' I said, shifting in my chair. At this statement, everyone at the table looked at me.

'All right! Not exactly mutual but it's … complicated.'

'Everything seems to be complicated with you.' Joe rolled his eyes at me.

'Leave her alone, Joe,' Dan said. 'Sometimes things are complicated.'

I threw Dan a grateful glance and made my excuses to leave the table, telling Mum to give me a shout when she wanted a hand clearing up. She told me not to worry tonight and that Joe would be helping her. Joe sighed without looking up and I left the house.

A little while later, a knock on the door was followed by Dan's voice.

'Oi. Grouchy Pants, can we come in?'

'If you must.'

Claire and Dan grinned as they entered the room holding coffee mugs. Apollo bounded up the steps behind them and steered his body past to get into the warmth as soon as possible.

'I guess you can come in too,' I said to him as he went straight to the radiator, turned around three times, and curled up on the dog bed I'd put there.

Dan and Claire took a seat and cosied up on the sofa. I gave

Claire a glance under my lashes. She'd been looking pale and tired ever since I got home and I'd made a comment about it to Dan, but he'd assured me she was OK. Knowing that this man would move the moon for her if she asked him, I took some comfort from this, but it didn't stop me feeling a little concerned. She was still helping out at the shop although more than once I'd taken over a task from her, under protestation, and sent her home. Swamped in a jumper that looked big enough to fit her husband, Claire snuggled into him as she caught my eye and smiled.

'We just wanted to check you were OK,' she said.

I flapped a hand. 'Yeah, I'm fine. Takes more than Joe's particular brand of bluntness to upset me.'

Usually.

'You know he doesn't mean it,' Dan said, giving his coffee a slurp.

'I think he means what he says. He was just towards the back of the queue when tact was being handed out. Honestly, I'm all right. And to be fair, he does have a point. You lot have all managed to find the right person without too much drama. Even Joe's found someone prepared to put up with him,' I teased. 'So I'm not sure what that says about me.'

'He just wants to see you happy. Just has a funny way of showing it.' Dan shrugged. 'Besides, it's not that people aren't willing to put up with you, is it? So, don't give me that.'

'I don't think my particular choices have helped. As far as Joe's concerned, he could have had a sister married to an F1 driver and free entry to races for life. And now with Cal ... I know everyone's very fond of him so hurting him was never going to go down well. I'm just hoping screaming hordes of women aren't going to come storming into the shop to tar and feather me!'

Claire giggled and Dan smirked. 'I should think they're actually breathing a sigh of relief. So far as they're concerned, Cal Martin is now back on the market again.'

I frowned at him. 'He was never off the market.'

Dan tilted his head at me. 'We all know he's still very firmly taken. In his mind, anyway.'

Keeping my head turned away from them, I sat down next to Apollo and began slowly, rhythmically stroking his shiny caramel fur, feeling my pulse calm with each pass. He gave a satisfied sigh and opened his eyes, checked that we were all still there, twitched his eyebrows a couple of times, and then drifted back off to sleep.

'He's not taken.'

'Lex. I've never seen you happier than since you've been home, getting stuck into the shop – and getting to know Cal. Even with Marco. Don't get me wrong. I like Marco, but there's something different about you when you're with Cal. And it's good.'

'All a bit late for that, unfortunately.'

'It's never too late.' Claire's quiet voice made me look up.

'No, of course not,' I replied hurriedly. 'I didn't mean with everything … I just meant with this. Me. Cal. That's all.'

I'd never give up hope on these two finally having the child they so desperately wanted. It was a bond that had strengthened the tie between Dan and me, and had forged a strong friendship between me and his wife.

'I know what you meant, don't worry.' She laid her hand gently on my shoulder as I went back to stroking the dog. 'But I'm not sure Cal's quite as ready to give up on things as you are.'

I plopped back onto my bottom, leaving the dog snoring contentedly. 'It's not that I'm giving up on him.'

'No. You're giving up on yourself, which is worse.'

I gave her a look up through my lashes. 'You know, I think I preferred it when you first started going out with Dan and would come here and not say two words.'

She grinned at me and for a moment, the tiredness went away, replaced by a radiance. 'Very funny. But you've got a good point. It was scary to me coming into a big family like this, especially to someone who'd never had any brothers or sisters and didn't have the best relationship with her parents either. You were already this tight family unit, and it was kind of terrifying to be launched into that. I worried that I'd feel the odd one out. That I wouldn't get the in-jokes, or might say the wrong thing.'

'No. We tend to leave saying the wrong thing to Joe. He's already so accomplished at it.' Dan said with a smirk.

'Oh, don't be mean. You said yourself – he's just looking out for Lexi in his own way. But my point is that the thought of meeting everyone, learning how to be a part of a large family, was quite intimidating. I had moments of wondering whether I should break it off with Dan because, even though you were all so lovely and welcoming, it was difficult for me. That's why I hardly ever spoke to start with. I'd be gripping Dan's hand under the table so hard I'm surprised I didn't break a finger.'

'You did. I just never told you.'

Claire spun to face her husband and caught the gleam of the tease in his eyes. 'Oh you!' She laughed, batting him on the thigh.

'Anyway, what I'm trying to say is that sometimes things are scary and you don't know if they're going to work out, but you do them anyway because the thought of not being with that person is far worse than anything else that could happen. I knew how important family is to Dan, and I was terrified I wouldn't fit in, you wouldn't like me, or a tonne of other possibilities I'd created in my mind. But I knew that somehow, we'd make it work. Whatever happened, we'd make it work. And we have. Even though we've had more challenges than we'd have liked, we still make it work because we know that together is where we are supposed to be.'

I sat for a moment and then launched myself at both of them, wrapping them in the biggest hug I could muster.

'I love you both so much.' My words were muffled by Dan's shoulder, 'but I'm not going to let you in again if you're going to make me cry.' The hug got tighter and Dan's shoulder got a little damper.

'Never give up on yourself, Lex,' Claire whispered.

'I'm not,' I said, shaking my head against my brother's arm, 'I just don't want to hurt them further down the line. And if it feels this awful after such a short time, what would it be like once I was completely in love with them both?'

'Right. Because you're not already …'

I pulled back and looked at Dan.

'What?'

'Lex. I held you when you were less than an hour old. I've been watching over you ever since and I know what makes you happy and what doesn't. You once said that I didn't seem excited about your wedding to Marco. It's because I never saw the spark in you that I was looking for. I know what marriage and family mean to you. I didn't want you going into something that maybe wasn't quite right for you.'

'What spark? And how come you never said anything?'

'The spark isn't something you can explain. You just know when you see it. And I didn't say anything directly, but believe me, I was keeping an eye on things.'

'Right. Well, I guess you were right.' I sighed.

'I didn't want to be.'

'I know. But do me a favour. If you see that elusive spark, whatever it is, give me a shout, won't you?'

Dan stood and put a hand out to help Claire up, gathering their now empty mugs to take back to the main kitchen in the house.

'I've already seen it, Lex. Everyone has.'

Chapter 15

The doorbell tinkled as Cal entered the shop, stopping to shake off the light layer of snow that had settled on the charcoal wool of his coat. It had been over a week since I'd seen him and it felt like a year. He gave me a slightly awkward smile. I returned it while making a desperate attempt to stop my stomach doing inappropriate backflips. Didn't it know we were just friends?

'Hi,' he said, approaching the desk. My stomach did another massive flip at hearing his voice. So no, apparently, it hadn't got the message.

'Hello,' I said, glancing across as the door rang again and a woman began trying to manoeuvre a trendy pram in.

'Hang on a sec,' I said, getting up to dash across to help her with the door.

Cal was already on it. When she was safely in, he headed back over towards me.

God, he was gorgeous.

Oh, flippin' heck. Now my brain was colluding with my stomach!

'Thanks for that.'

'No problem.'

A few moments' silence settled across us. I risked a glance

and my gaze bumped into his. A slightly crooked smile slid onto his face.

'At least it's not awkward or anything.'

'No. Because that would be awful.'

His smile spread and a laugh grew from it, breaking the bubble of discomfort that threatened to surround us.

'How is George?'

'Good. It's party central for him at the moment it seems. These kids have a better social life than their parents!'

'I've heard that.'

'He's looking forward to Christmas, of course.'

'I bet.'

'Although apparently our house isn't Christmassy enough, I'm informed.'

I grinned. 'Oh dear. Why's that?'

'Apparently it should be more like this shop.'

Laughing, I shook my head. 'I'm pretty sure that would be a bit full-on for your lovely house.'

'Not according to my son. So, if you have a moment between everything, do you think you could pick out some items to make the place acceptable to a five-year-old? Whatever you think. I trust your taste.'

'Famous last words.'

His laugh wrapped around me and I saw the woman with the pram smile to herself.

'I've actually got a day off tomorrow so I was wondering if it would be OK to come over to the workshop and do some work on the car?' I knew from Xander that Cal got into the work-shop a little less often these days, so I was desperately hoping tomorrow would be a day he had a mile-high pile of paperwork to go through.

'Of course. Like I said, any time.'

'Thanks. I can put together a box of extra decorations for you and bring it over at the same time.'

'That'd be great if you could.'

'No problem.'

Cal checked the expensive watch on his wrist. 'I'd better get off and fetch George.'

'Say hello to him for me.' I wasn't sure if it was just the parties keeping George away from the shop or if there'd been some extra manoeuvring from his father. Either way, I'd missed seeing him this past week. I'd missed seeing both of them.

'I will. He's been grumping about not having seen you.' The grey gaze settled on me and we both knew there was a whole lot more meaning behind the simple phrase than there sounded.

Unable to speak for a moment, I lowered my eyes and nodded in reply.

'OK. I might see you tomorrow then.'

I steeled myself and looked back up. He was waiting, a question in his eyes. 'Yes.'

The flicker of a smile played around his mouth before he broke the gaze and turned, his long legs striding purposefully across the shop. As he pulled the door behind him, he caught me watching. I wanted to look away but I couldn't. Cal met my eyes, raised a hand in the briefest of waves, and then he was gone.

The woman from before was approaching the counter with one of the wicker shopping baskets, currently decorated with tinsel, balanced on the hood of the pram.

'Good morning!' I said to the young mother, taking the basket from her. 'Did you find everything you were looking for or is there anything else I can help you with?'

She gave me a wide smile and thumbed at the door. 'Yes, I think so. Although, if you could tell me where I can get one of those for my sister's Christmas present, that'd be great.'

I smiled widely, joining in the joke, and began mentally repeating my mantra again. Unfortunately, it definitely didn't seem to be working.

The deep voice behind me made me jump and only luck stopped me banging my head on the open bonnet in a classically slapstick manner.

'My informants tell me you've had your head under there for the past four hours.'

I stood up, avoiding the bonnet, and turned to face Cal, who was leaning against a long workbench to my left.

'Sorry. Do you want to lock up? I can go. I got carried away.'

Cal gave a faint smile and shook his head. 'No. I just came out to see how you were getting on.' He pushed himself off the bench and came closer to the car. He leant one arm on the wing gently and lifted the other, resting it lightly on the edge of the raised bonnet. Unhelpfully, this gave me a perfect view of an ultra-toned triceps muscle, and a peek at similarly toned abs where his T-shirt rode up a little.

'Wow. You've really been getting stuff done. Don't hang around, do you?'

I wiped my hands on a rag I had dangling from my pocket. 'There's not a lot of time to hang around in the pit. I guess I got used to working at speed. Although, I've been given a head start. You've already made good progress on her from what I could see.'

'I was doing an order for some parts from a guy anyway. He deals a lot in Jags so it was no problem.'

I knew that being able to take advantage of Cal's connections in the industry was helping me enormously with sourcing the bits I'd need to complete the restoration properly. Even with things coming to a head last week and our friendship now looking decidedly worse for wear, I knew he was unlikely to charge me what he should for any parts and labour he used, if at all. Which was exactly why I now had, in the boot of my car, two cardboard boxes full of enough Christmas decorations to satisfy even the most – or least, depending upon which way you looked at it – discerning of five-year-olds.

'Well, thank you. I might actually get this done in time to take

Dad out on Christmas Day after all.'

Cal dropped his arm from the bonnet as I reached for the stay to release it. Shutting it carefully, I rubbed a couple of greasy marks from the paintwork and stood back. Its years of sitting in the barn at the back of our house had taken its toll and the once bright red had now dulled and succumbed to the odd scratch and mark.

'Once you're done, a respray would finish it off.'

'It would. But that might have to wait for a bit. Maybe that could be next year's Christmas present.' I wasn't about to tell Cal that I'd had to dip substantially into my savings this year. Work this past year had been fairly sporadic and not terribly well paid. I had convinced Mum and Dad and my brothers to pay me minimum wage, assuring them I could dip into my savings if necessary, as my parents were flat out refusing to take rent money. They weren't thrilled but had eventually agreed. The new job would give me a better regular income but it was still less than what I had been earning, and renting in the expensive area where the factory was located was going to take a substantial bite out of my monthly salary.

Cal looked thoughtful, running his hand over the curves, and I stared at the car, hoping it knew just how lucky it was.

'We've got the spray shop here. Just pick a colour and when you're ready, I'll get it done.'

'Cal, you don't have to do that.'

'I know I don't. But I'd like to.'

'Cal—'

'Your parents, your whole family, have done a lot for George and me since we moved here. So' – he stood back up to his full height – 'if your mind is doing something crazy again and going off into a panic, you can stop. I'd like to help out as a thank you for that. So I'd be doing it for them. Not you.'

'Right. No, of course. I didn't think …'

Cal slanted his gaze to me and I stopped talking. Of course he wasn't doing it for me. Why would he be?

The workshop was quiet now, the other mechanics having left some time earlier. I finished tidying my tools and tucked them in a spare space on the bottom shelf of the workbench.

'Are they OK there?'

'Sure.'

'I'll get out of your way now.'

'You're not in my way.'

He was doing that thing again, making the rest of the world disappear.

'No … I meant …' January couldn't come too soon for me. Truthfully I hated the thought of Christmas, and my time at home, being over but getting some distance between me and the sexiest man I'd ever met was probably a good thing.

'Oh! I have some decorations for you in the boot of my car. Like you asked?'

The smile transformed his face. 'Great! I'm getting asked twenty times an hour about them at the moment. I told George you were on the case.'

I laughed. 'No pressure then. Hopefully he'll like them. With a bit of luck, you won't think they're too much.'

'Hey' – he spread his hands as we walked to my car, him having now drawn the large doors closed and locked the workshop back up – 'it's only once a year.'

'Once you're finished putting all this lot up, you'll probably be glad of that!'

Cal waited as I lifted the boot lid. 'Is my house about to become a full-on grotto?'

I lifted out one of the boxes and put it into his waiting arms. 'I'm afraid so,' I replied, pulling out the second one.

'Do you want me to take that one too, or are you bringing it in?' I gave him a wary look under my lashes at the suggestion. 'George would love to see you,' he added.

I let out a sigh. 'That was a low blow.'

'I seem to remember you using him to get me to hand over

my keys when I was too tired to drive once before.'

'That was for your safety.'

'And this is for George's happiness.'

He raised his eyebrows, daring me to question him. OK. I could do this. If he could be casual about it all, then so could I. At least on the outside.

'OK.' I hefted the box up, turning slightly as Cal made a move to take it from me. 'I've got it. Lead the way.' Cal studied me for a moment, assessing. His mouth tilted at the corner just a fraction and I knew he'd seen straight through me. But right now, I didn't care. If George had missed me even half as much as I had him, then I was doing the right thing.

'Lexi!' George scooted along the hallway, leaving Martha looking on, and charged towards me. With perfect timing, Cal whipped the box out of my hands, allowing me to drop to one knee and hold out my arms for a hug.

'I haven't seen you for aaaaages!' George said into my shoulder, his little arms wrapped as tight as they could be around my body.

'I know. I missed you.'

'I missed you too!' he said, pulling back. 'I know Daddy missed you too because he hasn't been very smiley this week.' George gently lifted my plait and began using the end of it like a paintbrush on my shoulder. 'Are you and Daddy not friends any more?'

'Of course we are.' Cal stepped in and I flashed him a grateful look. 'Now, how about letting Lexi get up off the floor?'

'OK,' George said.

I stood and he snuggled against my hip.

'I'll be going now then, Cal,' Martha said, having quietly observed the scene as she wrapped up against the bitter evening. 'Nice to see you again, Lexi.'

'And you, Martha.'

She smiled but Mama Bear was definitely back in play. And I guess if George had noticed his dad wasn't quite himself, there was no doubt Martha had seen it too. I got the feeling that Martha didn't miss very much at all.

'There's some stew on the stove for you all. George had his earlier but there's some crumpets in the breadbin if he's a bit peckish before bed.'

George began pecking at my leg, giggling at the word. 'Peck, peck.'

I chuckled and rested my hand at the back of his head.

'May I have a crumpet while you have dinner with Lexi, Daddy?'

'Oh, I'm not staying for dinner, sweetie.'

Immediately, three sets of eyes focused on me. George's were pleading, Martha's assessing, and Cal's … Cal was just waiting to see my next move.

'Ohhh!' George clung a little tighter to my leg and his bottom lip stuck out as he peered up at me.

I fixed Cal with a look. 'OK, that's not fair.'

His mouth twitched with a smile. 'Nothing to do with me.'

I turned to Martha in vain. She was pulling on her second glove. 'It's very good stew,' she said, nodding and smiling at Cal as he opened the door for her. Derek's car sat waiting in the drive – the engine running – and Cal gave him a wave, which he returned. 'I made it myself. Good for warming up. Goodnight then, everyone.'

George separated himself momentarily from my leg, exchanged a hug with Martha, and then fixed himself back on to me. We waited until Martha was in the car, gave her a wave, and then Cal closed the door. Silence enveloped us … for about ten seconds. There was, after all, a five-year-old in the room.

'What are those?' George said, unpeeling himself from my leg and plopping down in front of the boxes Cal and I had brought in from the car.

'Decorations. Your dad said he thought your house could do with a few more.'

'That was my idea!' George grinned, his hands delving through

179

the contents of one box.

I'd had an idea that the little boy would be hands-on with this task, quite literally, so had been careful to include only non-breakable items in the choices I'd made. 'I think it was a very good one then!'

George began delving into the other box. 'Can we really put all these up, Daddy?'

'Why not?'

Quickly pushing himself up from the floor, his son began jumping up and down, cheering. It was hard not to get caught up in his festive joy.

'So, are you staying for dinner?' Cal asked casually, as he scooped George up and bounced him on his arm.

'Please say yes!' George added.

My stomach growled, echoing in the hallway. George giggled and a smile hovered around his father's mouth.

'Your tummy is hungry,' George said.

I let out a sigh, knowing when I was beaten. 'It does rather sound like that, doesn't it?' In truth, I was starving.

'Is that a yes?' Cal raised an eyebrow.

'Yes. It is. Thank you.'

'Good.' He put George back on the floor and sent him off to tidy up his toys.

'Did you want to go and wash up a bit before we eat?' He hesitated and I caught the smile he was trying to hide. 'I'm assuming you are actually wearing something under those overalls.'

I rolled my eyes and he laughed. There was still a hint of awkwardness but it seemed to have dissipated a bit, with little George being an excellent catalyst and I was glad of it. Atmospheres weren't my thing. I didn't even know they were a thing for years. They simply weren't tolerated in our household. People said what they needed to, it got discussed, debated, settled, and we moved on. We didn't tiptoe around on eggshells – we tramped right over them in great, hobnail boots.

'Bathroom's through there,' Cal said, pointing to a room further up towards the extension that appeared to house the bedrooms. I headed in and, locking the door, stripped off my overalls. Next came the jeans and T-shirt, and finally I yanked off the thermal vest and leggings I'd had on under both of them. Cal's workshop was heated but it was still a workshop and I'd needed the layers.

I knew this invitation tonight wasn't anything romantic. It was an attempt at repairing bridges, and preventing any extra collateral damage in the shape of our families. Finding a way to be together easily again, now we knew that being together as we might have once hoped wasn't an option.

I cast my eye over the discarded underclothing and smiled. Had I thought there was still the chance of something between us, probably the simplest and most effective option would have been to go back out there in my thermals. They were enough to kill even the most ardent passion stone dead. I had a quick splash around and pulled my T-shirt and jeans back on, bundling the rest of the items into a ball, which I then took back and left in a small heap by the front door, ready to pick up on my way out.

Following the trail of a delicious aroma, I was led into the kitchen where George was already sat at the table, tucking into a buttery crumpet, and Cal was stood in front of the hob, stirring a pan.

'That smells so good,' I said, wandering over and peering past him.

'Martha's an excellent cook. I keep telling her she isn't here to cook for me, but it seems to fall on deaf ears.'

'Are you complaining?'

'God, no. It's lovely food without exception. But she's George's childminder, not my personal chef. I don't want it seeming like I'm taking advantage of her.'

I laid a hand on his arm briefly. 'She doesn't think that. She cares about you, and I think she enjoys cooking. When she told me she'd made the stew herself, there was pride in her voice. I

181

think she enjoys sharing that talent with you, as well as George.'

'Maybe you're right.'

'I am right.'

He switched the hob off and turned to look at me. 'You seem very sure.'

'I know. Which lately is quite unusual, so make the most of it and enjoy Martha's stew.'

'If you pass me over those bowls, we both can.'

I handed him the bowls and we took them, now full of steaming stew to the table. George had finished his crumpet and was glugging a glass of milk. Putting it down empty on the table, he grinned at me and automatically I pulled a tissue out of my pocket and gave his buttery chin and milky smile a wipe.

'Thank you.'

'You're welcome.' And then I remembered George wasn't one of my nieces or nephews, and I was still on slightly wobbly ground with his father. I looked up tentatively, wondering if I'd overstepped, whether Cal had been about to tidy up his son when I barged in and did it before he could, but he was happily tucking into his stew and just pointed his spoon at the bowl, making an appreciative face.

A short time later, we'd both finished our bowls, and all three of us were sat on the floor, poring over the decorations I'd brought with me. George was playing with a stuffed toy reindeer, trotting him around us both as we pulled the last few items out of the boxes.

'You ought to be in bed, young man,' Cal said.

George stopped in his playing momentarily. 'Ohhh, but Lexi's here.' He gave his father a look that completely melted me but obviously Cal was made of sterner stuff.

'Five more minutes.'

George considered his dad, likely working out whether he could wangle longer, but experience obviously told him to take what he could get.

182

'OK. Can we put some decorations up before I go to bed?'

'We can.'

'And then can Lexi read me a story?'

Cal didn't look at me, and I could see the glimmer of concern on his face. 'We'll see. Lexi's had a busy day and is probably tired.' He stood, pulling me up with one hand and George with the other. 'Maybe another time.'

I kept my eyes off Cal and pretended to concentrate on considering where the decorations might look best in the room. I knew he was keeping a distance between me and his son. Being civil, and even friends again, I hoped, was acceptable but there was a line I wouldn't be allowed to cross and I understood. Agreed, even. We both knew it wasn't likely I was going to turn down the job I'd been offered, even though it was going to take all the reserve I had to leave the village again and walk into a new job, with everyone there knowing I'd screwed up and taking a demotion. But I would have to deal with that.

In my eyes, I hadn't screwed up. That was the one thing I was sure of. I was needed and I came. Sometimes your heart tells you what to do and you have to follow, whatever the consequences. It wasn't often I did that but in that instance, there'd been no question. I stole a glance at Cal and tried to tell myself that following my heart this time would absolutely be the wrong thing to do. I only wished it would start listening.

'Right.' Cal looked at the piles now in front of us. 'I literally have no idea where to even start with all this.' He looked down at me. With me in my socks, he was well over a foot taller, and George and I both craned our necks to meet his bewildered eyes.

'Well then, you're very lucky I'm here, because I know exactly what to do.' I grabbed one of the piles and held out my hand to George. 'Come on, you, how about being my little elf helper for those five minutes before your bedtime?'

'Yay!' George took my hand and began jumping along as I headed into the main living area and set to work.

When the five minutes passed, I saw Cal glance at the large clear-numbered clock hanging on the wall and then back at his son who was engrossed in helping me attach a garland to the mantelpiece. I caught his eye and he gave the smallest of nods. It was Saturday tomorrow so both of them could grab a bit of a lie-in if needed.

As I pressed the switch concealed at one end of the garland, which I'd secured away from any possibility of being accidentally pulled off, the entwined white fairy lights began to twinkle. George gave a little gasp of joy, his eyes wide with excitement. Small arms were flung around my neck and he hugged me. Automatically I cuddled him back. I knew all this was just going to make it harder when I came to leave and honestly, I didn't even want to think about that right now. I just wanted to enjoy the moment.

Raising my eyes, I saw Cal watching the scene, his expression unreadable. I knew his concerns but Cal and I weren't acting romantically towards each other. In fact, it was the opposite. He'd pulled completely back. There was no hint of the interest he'd previously shown, albeit cautiously. He was sticking to the plan. It was the best way forward. Even if my heart didn't agree.

Ten minutes later, George was asleep, having crawled up onto the sofa, and Cal was scooping him up, tipping him gently against his chest as he settled him in his arms. At least he wasn't going to have any awkward moments about the bedtime story now.

'Can I help at all?' I asked.

Cal shook his head, keeping his eyes averted from mine as he made his way across the room. 'I'll be back shortly. You don't have to do the rest. I'm sure I can work it out.' He conceded the slightest of glances as he left, and then they were both gone, heading up the corridor to the little boy's room.

'Right,' I said to myself quietly as I sat back down on my knees.

I trailed my fingers to and fro through one of the tactile wall hangings, thinking. Remembering the bewilderment on Cal's face earlier as he'd looked at all the decorations, I grabbed another pile and headed back into the dining area of the kitchen and set to work. By the time he came back ten minutes later, I was already well on the way into turning it into a grotto fit for a five-year-old elf.

'Blimey. How long was I gone?'

I laughed. 'I'm good at cars, and I'm good at this.'

Cal looked around. 'You can say that again. How do you know what to do with all this?' He took a chair at the table where the rest of the supplies were piled and began rifling through them.

'That little shop of ours has taught me a lot about decorating for Christmas. I grew up doing it. And my parents love Christmas so there's always been tonnes of stuff to put up at home. I guess I learned by osmosis through them.'

Cal stood, taking the end of the garland of stripy candy canes I was currently stretching to reach and secure.

'Where do you want it?'

I looked up. 'It's your house. I was just passing the time.'

Cal looked around. 'It's been time well spent. If you have a little more, I'd actually be grateful if you didn't leave me floundering with all this stuff. Honestly, I haven't a clue. I'm not very good at all this. George was right. Our decorations were a bit sparse. I could do a tree – although to be fair Martha's done that for the last few years, which is why it doesn't look like a Christmas department threw up on it. I provide the tree and she does the rest with George.'

'That's lovely though.'

'I did come in in time to help him put the star on the top.' There was something in his face that made me stop.

'You can only do so much, Cal. You're only one person.'

'Yeah. I know. I just … The older he gets the more aware of stuff he is. Christmas, I mean. I want to get it right for him.'

'There's no right and wrong when it comes to Christmas. You just do what you feel.' He was still holding the end of the garland so I gently held his arm and guided it into the place I wanted it fixed. 'There. That's perfect.' We both stood back and looked.

'It is,' Cal said. He reached up and tapped one of the candy canes, sending the rest gently swinging too.

'What if you don't feel anything about Christmas?'

I stopped searching through the decorations. 'What do you mean?'

He shrugged. 'I just don't get all the excitement about it. Obviously it's been easier since George arrived because he's naturally excited but I still don't really get it. We've actually gone abroad mostly.'

'Oh.'

He lifted a rather mischievous-looking angel from the table. 'Where am I putting this?'

I pointed to a space on the deep windowsill of the breakfast nook. He put it down, and glanced over his shoulder to check with me on the position.

'Just to the left a bit and that will leave us space for these.' I picked up the other decorations I'd put aside for the space and put them into Cal's outstretched hands.

'Why do you go abroad for Christmas?'

Cal took a deep breath in. 'It's easier.'

'Than what?'

He opened his mouth then closed it again. 'I don't know. It seemed like the best option. It's not like we have family or anyone to celebrate with and at least if we're at a place with a kids' club, George gets to mix with others and have fun on the day rather than sitting here with just me.'

'Oh, Cal.'

He frowned. 'I'm not looking for sympathy, Lexi. You asked a question and I answered it.'

I took the next ornament from him. 'I wasn't pitying you . I was just …'

'What?'

'Thinking how wrong you are if you think George wouldn't

have a good time if it was just you. Anyone can see how much you do for him and how much he adores his dad.'

'Thank you,' he said eventually, following my lead and beginning to put some of the other ornaments out.

'Did you not have any good Christmas experiences growing up?'

Cal concentrated on positioning the ornaments. For a moment I didn't think he was going to answer but then, without looking at me, he spoke.

'There was one year. One particular family who fostered me. Actually, it was the dad there who helped spark my love of cars. He had this beautiful old D-type he'd restored.' He glanced down at me. 'You'd have loved it.' I smiled. He was right. I would have. 'I was only with them one Christmas but it was amazing. I guess it's that one I try and remember when I've done things at home for George.'

'There's only one you remember?'

'No. There's only one I want to remember.'

I looked up but he'd turned away, reaching over to the table for the next part of our decorating journey. 'I assume this fairy light net is to go on this wall?' He pointed at the one next to the window, which currently just held one large, colourful picture. The lights would just stretch across it without damage and it would finish the breakfast nook perfectly.

'It is. See? You're a natural!'

Cal laughed. 'I'm not so sure about that. It was more a case of elimination. It's not going to fit anywhere else in here.'

I shrugged. 'I like my version better.'

He gave a little chuckle and began fixing one corner of the net to the wall, just below the ceiling.

'So if things were good with that family, how come you only got one Christmas with them?'

Cal moved to the other corner of the net as I spread it out, making sure it was even. 'You ask a lot of questions, don't you?'

I sat on the floor and began fixing the bottom corner. 'I was always taught that asking questions was how you learned.'

He turned and looked down at me sitting on the floor. 'And exactly what is it you're hoping to learn here, Lexi?'

I shook my head. 'I don't know. I'm interested.' I scooted on my knees across the floor to the other corner.

'Why?'

'Why what?'

'Why are you interested?'

I fixed the corner, let out a sigh, and stood up.

'Because it's my nature to be. Because I think you're an interesting person and I like talking to you, and I'm always curious about what makes people who they are. I'm not trying to break into any locked corners of your mind, Cal. I'm just … nosy, I guess.'

The tension that had threatened broke with Cal's laughter. 'You're not nosy. And I'm sorry. I didn't mean to snap. I've spent too many years keeping myself to myself. I'm realising that's not how things are done here.'

I grinned. 'No. Not exactly. But I am sorry if I've asked anything I shouldn't have.'

'It's fine. And in answer to your question, unfortunately the family ended up having to stop fostering when one of their elderly parents became ill.'

'Oh no. I'm sorry. It sounds like you were happy there.'

'I was. Which hadn't been the case very much' – he gave me a look under his lashes – 'so it was a bit of a bugger really. But I'll always be grateful to them for that time.'

'Are you still in contact with them?'

He shook his head. 'No.'

'That's a shame. I'm sure they'd love to see you and how well you're doing, especially if that's where your first taste of falling in love with cars began.'

Cal ran a hand over his jawline. 'I've never even thought about it.'

'Will you now?'

He laughed again, shaking his head. 'Don't push it.'

I held up my hands, grinning. The seed was planted. Whether it grew now would be up to Cal.

'So, enough about me. Tell me about your Christmases. They were obviously very different to mine.'

They certainly were, and as together we finished the rest of the rooms, I told Cal all about the busy, noisy, laughter-filled Christmas celebrations I looked forward to every year. I'd only ever missed one when Marco had booked a surprise trip to spend the season in Monte Carlo, seeing friends and lunching with his own family. It had been incredibly different from what I'd been used to – it was glamorous, and formal and expensive.

I'd done my best to enjoy myself but I hadn't relaxed the entire time. It was perfect for some, but I wasn't one of them. I needed the chill of the air, the warmth of laughter, and the utterly relaxed atmosphere of opening presents in your pyjamas and nobody caring if you never quite got to the point where you got out of them. That was something you definitely couldn't do in Monte Carlo.

'No wonder you get excited about it. I wondered when I came into that shop whether you ever got fed up with going in every day for months, being surrounded by Christmas, but I can see now that you probably don't.'

'Not at all. I love the shop at all times of the year, but it really does make the best little Christmas shop.'

'I'd have to agree.'

I gave him a smile and put the remaining child-friendly items back into one of the boxes, giving Cal some ideas as to where he could put them up in George's room tomorrow.

'I should probably get going. Have you seen my phone?' Unlike some, I wasn't surgically attached to my phone and had a habit of leaving it in various places.

'Hang on, I'll go and look.'

While Cal set off searching, I balanced against the door and began to pull on one of my boots. Before I got a chance to even get it on, he was back.

'Here.' He handed it over and I gave the screen a quick flick over, just to check I hadn't missed anything important. There were four missed calls from various members of my family and a text from Dan.

Call when you can.

Chapter 16

'Lexi. What is it? You've gone white.'

I shook my head. 'I don't know. Did you get any calls?' I comforted myself that if it had been anything serious, someone would have rung Cal to see if I was here. I'd told Mum I was going to work on the car this afternoon at Cal's workshop, although staying longer had been unplanned. But I know they would have tried if they'd had to.

'I don't know. I was stuck to it most of the afternoon so I left it in the office charging. Let me go and get it.'

I nodded briskly, and Cal put an arm around me. 'I'm sure everything's fine. Don't worry, OK? Wait here a minute.'

When he returned, I could see that everything wasn't fine.

'What?'

'I've got some missed calls too, and a voicemail from Dan asking me to get you to call him if you were here.'

'Oh God.' The words were barely audible and Cal's arms were back around me. 'I need to get home.'

'You're not driving like this. Let's get some information first. Give Dan a ring.'

I stared at my phone. I'd been here before. Wanting news but afraid at what it might be. First Dad's heart scare and then Marco's

191

accident and now … who?

'Lexi.' Cal's voice was soft. 'Do you want me to do it?'

'No. No, I'll do it. Thank you.'

I selected my favourites and tapped Dan's name. The dial tone began to ring in my ear.

'Lex? You all right? We couldn't get hold of you.'

'I'm fine. I'm at Cal's but his phone was charging in another room. What's wrong?'

'OK. Good. It's Joe. He's had a bit of an accident.'

I felt my legs buckle and then Cal's arms were strong around me, holding me, supporting. Words wouldn't form.

'Are you still there?'

I swallowed hard. 'How much is a bit?'

'Don't go worrying now. He's all right. Just a bit bumped and bruised. Hit a patch of black ice and came off the road.' Dan obviously heard the hitch in my breath and repeated himself. 'He's all right, Lexi. OK? They took him to hospital and he's been checked out thoroughly, and he's back at home. We just knew you'd want to know and didn't want you hearing something half-baked somewhere.'

'You sure he's all right? Can I speak to him?'

'You're best off leaving it tonight. They gave him some fairly strong painkillers so I imagine he's asleep. You of all people know how tiring worrying can be. You can pop round in the morning and see him.'

'But you're sure he's OK?'

Dan's laugh drifted down the line. 'I'm positive. Now go back to doing whatever it was you were doing.'

'I was just leaving actually. I've been helping George and Cal decorate the house some more.'

'You're leaving now?'

'Mmhmm.'

'OK. Is Cal there?'

I looked up, meeting Cal's eyes, his expression serious, his arms looser now, clearly having felt some of the initial tension drain from me.

'Yes.'

'Can you put him on?'

'Yes. Hang on.'

I held the phone up a little. 'Dan wants to speak to you.'

Cal took the phone, keeping his other arm around me. 'Hi, mate. Everything all right?'

Dan obviously gave him a quick synopsis of the evening's events. He listened, brow creased for a few minutes.

'Yeah, she's all right.'

Dan said something else but I couldn't quite hear. My whole body suddenly felt weak and tired and without thinking, I rested my head on Cal's chest. His arm tightened around me. Somewhere in the back of my mind, a warning bell went off but I didn't care. Right now, it felt like exactly where I should be.

'No. I thought the same,' Cal said, agreeing with whatever it was my brother said. 'Right. Good. Speak to you soon. Night, mate.'

Cal ended the call and replaced his other arm around me, before leaning back, waiting for me to meet his eyes.

'He's OK, Lex.'

'I know. I just … I can't bear to think of anything …' And then I burst into tears. Cal held me tighter for a moment and then, bending and slipping one arm under my legs, lifted me as easily as he had his son earlier.

I didn't do this. I didn't just blub on people but I couldn't help it. Joe and I bickered more than the rest but we loved each other just as much and just as hard. I was crying with relief as much as anything, and now I'd started, I couldn't seem to stop.

'I should get home,' I managed to get out between hiccups and sobs.

'Not right now, you shouldn't,' Cal replied, his voice gentle as he sat us both down on the squishy eggshell-blue sofa, transfer-ring his arms so that they held me tight against him.

I nodded in disagreement and carried on sobbing. Cal said nothing, just held me and waited.

After a few more minutes, I felt the wracking sobs begin to ease a little and after a few more, I was almost back in control, but completely exhausted.

'I'd offer you the guest room but I don't think you'd take it.'

I moved my head from side to side but didn't look up. 'No. But thank you.'

'You're welcome.' He dipped his head down, trying to meet my eyes. 'Better?'

I was in no doubt about what a state I looked like right now but I was past caring.

I nodded against his chest, finally meeting his eyes.

'I really should go this time.'

'In a minute. Dan didn't want you driving straight away, and I'd already decided on that the moment you picked up your phone.'

'I'm OK now though, really,' I said, trying to convince myself of the words.

'No. I think you're better than you were, but I don't think you're OK.'

I scooched myself off his lap, breaking the encirclement of his arms, and sat next to him, cross-legged. 'I am, really.'

He watched me for a moment and then dropped his gaze to his lap. 'So I assume that means you don't want to talk about it.'

'About what?'

'The fact that all that wasn't just about Joe.'

I swallowed, wanting to lie and not being able to.

'It just brought it all back.'

'I think that's natural.'

I shuffled position. 'Anyway, you're a fine one to talk about wanting to discuss things. You're not exactly big on sharing much about yourself.'

'Point taken. But I'm working on that.'

I looked up from where I was fiddling with my jeans hem. 'Are you?'

'Yes.'

I thought about it for a moment. 'I think that's good.'

He gave a little laugh. 'Well, you're the one who inspired me, so I'm glad.'

I frowned. 'Me?'

'Yep.'

'When you say inspired, do you mean I was the only one who kept sticking my beak in?'

Cal laughed harder this time. 'No. That's not what I mean.'

My head thumped from crying and I was completely drained. I couldn't even begin to have the energy to think about how I'd inspired Cal so I just took it at face value.

'OK.'

'I'm going to make us some hot chocolate,' Cal said, pushing himself up from the sofa. As I began to move too, he turned. 'You stay there and rest.'

I didn't want to stay here. I didn't want to be alone with my thoughts right now.

'I want to come with you.'

Cal frowned momentarily, assessing. Without a word, he put out a hand and helped me off the sofa, not letting go until we'd reached the kitchen. 'Here. Sit down.'

Doing as instructed, I sat at the table and watched him move efficiently about the kitchen, grabbing mugs, grating chocolate, heating milk.

'Wow. Proper hot chocolate,' I said, letting my head slide down to rest on my arms on the table.

'Certain circumstances demand it.'

'And this is one of them?'

'Yes. I think so,' he replied, his eyes flicking to me briefly before focusing back on the pan in front of him. Minutes later, two steaming mugs stood ready, and a plate full of mince pies sat next to it.

'Have you been baking?' I asked, looking with interest at the slightly misshapen treats.

'Hmmm. George wanted to do some the other day so we had a go. I think he ate half the mix before it got anywhere near the tin and decided after one bite that he didn't like mince pies after all. I misread the recipe as to how many it served so I've got bloody loads of the things. Feel free to have one. Or five.'

I let out a giggle and some of the tension seemed to leave his shoulders. I snagged a pie and bit in. 'These are lovely!'

He grinned. 'You really don't have to eat them.'

'No, seriously. They're good!'

I caught the little smile of what might have been shy pride before he bent and threaded his fingers through the handles of the mugs. 'Let's take these into the snug. It won't take long to build the fire back up in there, and it'll be warmer.'

'Are you cold?'

'No. But you're shivering.'

I realised I was but hadn't noticed. Everything felt numb.

'Come on. I'll take these.'

I followed him through and a few minutes later I was sat on the cosy sofa, a blanket over me and fire crackling gently in the grate, warming up the already snug room. Silently, we sipped our drinks and I felt the soothing heat from it spread inside me.

Neither of us spoke as we drank but the room and the company were soothing. Gradually the tension began to release from my body, with the drink and pastries helping to settle my insides and sugar levels.

'Thank you,' I said, facing Cal as I sat round a little on the sofa.

'You're very welcome. I'm glad you were here and I could help.'

'I don't normally go to pieces like that.'

'You didn't go to pieces.' His hand went to mine and I let it.

'I don't know if getting a phone call or seeing it happen in the moment is worse.'

'I don't suppose either is easy.' Cal's hand tightened for a moment.

'I know you watch Formula One. Did you see the race where Marco had his big accident?'

Cal nodded. 'I did. He was lucky to come away from that, I think.'

'He was,' I said, my voice breaking and tears threatening once again, emotions I'd been working to keep in check having free rein after the shock of earlier.

The memories of that day at the track, and later the hurt on Marco's face when I'd told him I was leaving, and the knowledge of exactly what it was I was pushing away right now were all colliding in both my head and my heart.

Cal was right. Marco had been extremely lucky that day. The memory of it still brought a chill to my spine. Sitting in the pit garage, we'd all watched in mute shock as a clip with another car had sent Marco careering off the track at speed, a freak chance causing the car to flip in almost every direction, finally stopping when it hit a crane that had been positioned to remove another car that had come off..

The impact caused Marco's car to halt with such suddenness, it had literally dropped to the ground like a stone. A silence like I had never known – and hoped never to again – had descended over both the paddock and the grandstands. We all knew that despite the incredible steps forward made in the racing industry in terms of safety, it was still a highly dangerous sport. You couldn't hope to account for every single possibility. There was always that chance. That freak moment.

Everyone had just stared at the screen, hoping for the best and fearing, almost knowing, the worst. Nobody came to a halt that suddenly, that violently, and survived. At least, not intact. It had happened once before and ended in tragedy. In that moment, the world was watching and wondering how it could have happened again. I'd gone out the back of the garage, thrown up, and sat hugging my knees, waiting for news. Wanting it, but at the same time, not wanting to know.

To the shock of everyone who'd witnessed it, Marco survived the crash. Bruised and out for several races, he defied the odds and, although not literally at the time, he had walked away. When I'd first seen him in hospital, I hadn't known whether to hug him or punch him for scaring the life out of me so completely.

But the look he gave me, the look he'd kept hidden from the press and from most of his other visitors, had me rushing across the room to embrace him. He knew just how lucky he'd been, and it had scared him. It brought home that despite everything, despite all the accidents every driver had walked away from as they'd gone from karting, transitioning through every stage to reach the top level they now drove at, they were all just as fallible as anyone else, no matter how much skill and protection they had.

'Marco and I had been seeing each other for about a year by then. We were having fun, enjoying each other's company but neither of us had serious plans. It was kind of hard to make those sort of plans – our lives were so busy and chaotic, and Marco was never one for serious. He loves that life. The racing, of course, but also the glitz of it. The parties. All the beautiful people. I never felt comfortable with all that.

'But everything changed that day. Marco knew just how close he had come, and it was as if with that knowledge came a wish to make the most of every moment he'd been given. A few days after the accident, I was sitting next to him on the bed in the hospital room, and he asked me to marry him.

'I never should have said yes to his proposal,' I told Cal, who was listening quietly, his large, warm hand still wrapped around mine, providing comfort but not pressure.

'We were both so caught up in the emotional aftermath of something that we knew could have ended very differently.'

'You didn't love him?'

'I did. But I realised after a while that it wasn't in the right way. Or if in the right way, maybe just not quite enough. Not in the way I really should have if I was going to make a commitment like that. It wasn't fair on me and it certainly wasn't fair on him. He deserved so much more than that from me.'

'It can't have been an easy time. You shouldn't be so hard on yourself.'

I pulled a face, sniffed, and blew my nose.

'Can I ask you something?'

I smiled and rolled my head, now resting on the back of the sofa, to face him. 'It would be a little hypocritical of me to say no, wouldn't it?'

He returned the smile and held my gaze. 'Is what happened with Marco why you're frightened to let something happen between us?'

I couldn't stop the tear that trickled down the side of my cheek, nor the one that followed. 'You have to believe me, Cal. I'm not right for you. It won't work.'

He lifted his hand, the slightest touch brushing away the tears. 'I know you say that it's because you'll be going away, and that it will be hard to see each other, which I understand. But I think you like me.'

I knew the look on my face confirmed his statement.

'And I really like you, Lexi. More than I've ever liked anyone else in my life. More than I've ever let myself like anyone. In fact, I'm pretty sure it's more than that. Which is why I'd rearrange the stars to make it work with you. So you have to give me more reason than you have to convince me that it won't.'

'Cal. I can't have children.'

I saw his Adam's apple bob and faint ridges appeared on his forehead. Silence drifted over us for a moment. I stepped in before he could. 'At least not easily. I have endometriosis, and the likelihood of me conceiving a child … Well, it's not great.'

Somehow, I felt that framing the information in a more casual, detached way might help the situation feel a little less painful. That it might, by association, allow me to be a little more detached too. But I knew I was kidding myself. The pain of that knowledge, and what it meant, tonight especially, was as real and raw as the moment the doctors had first told me the results and what that meant for me.

'Are you still in pain?' Cal asked.

I gave him a wary look and he pulled a face.

'When I found out George was on the way, you wouldn't believe how many online rabbit holes I fell down,' he said, explaining his knowledge.

'Sometimes. It's not so bad at the moment.'

'But they think it will come back?'

'They, and I, know it will.'

'How long have you had it?'

I looked down at where he'd kept hold of my hand and distractedly traced my finger along the fine, silvery scar on the back of his. 'Quite a while. I was still living at home when it all started.'

'Did you know what it was at the time?'

I shook my head. 'I didn't even know it existed. That might sound a bit ignorant, I guess, but I just had different interests and girls' and women's magazines – places I might have accidentally discovered stuff like that – weren't exactly my reading matter of choice.'

'Why doesn't that surprise me?' Cal's voice was soft and, in the low light, I could discern the slight curve of his mouth.

I gave a little shrug and returned the almost-smile.

'So, what happened? How did you find out that's what you had?'

'I'd tried to hide how bad it was from my parents. I wasn't one for scouring the internet when it came to medical stuff, and as it was often centred around that kind of time, I just assumed it was kind of normal in a "really bad period pain" way. Anyway, one day the pain came on so severe and so sudden, I didn't have time to get out of the kitchen and ended up curled up in a ball, sobbing. Dad picked me up, and they took me to A&E. I was referred and found to have a severe case of endometriosis. They booked me in for surgery and I was put on the contraceptive pill to try and help keep it in check.'

'You weren't on that then?'

'Not then, no. But the trouble was I felt absolutely awful on it. They kept trying different ones. Some gave me such awful headaches, I could barely see. Another I persevered with for ages, but I spent most of the morning feeling sick every day I was on it. It was a nightmare trying to find one that agreed with me.'

'Did you?'

'Not especially. I just ending up sticking with the one that made me feel the least terrible. It wasn't ideal but I didn't have a lot of choice.'

'And did it help?'

'I suppose it did. I still had to go back in to hospital a couple of times when it got bad.'

Cal nodded, thoughtful for a moment. 'Something tells me there's more to the story.'

I raised my eyes to meet his as I let out a sigh. 'It's not something I really talk about. Only a few people know, outside my direct family.'

'It's nothing to be ashamed of, Lexi.'

'I know. And I'm not. I'm just … not used to talking about it much.'

'That's understandable.' He caught my chin with his forefinger and tilted it up from where I had gone back to studying his hand. 'But so far I haven't heard anything that makes me think we can't make this work.'

'That's because you haven't heard the whole story.'

'Then tell me,' he said, softly.

I shifted in the seat, and Cal sat back a little, giving me the physical – and mental – space I needed to get the rest of the story out. He wasn't demanding in his request. He was asking me to share and, bearing in mind he'd offered to let me into his life and share him and his son and I was hell-bent on rejecting him, I knew that he deserved an explanation.

Something deep inside of me wanted him to know that I wasn't shutting us down because I wanted to. I was doing it because I had to. For him. For George. And for me. Doing it now was painful enough. Doing it further down the line meant risking far too many hearts. As it was, mine was already feeling more bruised than it should after such a short acquaintance.

'When I told Marco about everything, when we got engaged, he wasn't worried. He was adamant that he wanted kids at some point and just as adamant that we'd have no problem. After his accident, he was sat at home and I guess as he wasn't rushing around at a million miles an hour like he was used to doing in his life. Having had to slow down and accept that he needed the recovery time, he began to notice just how grim the pill made me feel. I'd moved in at that point, partly to keep an eye on him and partly because we were both swept up in this new phase of our lives, and it seemed a natural step.

'Being in close proximity all the time, I wasn't so able to hide feeling ill from the medication as I was used to doing with everyone. Marco suggested me coming off it just to see how things went.' I glanced at Cal. 'I expect you're thinking we were rushing into things?'

'I'm not thinking anything except how lucky he was to have you, and I'm trying not to focus on that too much right now.'

'Opinions change.'

'Mine won't. Just so you know.'

I met his eyes and knew he meant every word. But I couldn't let myself think about that. We'd all move on in time, I told myself in what I hoped was a convincing manner. Cal, I was sure of; me, on the other hand, was less guaranteed.

'So, the first couple of times, we used protection …' I looked up at Cal. 'This feels so weird telling you all this.'

'It's fine. I want to hear it all. And I think you need to tell it.'

'So, the first time we didn't use something was a bit of an accident. Late night, too much wine. You know how these things happen.'

He bent his head down and gave me a look.

'Oh yeah. Good point.' Little George was a prime example of "how these things happen". Of course Cal knew.

'Anyway, nothing happened that time, or after a few more times. And then I suppose, somehow, we transitioned to actually trying in earnest for a baby. But every month was the same. I ended up going back in for more endometriosis surgery at one point and during the follow-up, Marco asked the surgeon if there was a reason I wasn't getting pregnant. He hadn't discussed it with me, just blurted it out there and I felt like he was putting the blame squarely on me, which I know now that he wasn't. It's just the way he is. When things aren't going right with his car, or in his life, he wants to know why and how it can be fixed. He's used to getting data and using that to make things better. Except this wasn't something that could be made better just by having the information.'

'Had he ever got himself checked out?'

'Huh?'

'Your fiancé? Had he ever got himself checked out?'

I shook my head. 'It wasn't him, Cal. It's definitely me.'

Cal opened his mouth to say something else but seeing the look on my face, closed it, gave my hand a little squeeze and encouraged me to go on.

'Anyway, the consultant told us that I was starting off at a bit of a disadvantage because of the severity of my endometriosis, even though I'd been taking the pill to help control it, it had certainly lowered my chances of conceiving. At least naturally. Marco brought up IVF and the possibilities with that, and while the doctor said it was an option, he also emphasised that we shouldn't give up hope and just keep trying naturally.'

'I imagine that the stress of it all wasn't exactly conducive to romantic nights in?' Cal, astute as ever, was exactly right.

'No. Not really. I could tell walking away from the appointment that something had changed. You know when you just feel a tiny shift in the way things are? Nothing you can exactly put your finger on, but there's… something.'

'And had it?'

'Yes.' The word came out sadder than I'd intended, and I cleared my throat of the lump that had popped up as I went back to that day in my mind. 'Our relationship had already changed by that point. What had been a fun-loving one had turned stressful, and we were arguing more and more. We'd argued before over things, even when we were just friends. Well, Marco never called it arguing. He called it having a healthy discussion. Which, I suppose it was usually. Kind of like the arguments I have with my family. But these were different. These were definite arguments.'

'Was he supportive?'

I nodded. 'He was. But I knew it was taking its toll on him too. The constant disappointment month after month. After the accident, Marco got this renewed zest for life. I think that's why he proposed when he did. He knew he'd been given a second chance. But the longer we were together, the more I saw that life, that joy that he'd always had in his eyes, start to dim. It was awful knowing I was the reason for that.'

'Lexi. It's bound to be hard, and I doubt it was a picnic for you either.'

I moved my head in a way that suggested he might not be too far off the mark with that assumption. 'In the end, I told Marco that it was over, and that I'd be gone by the end of the day.'

'How did he take that?'

Memories flooded in and I could feel tears pricking at my eyes as I remembered it all.

'Not well. As far as he was concerned, this was just par for the course. He accepted that the problems conceiving had been difficult but told me he'd been looking into IVF and he was sure that would work for us. Being who he is, he had access to the best doctors and treatment centres, and he might have been right. It might have worked. He was convinced that our relationship had just been going through a rough patch, like everyone does, which of course is true. But it wasn't just a rough patch. I knew that, and I think Marco did too.' I stopped for a moment as I rummaged in my pocket for a tissue.

'He wanted to work things out?' Cal asked softly as I swiped at my eyes.

I nodded. 'He did. But Dan and Claire have been through IVF and I know how hard it was for them. What a strain it puts on things, on top of everything else that's already going on. A relationship has to be incredibly solid to survive that. Ours was already fracturing, and I knew it wouldn't survive that. But that wasn't the only reason I walked away. I loved him but I couldn't deal with it all. The side of the life he loved: the publicity, the constant questions. Never being able to just chat to someone casually in case they were actually a pap trying to get some sort of scoop. I couldn't adapt to all that and in my heart, I knew I couldn't make him happy.'

Cal remained silent.

'I couldn't make you happy either,' I said miserably, leaving the tears to flow unchecked.

'I disagree,' he countered, his voice calm. He lifted his free hand and, cupping it around my face, brushed my tears away with his thumb.

'Cal! Look at the state of me! Do you think I'd be doing this if I thought it could work? Putting myself, and you, through this? I care about you way too much already, which is why I have to tell you all this. To make you see it won't work. It can't. It's painful enough now, and I don't want to think how much worse it would be if we let ourselves start something and I ended up completely head over heels for you. It has to be this way. I can't give you the family you need and deserve. You missed out as a child and I'm not going to be the one to make you miss out as an adult.'

'You're already making me miss out. I'll be missing out on you if you're determined to end something before it's even begun.'

I shook my head. 'It's better this way.'

He gave me the stormy look I'd seen the first time I met him.

'I know you don't think that at the moment,' I said, 'but you will.'

He opened his mouth to argue, but I stopped him. 'Cal. I hurt people. I don't mean to, but I do. I hurt people I care about, and it's awful knowing that someone is suffering and you're the cause of it. It was bad enough with Marco but I know that with you, it would be so much worse. I just can't take the risk.'

'Life is all about taking risks, Lexi. You're the last person I thought I'd ever have to say that to. I've heard quite a few of your daredevil tales from your family.'

'That's different. The worst thing I ever did then was break an arm. Taking a risk on this could result in something far more important getting broken, and to me, that risk is just too great. I'm sorry.' I rested my head on his shoulder for a moment. 'You don't know how very sorry I am.'

Chapter 17

'Just lunch. Surely you have time for lunch?' Marco's charmingly accented voice drifted down the phone, and I could almost see the perfect, wide smile he was so well known for.

'An hour. That's all.'

'Hmm, OK. It will be plenty long enough to tell you what I need to, but it's still not long enough for me personally.'

'It's practically Christmas, Marco. One of our busiest times.'

'It sounds so strange listening to you talk about this. It's like a different life.'

'It is a different life,' I replied quietly.

'And do you like it, this new life?'

'It's … different.'

'So you said.'

'Can we not leave it at that then?'

Marco made the audible equivalent of a Gallic shrug.

I sighed in response. 'I don't know, Marco. I guess I do. I mean, yes. I do. But I also know it's not what I'm supposed to be doing.'

'Supposed to be doing?' he echoed.

'Yes. You know. The racing. It's what I'm trained to do. What I'm good at.'

'Forgive me if I mention that you sound less than enthusiastic about what you are "supposed to be doing" then.'

'Oh. Ignore me. I'm just tired. And I guess it's a little frustrating that I'm going to this team several steps below where I'd worked myself up to. You must understand that.'

'I do. Completely. So, you'll meet me for lunch?'

Marco had reserved a table at a ridiculously exclusive restaurant about a half hour drive from the village. As much as I enjoyed spending time with Marco, especially having lost his friendship for a time, the shop was busy and I didn't want to let my family down either. A lunch hour at the pub would have suited me but that wasn't Marco's style, and when I explained it to my family, they immediately rallied round and my afternoon shift at the shop was soon covered.

They didn't ask but I hadn't missed the hint of concern in a few of their expressions when I'd said I was meeting him, but I wasn't entirely sure what it was they were worried about.

Unlike many people, my family – thankfully – weren't the type to be impressed by either fame or fortune, illustrated by the fact that Joe had given a little raise of his eyebrows and my mum had just said, 'Oh, that's nice.' Joe had never been able to keep his thoughts from showing on his face and my mum was terrible liar. It's where I got it from.

'It's just meeting up with a friend. Nothing for anyone to get excited about.'

'No one's excited,' Joe replied, before heading past me on the way to the office above the shop.

I stood and blew out a sigh. Dan stood from where he'd been sat warming his feet on the Aga door and emptied the remnants from his mug down the sink before popping it neatly in the top drawer of the dishwasher.

'Don't worry about him. Cal's a good friend and everyone knows how he feels about you.'

'And despite appearances, Joe's enjoying having you back. He's under the impression Marco's got plans to whisk you back out of everyone's life,' Mum said.

I threw up my hands. 'Oh, for goodness sake! Mum, is that what you think too?'

'I don't know, darling. We all know he was broken-hearted when you left.'

'Which is exactly why we're now just friends. And I'm lucky he's even talking to me these days. I hurt him badly and I'm not about to do the same thing again – to him or anyone else! Honestly, the last thing Marco is going to want is to start something up again with me. We both know it was a mistake. It's completely over! I am certainly not about to swan off to Monte Carlo to live with Marco.'

'Nobody's saying you are.' Dan's tone was even and calm, in complete contrast to mine.

'That's exactly what they're saying!'

'Lex. It isn't. We're just loving having you back in the fold, so to speak. That's all.'

'So why is everyone being so weird about me meeting Marco for lunch?'

'Because it's a long way for him to come just to have lunch.'

'Not for him it isn't! These people don't live their lives like we do. He'll go to Capri just for a party! This is nothing to him.'

'All right. Then drive carefully and enjoy yourself.'

'I will. And thanks for covering my shift for me.'

'You're welcome. Now, I'm just going to pop home and check on Claire. She's feeling a bit tired again today so I've told her to stay in bed for a bit.'

'Is there anything I can do?'

'No, but thanks.'

'OK. Just let me know if you need anything.'

'Yep, will do. Thanks, Lex.'

*

Marco had offered to pick me up, but I opted to meet him there rather than having him double back on himself to get me. He'd promised that he didn't mind but I'd insisted. Now as I parked my sporty little Fiat among the assortment of super and luxury cars decorating the parking area, I tried to keep up with my resolve that this had been a good idea. I'd been to some pretty nice places over the years but it had usually been either with Marco or as a group, and now it was hard not to feel a tiny bit intimidated at the thought of walking in this place on my own.

I undid my coat and straightened my dress, hoping to goodness it was the right thing before wrapping my coat back around me to keep out the cold. My fun little roller skate of a car looked cool, if incongruous, tucked between a huge Bentley and a rather beautiful Noble. I gave it a comforting pat on the roof.

'You're just as good as them,' I said quietly, the pep talk not entirely only for the inanimate object I was leaning on.

'I'm glad to see you haven't lost your car-whispering skills.' The cool French accent drifted across the still air, the damp of the morning clinging to the rest of the day. A tone of amusement laced the words.

I jumped, my hand flying to my chest. 'Bloody hell, Marco. How many times have I told you not to creep up on me?'

His laugh was relaxed, his eyes shining with the joke and my remonstration.

I looked down at the ground. It was gravelled. 'How the hell did you even manage to be that quiet on this?'

Marco hugged me, placing a kiss on both cheeks, one hand staying at my waist. 'That, my beauty, was entirely down to you. I did call you but you were off in a little world of your own.'

I wrinkled my nose as I looked up at him. 'It's a bit posh. I was psyching myself up.'

'And are you psyched now?' He was making fun of me, but I knew it was meant in fun. There were a lot of egos in the paddock, and of course, Marco had one too. He had to. It was

210

part of having the desire to win, to challenge, to fight in such a competitive world. But luckily his wasn't the size of a small planet like some. Working with him had been enjoyable but I knew some engineers struggled at times with other drivers who had a tendency to believe their own press more than Marco did.

'I think I'm as psyched as I'm ever going to be.'

He grinned down at me. At six foot one, he was close to being ineligible for the type of racing he'd chosen. Any bigger and he'd likely not fit in the car. Although …

His smile faded. 'You're looking at me funny.'

'You've put on weight.'

He slowly raised one eyebrow at me. 'And if I had been the one to say that, I'm pretty sure I'd be on my knees by now, clutching some items very dear to me.'

I squeezed his arm and laughed. 'It's a possibility. But you're far too polite to say such a thing.'

'Whereas you, apparently, are not.'

I shrugged. 'You get what you get with me. You know that.' I winked.

Marco studied me for a moment. 'Yes. I do.'

'Anyway, I meant it in a good way. It suits you. You always were too skinny for your height.'

Marco indicated the way and hooked my arm over his as we headed towards the large Jacobean house where our table awaited.

'You know what it's like with trying to get everything lighter all the time. Including the drivers!' He pulled a face.

'I know. I just always had an urge to feed you cake.'

'I would have taken it if you had, damn the consequences!'

'You look good for it.' We stepped through the large wooden door and into a marble-floored hallway.

'Thanks. I feel good for it. At last.'

His tone caught my attention. 'Marco? Did something happen?'

'Ah! Mr Benoit. It's so good to see you back. Your table is waiting.'

Marco nodded at the maître d'. 'Thank you,' he said, then turning, he gave me a quick squeeze and dropped a kiss on the top of my head. 'Everything is good. And, hopefully about to get even better. Come on. I'll tell you over lunch.'

The food was amazing and I could see how the place had kept its stellar reputation, not to mention several Michelin stars, for so long. The menu didn't have prices and frankly, I was kind of glad. In all likelihood, I'd have probably just ordered tap water if I'd known what they were charging. When Marco had suggested this place, I'd countered with my own classy suggestion of Pizza Express, which would at least have given me the option of paying half the bill. He'd pretended to think about it and then rejected it, along with my argument of wanting to pay half.

Marco had insisted that as he was going to be asking me for some advice at some point during the meal, that it was a business lunch. And because he was the one asking for help, then he should also be the one to pay. It was pretty thin reasoning to my ears but he clearly wanted to eat here so I'd accepted his terms, albeit grudgingly.

'So. What's this advice you wanted?' I asked, finishing the last of my cheesecake. It had been passion fruit and something else with a fancy name that I hadn't been entirely clear on. What was clear was that it had been delicious and I'd happily have eaten it all over again given the chance. It had also been good to see Marco digging into proper food and enjoying it, rather than some of the meagre portions he'd often had to restrict himself to, to maintain the weight needed for the car.

'You haven't heard anything then?'

I frowned at him. 'Heard anything about what?'

Marco looked at me. 'Anyone else, and I'd think they were playing me. But you, I give the benefit of the doubt when it comes to honesty.'

I gave him a look. 'Wow. Thanks,' I replied flatly. 'And for your information, I am being totally honest. You're going to have to give me more of a clue as to what you're talking about before I can tell you whether I've heard anything about it or not.'

'How in touch with the world of F1 are you at the moment?' he asked as he signalled a waiter for coffee.

I shook my head. 'Honestly? Not at all.'

I saw the shadow of surprise flit across his face.

'I know. I never thought I'd want a break from it either. But actually? It's been really nice. I'll always love the sport but I gave it a lot, and spending the past year banging my head against a wall trying to get back in was hard. I've got this offer so I'll catch up then, but for now, I've kept out of it all, purposely. Going home and getting involved with the shop again has been different, that's for certain, but it's been good. And I've loved being close to everyone again, knowing I'm not rushing off in a couple of days and having to try and cram everything in.'

'You sound like you'll be reluctant to go back, if you take this other job.'

I fiddled with the sugar tongs, which was probably against etiquette but I had a fidget gene so by my reasoning, that excused me.

'I will, in a way. But it's sort of like when you've had a lovely holiday and you know you've got to go home, but you don't want to. You know it's going to happen and once it does, it's fine. But until then you want to make the most of the holiday.'

'What if you had a better option?'

'Huh?' I was pretty sure saying 'huh' in such an establishment was another social faux pas but oh well.

He studied me for a moment.

'Marco, what's going on?'

The smile he was so well known for spread across his handsome features. 'I have some news …'

*

213

Marco walked me back to my car. The light was already gone and the damp air of earlier had grown colder and now seeped down collars and up sleeves until it made its way to our very marrow, chilling us from the inside out. I shivered and wrapped my coat tighter. Marco gently tugged my collar up.

'An apartment in the south of France doesn't seem like such a bad idea now, does it?'

I gave him a look through my lashes and he laughed. 'I have to try.'

'Of course.'

'But you will think about it?'

I nodded, not quite meeting his eyes.

He caught my chin with the side of his forefinger and tilted it up. 'But I think you may have already made up your mind?'

I wrapped my hands around his. 'No. I promise I haven't. I will think about it. It's a lot to think about, and very unexpected, so it's taken me by surprise.'

'I'm sorry to have … sprung … is that the right word?' He furrowed his brow for a moment and I nodded. 'OK. Good. Yes, to have sprung it on you. I did think you might have heard something. You know how the gossip mill is always working in racing.'

'Oh yes, that's for sure.' We both knew all about the gossip in the paddock and beyond and had always done our best to ignore them.

'But you'll think about it?'

I laughed and gave him a gentle tap on his arm. 'I said I would! Stop hassling me!'

He grinned. 'Actually there's something else I'd really like you to think about too, if you get time?'

'Something else? You didn't think that was enough?'

He did the Gallic shrug thing. 'It's something I've been wanting to talk to you about for a while but it never seemed the right time.'

'OK. Let's hear it then. May as well get all my thinking done in one—'

214

I jumped back from Marco's kiss in shock and whacked my hip on a gold-wrapped, pimped-up, and frankly quite hideous Range Rover, which only served to add insult to injury.

Marco shoved his hands in the pockets of the made-to-measure wool car coat. 'That wasn't exactly the reaction I was hoping for.'

I opened my mouth to reply but my thoughts hadn't yet formed into anything cohesive so I clamped it closed again. Turning away, I began crunching over the gravel towards my car as I waited for my brain to come up with something. Anything would do!

'Lexi. Please wait.'

Marco's longer strides, together with the bonus of not having to fight with thin heels on gravel, meant that even though I didn't wait, he was soon beside me. He reached his hand out and caught mine as I laid it on the door handle, ready to pull it open. Keyless entry had its benefits when it came to making quick exits. Beautiful but impractical heels didn't.

'I'm sorry. I didn't mean to surprise you quite that much.' When I remained silent, he continued, 'I suppose I wasn't thinking it would be that much of a surprise. I thought you knew that I'd always wanted to give us a second chance.'

I gave a thoroughly unladylike snort of laughter. 'Yeah, it was really easy to tell that from the string of women that filtered through the pit garage after we'd split up!'

'They're different.'

'You can say that again.'

'But that's why I can't stop thinking about you. Because you're not like them at all.'

'OK, seriously. You need to stop while we're still friends. All the women you date are ridiculously stunning and although I pride myself on not being vain, being told I'm completely the opposite of gorgeous isn't what my ego needs to hear right now.'

'That's not how I meant it. I loved that I could talk to you about anything, have fun with you, enjoy watching you eat dessert! Do you know how long it is since I dated a woman who ate dessert?'

'Marco, you can't enjoy dating women who have amazing figures and then moan that some of them don't eat as much as you'd like them to!'

'You have a great figure and still eat.'

'Flattering as that might be, it's also complete bollocks. They're models and actresses and spend half their day working on their bodies. It's a completely different thing.'

'I also love the fact that you're not afraid to tell me when you think I'm talking bollocks. Even when I'm not.' He grinned and I couldn't help but smile.

'Marco, what were you thinking?' I asked, my voice soft.

He tilted his head and gave me a sad look. 'I was thinking … hoping that you might feel the same way about me as I still do about you.'

I dropped my gaze and shook my head, lifting both to meet Marco's. 'I hurt you before and I couldn't bear to do it again.'

'Things would be different this time. I know you didn't enjoy all the same aspects of life but, if you want to know a secret, I'm a little tired of that side of it all too. Perhaps I am finally growing up.' He gave a wink. Not everyone could pull off a wink. Marco, of course, did it with charm.

'Marco, I just don't fit into your world. I never felt like I fitted there.'

'That's exactly why you're so right for me.'

'But I'm not. We both know that. We're great together in the good times but not so good in the bad times. It needs to be strong in the good times and the bad.'

I saw his back stiffen as the realisation settled. 'There is someone else.'

I nodded. 'Yes. I mean, no …'

Marco frowned at me. 'You seem confused.'

I sighed.

'If he doesn't return your affection then he is an idiot. Believe me, it takes one to know one.'

'It's not that. I just can't risk hurting someone else like I hurt you. And you were never an idiot, Marco.' I squeezed his arm.

He waggled his head, maybe yes, maybe no. 'I never should have rushed you. Maybe if I hadn't …'

'There's someone out there much better for you than me – you know that. Someone who likes all the glitz and knows what to do with all those forks at the posh dinners. Someone who fits into your world so much better than me.'

'You fit fine.'

'Not really, Marco. We've proved that we're better as friends. And the problems that put our relationship under pressure? They haven't gone away and I can't risk losing your friendship, or hurting you like I did before ever again.'

'I think I've learned a lot about myself since you left. I think you taught me a lot about myself. I'm stronger than I was, and I think we could make it work this time.'

'Marco, please don't think I don't care.'

He regarded me for a moment. 'I have a feeling that whatever I say, you're not going to change your mind, but will you at least think about it? I promise, it'll be different this time.'

'Oh, Marco …' I sighed sadly, the words sounding thick as I struggled with the emotions tumbling through me.

He gently cupped my face, wiping a rogue tear away with his leather-gloved thumb. 'Don't cry,' he said, pulling me close, 'I never meant to upset you.'

'I always promised I'd never hurt you or anyone like this again, and I've still managed to do it.'

'No, no,' he said, gathering me into him and rocking me in a gentle motion as if soothing a child. 'I just had to ask. And you've said you'll think about it. That's all that can be done. I would never want you to do something that will make you unhappy. I've seen you unhappy and it broke my heart. I've learned from that, I promise. And I've already seen that going home, working in your family's business, all that has the possibility of making you happier than I've ever seen you.'

'You've seen?' I asked, pulling back to look up at him.

'I had been thinking about you. And then I saw the photos on social media.'

'What photos?'

'The ones of the Christmas event on your family's business account. You were dressed up like a little elf. So cute.' He laughed and cuddled me again. 'In one, you were talking to a man. Tall, very good-looking.'

I knew getting Mum that camera with the zoom lens was going to come back to bite me one day. Social media wasn't really my favourite thing, and my brother Matt tended to take care of that for the business, although Mum had rather got into it, and loved adding photos. The one Marco had seen being a case in point.

I tried to be casual about it all. 'Late-night shopping events can be busy. I spoke to lots of people.'

'Were they all gazing adoringly at you like he was?'

I snapped my head up. 'What?'

'Tall, muscular, dark. There was a child with him in one of the photos. Is he the man you're not sure if you've met or not?' His mouth was teasing but there was hesitation in his eyes.

'He is. But he most certainly wasn't gazing at me, adoringly or otherwise.'

Marco gave me a look that I knew of old. It meant 'you can say what you like but I'm sticking my heels in on this one'.

'Anyway, it's complicated.'

'I saw the way he was looking at you. There's nothing complicated about that.'

'There really is.'

'Is he married?'

'No! Of course not!'

'Then he's single.'

'Yes.'

'And so are you.'

'Yes.'

Marco spread his hands. 'So, where's complicated?'

I gave him a look under my lashes. 'You, of all people, know there's always more to it than that. Anyway, those photos don't mean anything.' I blew my fringe up and ran a hand back over my hair. 'It was just a fun evening. Everyone was smiling and laughing like that.'

Marco leant his forehead against mine. 'No, Lexi. Not like that. Believe me.'

He released me and opened the door of my car.

'The other offer still stands. Think about it. Take your time. But really think about it. I know you say you're happy doing what you're doing right now, but we both know where your talents lie and that things would be different this time.'

I glanced at my phone to check the time. 'I ought to get back before I hit too much traffic. Thank you so much for lunch, and it was so wonderful to see you.' I took his hand for a moment. 'I promise I will think about it, honestly.'

'Good.'

Clicking my seatbelt into place, I looked up at him.

'You know, Lexi, sometimes complicated is worth it. Just remember that.' With that he closed the door and stood back, allowing me to pull out.

Waving in the mirror as I turned off down the long avenue of the driveway, my mind began to start attempting to process everything from the meeting, but as I pulled out of the entrance to the grounds and onto the main road, the weather began to worsen and hail began bouncing off the bodywork and wind-screen. My concentration shifted to the road and traffic, with all other thoughts sidelined. For the moment, at least.

Chapter 18

George came barrelling towards me, gave me a big hug, and then charged off into the fray that was my nephew and nieces. The last we saw of him was a blond head bobbing about in a ball of giggling arms and legs. Cal watched for a moment, but as George hadn't given him a backwards glance as he piled into the game, he seemed to accept that his son was happy and safe and would come and find him if he needed him.

'Man, they're loud.' Cal laughed as we both took a seat on the sofa in the next room.

I gave a chuckle. 'They can be.' I held up my hands. 'Welcome to my world.'

Mum wandered past with a beer in one hand and a tray of canapé-style snacks in the other – a precursor to the party dinner for my youngest brother's birthday.

'I'll take those, Mum,' I said, beginning to rise from my seat and reach for the tray as she handed Cal a drink.

Mum lifted the tray away from me with the expertise of a waitress in a busy Parisian brasserie.

'Oh, no you don't. You stay here and talk to Cal. I'm just fine.'

'He doesn't mind, Mum. Let me help. Please!' I fixed her with a private look. I had my pride but there were occasions I wasn't above begging, if only with my eyes. Now was a prime example.

'I mind,' Mum said, completely ignoring my pleading look. 'Now, do as you're told and stay put.' She whipped a paper plate from the stack on a nearby end table, plopped an assortment of nibbles from her tray onto it, and placed it on my lap. 'Here. Eat. Talk … etc.' She gave us a wink and glided off, serene and gentle in the midst of the chaos around her, as always. And loving every minute.

'Right. Good. At least this isn't awkward or anything then,' I mumbled and risked a sideways glance at Cal. He returned it with a small smile before turning away and beginning to make inroads on the food Mum had put in front of him.

Pretending to be distracted from conversation by our food, we watched as Mum stopped by Dad and Dan and they both took some goodies. As she left, Dad tapped her on the bum. Dan looked over at me, and we exchanged an eye roll just before George and my nephew Harry launched themselves at Dan and began crawling all over him and battling to be crowned the King of Tickles.

Cal looked over, his face showing some concern. 'I should get him—'

I put my hand on his arm. 'He's fine.'

'Oh, I know! It's not George I'm worried about. It's Dan! It's all very well my son clambering over me, but he really needs to learn not to do it to others. They might not appreciate it.'

I watched them for a moment, joining in with the laughter emanating from all of them.

'Do you think Dan looks like he minds?'

'Well, no but …'

Claire, who had been nearby, came and leant on the armrest next to me.

'Hi. You feeling better?'

'Yeah. Thanks.'

She was still looking a bit peaky to me but I let it go. Dan worshipped his wife and if he thought there was anything up, he'd be taking care of it.

Claire smiled over at Cal. 'Please don't worry. Ever since the children became friends with George, he's like one of them, and Dan treats them all the same and loves them all the same, as if they were his own. So long as you don't mind, then I can assure you, being trampled on by small people always brightens his day.'

She gave us a smile and I took her hand briefly.

'Ooh!' I squinched up my face. 'You might have to revise that last comment.' All three of us looked over to where the two boys were now sat on my dad, one on each knee, watching Dan whose eyes were watering as he sat quietly with his knees drawn together and a pained look on his face.

'Oh dear.' She pulled a face but the grin shone through. 'Silly bugger. I've told him he needs to wear a cup.'

'Please send on my apologies if it turns out to have been my child damaging the family jewels,' Cal said.

Claire laughed, gave my hand the tiniest of squeezes, and headed over to offer moral support to her husband.

Cal frowned. 'That looks painful.'

I waved a hand. 'He'll get over it.'

We managed to keep things light and friendly between us, if not entirely natural. Although I'd wanted to give him an explanation, I still wasn't sure how I felt about my outpouring the other night and I was more than a little relieved when Mum called us all to the dining room.

'Dinner's ready!' she hollered in a voice that belied her delicate stature. It still amazed me that this slight and very feminine woman had produced men the size of my brothers. I'd got my build from Mum but the grease-monkey side of me was all Dad.

Cal was sat next to me. My family were not only generous, but also had a wide streak of persistence.

With dinner and pudding demolished and the kitchen now looking like a small war had taken place in it, Mum and I returned to the dining room bearing a very large birthday cake. I'd tucked my hair down the back of my dress so that it didn't dangle in any of the thirty-four candles as we placed it carefully in front of Joe.

'Make a wish, darling!' Mum chirped, landing a big kiss on her youngest boy's temple as she said it.

Joe grinned and laughed at some of the suggestions being helpfully offered as to what he should wish for. I slanted my eyes to Cal for a moment and saw the joy in his face at being a part of it all. Returning my gaze to Joe, I watched as he cast a glance at Dan and Claire before returning his focus to the cake. With an enormous breath, Joe blew out every single candle. I knew exactly what he'd wished for. I only hoped that it came true.

Despite its size having required two of us to lift it, the cake was nearly now all gone and so was much of the wine, which accounted for the fact the volume had kicked up another notch or two. Looking down the table to where the kids were all sat, George seemed to be thoroughly enjoying himself and as Cal's deep laugh burst next to me at the conversation he was immersed in with Matt, I guessed Cal was too. Across from me, Joe and Dan had inevitably turned the conversation to cars and racing and having dealt with touring cars and rallying, had now moved on to Formula One.

'You know it's a pain in the bum not having any inside gossip any more, Lex.'

I gave them a quick eyebrow raise. 'Sorry about that.'

'Don't you know anything about what's going on? Who might be the team to back this year?'

'You should back the team you choose because you support them, not just because they're winning.'

'When you're having a little flutter on the championship, that thinking – although noble – isn't exactly the best strategy.'

'Oh, Joseph, you know I don't like you betting.' Mum frowned at him.

'It's just one thing, Mum. I do it every year for a bit of fun.

That's all.'

'I guess there's no point betting on Marco Benoit to win the driver's championship again though,' Joe said.

I felt Cal's eyes on me for a moment as I squished up some cake crumbs on my plate with a fork.

'You don't reckon he'll do it again then?' Dan asked.

'Bit hard if he isn't even driving.'

'You think he's definitely retiring then?'

'That's what the rumour mill is saying. Nothing's actually been announced yet but according to some of the sites, he's quitting driving and starting up his own team. Been cherry-picking the top staff from other teams to join him.'

Dan looked over. 'Any of that true, Lex?'

I rolled my eyes. 'I've told Joe before half of the stuff on those sites is just made up.'

'Which means half of it isn't,' he countered. 'So is it?'

'What?'

'True?'

I shrugged.

Dan and Joe each gave me one of those looks that can only ever be exchanged between siblings.

'So, when you met him for lunch the other day, he didn't tell you anything or offer you a job?' Joe asked.

Beside me I felt Cal stiffen. When I didn't answer, Dan prompted me.

'Did he then? Offer you a job?'

I took a swig of wine in an effort to stall and seem casual about it all. Ordinarily I would have been doing cartwheels at an opportunity like Marco had offered me. But something had changed since I'd been home, and none of the decisions I was making seemed to feel as right as they should. I'd caught the look on my mum's face when Joe had asked if Marco had offered me a job. All of which meant that I was now feeling the very opposite of calm and casual. Shit.

224

The chatter from the adults had now subsided and pretty much everyone was looking at me, waiting for a reply. Everyone except Cal. He had his head down and was studying the pattern on the plate with the intensity of a man memorising it for forgery purposes.

I cleared my throat. 'As a matter of fact, he did. But I haven't taken it yet.'

'But you're going to?' Joe said.

'What did he offer you?' Dan asked.

I let out a sigh. 'Chief Race Engineer for his new team. He's announcing his retirement and the new team in a press conference tomorrow.'

'Chief Race Engineer,' Mum echoed. 'Well, that's marvellous, love. It's what you've always wanted, isn't it?'

I looked across the table to her. 'Yes.'

Her eyes filled with tears. 'Well, there you go then.'

'Oh, Mum, please don't cry! I haven't even accepted it.'

'But you have to if that's what you want, Lexi.' Her bright smile, although genuine, clearly took some effort.

'Oh, Mum.' I shoved my chair out and hurried past Cal whose body was now practically humming with tension. I scooched down beside my mum, wrapping my arms around her waist as I'd done when I was a child. Just as I still was to her. Her youngest. Her only daughter. Her baby.

'Honestly, I'm fine! Don't take any notice of me. I knew it was just a matter of time. But you did seem to be in two minds still about the other job because it put you back down the ladder. I suppose I had my hopes ...' She dabbed at her eyes with one of the Christmas-themed napkins. 'I've just got used to you being here again and incredibly selfishly, would love you all to be here all the time, but of course, it isn't possible and it's just me being a silly old duck.'

I squished myself up against her and she bent and kissed the top of my head.

'You're not silly or old.'

'To be fair, she's not a duck either,' my dad added, doing his best to lighten the mood. Mum giggled and flicked her napkin at him.

'Please don't get upset, Mum. It was just a conversation. And I told him how happy I am here at the moment.' I risked a glance at Cal but he'd switched to studying his water glass.

'Lex, you have to do what's best for you,' Dad said. 'Whatever it is, we'll all support you.'

'Auntie Lexi?'

'Yes, Harry?' I stood up, glad of the diversion from my nephew.

'Does that mean you're going to miss my birthday party again?'

Excellent. Like I didn't feel enough of a shit. His mum shushed him and gave me an apologetic look.

'No, Harry, sweetie. You know I'll always do my best to get to all your parties.' I gave what I hoped was a winning smile and prayed for someone to change the topic. Dad made reference to the latest Netflix hit series and the conversation veered quickly, and thankfully, away from me as I retook my seat.

A short while later, Cal excused himself, saying he had some work to catch up on. He thanked my parents for having him, checked that George was OK and happy to go ahead with his sleepover at Harry's, and then said goodbye to the others. As he wished my brother a happy birthday, Joe swept him into a massive hug and landed a big smacker on his cheek, making him laugh. Cal caught my eye, a faint smile on his lips. Joe was so going to feel like crap tomorrow.

With no pretence at subtlety, my family then disappeared back into the living room, herding a few children who were still up way past their bedtime, leaving Cal and I standing together in the kitchen.

'Sorry. They're not very good at subtle.' I pulled a face and tried to smile, but it felt awkward. 'They mean well, and they'll get used to it.'

'Used to what?'

226

'Us.'

'You mean the non-us.' I met his eyes, hoping for a flicker of amusement but there was none.

'Congratulations on the job offer.'

I nodded.

'I assume you will take it?'

'It's a much better package than the other team is offering. Marco's going to be far more flexible about emergency time off and holidays. He's not the type to be taken for a fool but he realises people have families and that life doesn't always go to plan.'

'That's for sure.'

I looked at him but his head was down as, having shoved his feet into his boots, he now concentrated on pulling on black leather gloves.

'If it's what you want, you should go for it. Assuming you feel you can work with Benoit?'

'Yes. We're lucky. We managed to get past the mess we made of things,' I said, studying my socks. Marco's offer of a job had been a surprise, but his other request had been an even bigger one.

'He wants you back.'

'What?' My head snapped up and met Cal's stormy grey eyes. 'No. I got offered a job because I'm damn good at it!' I felt the blood rush to my face, partly because Cal was accurate in his assumption but also in annoyance.

'I wasn't suggesting that was the only reason for him coming to you. I just wondered if it were one of them. Your blushes gave me the answer.'

'I'm not blushing. I'm cross with you for being so misogynistic as to think there has to be another reason for me being offered the position!'

Cal held up his hands. 'I wasn't thinking that at all!' He paused for a moment. 'OK. Yes, admittedly it did sound like that when I said it. But I didn't mean it to.' He gave a brief smile and laid a hand on the door handle. 'Besides, it's none of my business.

227

I'm sorry. I ... I shouldn't even have said anything. Night, Lexi.'
He pulled open the door and quickly stepped through, closing it
behind him before I'd even had a chance to respond.

Was Marco right? Was complicated worth it? Cal and I weren't
together but right now we didn't exactly feel like friends either.
I didn't know how I felt. Actually, that wasn't true. I knew I felt
totally miserable. Stuffing my feet into a battered pair of Ugg
boots by the door, I stepped out into the cold.

'Cal!' I called, the wind swirling my words around and whisking
them away. He was nearly at his car. I followed quickly and called
again. This time he turned. The moonlight showed a frown on
his face as he did so.

'Lexi, get back inside. You'll freeze!'

'I'm fine,' I said, my mind occupied with other things.

Cal waited, not saying anything, just looking at me. 'Did you
want something?' he prompted eventually.

'I ...'

I really did. But I couldn't have it ...

'I ... heard Mum had invited you both to Christmas dinner.'

The frown remained. 'She did.'

I nodded. 'I ... umm ... I hope you'll come. I think you'd enjoy
it. I know George would.'

'I'm sure we would, but I haven't decided yet. You should get
back inside.' With that he turned and crunched the last few steps
over to his Land Rover. I remained where I was. He stopped at
the door, let out a sigh, and dropped his head forward, leaning
on the frosty glass of the car's window. 'It's not that simple, Lexi.'

'What isn't? It's just dinner.'

He turned, catching me in that heady gaze.

'It's not just dinner though, is it? It's being here. Being with
you, pretending I'm OK with it all, and you know what?' He threw
up his hands. 'I'm not. I'm not OK with it at all. Not remotely. I
hate it. I hate this friends-but-not-quite-friends thing. I can't do
it. I can't pretend not to feel what I do for you.'

I could feel the cold biting into me but I didn't care.

'So … you want me to keep out of your way?' I asked.

Cal stared at me for a moment then laughed, but it was sad and hollow

'No, Lexi. What I really want is quite the opposite of that. What I want is standing right in front of me.'

'Cal, we've been over this.'

'No. You've told me why it won't work and I countered that by telling you that I know it will.'

'Nobody knows something like that for sure.'

'I had a lot of time to study a whole lot of relationships growing up, and yes, you're right. Maybe no one can know for certain but I've got a damn good idea about this one. You're all that I need.'

I shoved my fringe out of my eyes. 'You can't say that, Cal. You can't say to someone that you'd love a big family and then go, oh, actually it's fine, I don't want that after all. It's just lying. To yourself. To me. To everyone. It's not exactly a great foundation for a relationship.'

'I'm not lying, Lexi. Yes, I would love a big family but the thing I love the most, the thing I want the most, is to be with the woman I love. The woman I can't stop thinking about. The woman who's driving me crazy at this moment because she won't let herself believe that she's enough. And that anything else is a bonus. Thanks to that mile-wide streak of generosity your family seem to possess, George and I have already gained a big family. The times I'm with you …' he gave a sad smile '… it's wonderful. I feel like I have everything in that moment. I've never felt a part of something so much as I do when I'm with you and your family. As a child, I'd lie awake and pretend I was part of something special. And then I was. It just took a little longer than I'd hoped for but the bonus of it is that it comes as a package with the most beautiful, kind, funny, and feisty woman I know.'

'It's not the same, Cal, and you know it.'

'Oh my …' His jaw set as he raked his hands through his hair.

'What do you want me to say, Lexi?' he said, his voice breaking with exasperation and hurt.

I felt the tears I'd been holding onto prick my eyes but I concentrated on keeping them in place.

'I love you. I want to be with you. Yes, I've thought about having more children, but it was just that – a thought. I had no intention of even getting involved with anyone seriously for a long while yet! My plan was just to concentrate on George and my business. And then I walked into that little shop, just like I've done a hundred times since we moved here, and came face to face with this gorgeous woman about to let fly with a series of expletives in front of my five-year-old. And you know what? I was pretty much lost then and there.'

I wanted to say something, but no words would come. My mouth was dry and my head was spinning at the realisation that Cal had just said he loved me. No matter how much I tried to deny it, I knew I loved him too. Which should make this all so simple. Instead it made it more complicated than ever.

Cal's hands moved to my face, one resting gently each side. 'Lexi. Look at me.'

I did as he asked.

'I want you in my life. I want you in George's life. I want you. I don't care about anything else. We'll deal with it as it happens.'

'The main problem is that it doesn't happen. I … care about you … very much, and I can't bear to think of you resenting me down the line when things don't work out like you planned.'

I held back, forcing myself not to say the words. Telling Cal Martin I loved him wouldn't do either of us any good. Better for him to think I cared less than he did. Maybe it would help him deal with it a bit easier.

'Jesus, woman! You're impossible! I love you so much, it's driving me mad because all I can think of is you. All the time. And I will never, ever resent you. We might not be able to have any more children and that's the situation. We still have George, who thinks you're the greatest thing since sliced bread, and you have so many nieces and nephews I've lost count, plus there'll soon be Giselle and Xander's baby, which I believe you're already godmother of.'

I smiled at the thought of all the little people I loved so dearly, as well as those I was yet to meet. But something still tugged at me.

'It's not the same though, is it?'

'No,' he said, softly, 'it's not the same. But whatever happens, we will have an amazing and very full life. I promise you that. I will never resent you. The only thing I want to do is love you. But I can only do that if you let me. If you're going to go into something expecting it to break, then it will. But if you let go of everything else, give yourself over to it, I guarantee you'll be amazed at the things that can happen. But you have to believe in me, Lexi. And you have to believe in yourself. And right now, I'm not sure you believe enough in either one of us.'

His voice was soft now and his eyes glittered in the moonlight. I wasn't sure if it was from the vicious north wind that blew into my back, and onto his face, or from something far worse.

'Now, go inside before you freeze to death.'

'Cal …'

He unlocked the door and put a booted foot up, ready to haul himself in.

'Go inside, Lexi. Please.' Sliding behind the wheel, he kept his eyes away from mine, closed the door, and pulled the vehicle out of the drive, onto the road. The sound of the engine faded and the night closed back around me. I looked at the door to my flat and put a foot on the bottom step before remembering that my key was in my coat, which was inside the house.

Plodding back over to the kitchen door, the boots' foamy soles squelching in the damp, I wrapped my arms around myself, trying to stop the shivering that was now wracking my body. My teeth chattered and my eyes were streaming. Stepping into the kitchen, the warmth hit me and Apollo lifted his head briefly from his spot by the Aga to check who it was. He looked so comfortable I didn't blame him for not getting up. He looked so well settled, I doubted he'd have moved even if I'd been a burglar, intent on clearing the house.

'There you are,' Mum said, coming up behind me, 'I didn't know if you'd gone – Lexi? Whatever is the matter?' she asked, scooping my hair, damp from the cold, back from my face. 'Goodness, you're freezing!' Concern showed on her face as she pulled out a chair from the kitchen table and gently pushed me down into in. Crouching before me, she rubbed my arms, calling for my dad as she did so.

'Mum, I'm fine,' I said. She ignored me and called my dad again. The fact my body was shaking and I could feel tears dropping off the edge of my chin in a steady run didn't really aid my cause.

Dad wandered in, his relaxed look changing the moment he saw me.

'Grab me a blanket would you, love?' Mum instructed him, and he returned moments later with a thick and cosy one, which he then proceeded to lay around my shoulders, cuddling me into him as he did so. I reached my arms out and wrapped around his waist, unable to control the tears that continued to fall.

'You're like a little ice pop,' he said, moving me off the chair and then pulling me back onto his lap, tucking the blanket back around me. It didn't matter that I'd turned thirty. I would always be my dad's little girl. My parents had always been here for me. Whether I'd fallen out of a tree, or my heart was in pieces, I always had someone who would wrap their arms around me, rock me, and tell me everything would be all right. I'd never had to comfort myself, never had no one to talk to, laugh with, fight with. I was in pain, and I was sat in my dad's arms, feeling safe and loved. I knew that Cal was hurting too, and he had no one. He was alone.

'Mum?' I said, sniffing in a most unladylike manner.

'Yes?' she answered, handing me a tissue. I blew and then stood up, keeping the blanket wrapped around me, the chills still not quite ready to leave me.

'Would you mind doing me a favour?'

Chapter 19

'Lexi!' George's excited call shot a current of happiness through me, the strength of it surprising me.

I turned from where I'd been arranging cuddly turkeys wearing Santa hats on a shelf. Bit odd, I know, but they'd been a surprisingly good seller. George thumped into me and cuddled my thighs.

I tried to keep the sadness out of my smile as I stroked the top of his head, his hair fine and silky under my fingers. Cal hadn't been in the shop for a couple of days. I knew he'd been working on the festival floats and the shop was humming with business but it didn't matter. Every day I didn't see George and Cal felt like for ever. But it would get better, I told myself. For all of us.

'I'm sure you've been super busy getting ready for Christmas, just like Father Christmas. Although' – I looked down and met George's wide and curious stare – 'I think you're a tiny bit too small to be Father Christmas. So, I'm thinking you must be an elf.'

George giggled and let go of my legs. 'I'm not an elf. I'm George.'

'Yes. An elf called George.'

I tickled him and he giggled more. 'I'm not an elf; I'm a boy! Daddy! Tell Lexi I'm a boy not an elf,' he called out, wriggling and giggling in my arms.

I looked up. The door had been chiming merrily away all

morning. The shop had been so busy in the past few weeks that the bell had become merely background noise and I'd stopped taking much notice of it. Apparently, this time I should have. I'd thought George was over playing with Harry this morning and had been expecting my sister-in-law to be with him but instead, Cal Martin was standing there, looking as gorgeous – and as far out of my reach – as ever.

'Sorry, George, you had to find out sometime.' He scooped his son up and balanced him on his hip. 'I was out watching Father Christmas delivering presents to all the good little girls and boys one Christmas Eve and I saw this tiny elf tumbling down, having fallen off the sleigh. So, I quickly ran and caught him. And there you were!'

George studied his father's calm, serious face for a couple of seconds. And then he burst out laughing. 'Daddy! That's not true!'

'It's not?' Cal replied, a look of extreme surprise on his face.

'No!' His son giggled.

'Oh. Then I suppose you really must be a little boy then.'

'I am!' he said, flinging his arms around Cal's neck. 'I'm your little boy!'

Cal wrapped his arm around his son, placing one large hand on his back. 'Yes, you are.'

Remembering that the turkeys I'd been displaying were suddenly in dire need of attention, I turned away from the happy scene and fiddled about with them, moving one then putting it back and basically faffing, keeping my face away from the familial tableau behind me. It was easier that way.

'Lexi, am I allowed to play on the rocking horse?'

'Of course, sweetie,' I said, keeping my attention on the long-completed task in front of me. Little feet took off running across the floorboards. I hadn't heard Cal leave and by the way my neck was tingling, I was pretty sure he was standing right behind me.

'How are you?' His words were soft but guarded.

'Good, thanks,' I lied. 'You?'

I heard him shift his weight. 'Unless you're going to start stuffing those things, I think that display is pretty much perfect.'

Busted.

I gave a turkey one last prod and faced Cal. I didn't have to ask him how he'd been. His face told me everything I needed to know. Shadows lurked under his eyes and he was about three days late for a shave. His gaze fixed on me, and like it had the first time I'd met him, it made everything around me fade into the distance.

'I had a visit from your mum after Joe's party,' he said, the softest of smiles hovering on his lips.

'Oh?'

The smile widened a little. 'You're probably the worst liar I've ever met.'

I let my gaze drift back to the turkeys.

'If you start fiddling with them again, I'm going to buy them all just so you have to look at me.'

He laughed when I pulled a face, as if considering the economic side of that option, and a little of the ice that was between us cracked.

'Thank you for asking her to come and check on me. That was kind of you.'

I shook my head. 'I don't know how you coped without having someone. I always knew I was lucky with my family but you've helped me see just how much. And as I was responsible for you feeling … sad, I just thought you might feel a bit better if you knew you weren't alone.'

'I know I'm not alone, Lexi.'

'Oh! No, I mean, of course you have George. I just meant …'

'Like a mum. Or dad.'

I nodded.

He reached around me and took one of the stuffed turkeys from the shelf and began turning it over in his hands. 'It was nice. I … I guess I always thought I was OK. That I'd coped this

236

long. Whatever came along, I could deal with it. On my own. And for the most part, I have.'

'She said you were a little reluctant to let her in.'

'It was getting late and it was Joe's birthday.'

'Joe was past knowing who his mother was by then, let alone where she was.'

'Yes, that's pretty much what she said.' He smiled. 'And she can be pretty persistent.'

'This is very true.'

'Are you having that?' I said, pointing to the turkey.

'Yes. I think so. There's something oddly endearing about it.'

I took another off the shelf and handed it to him. 'On the house. You can't just have one. It'll be lonely.'

Cal raised an eyebrow. 'Have you been sniffing the cinnamon sticks?'

'No. Not today.' I smiled, shoving my hands in my pockets, glancing over at where Claire was ringing up items on the till for a couple of customers. The last few days had seen her colour improve and I was happy to see her back taking part in the bustle of the shop, not just because it helped ease the load but because I loved spending time with her. I looked back up at Cal. 'I'm sorry I hurt you. You don't know how much I wish things were different but they're not. And I can't make them different. But Mum and Dad love you and George as if you were their own, and my brothers think the world of you. I don't want … us … to mess up the rest of it. So, please don't let it. Don't stop seeing them just because you might not want to see me, will you?'

He reached out and brushed my fingers with his own, before shaking his head. 'No. I promise.'

I let out a breath I didn't even know I'd been holding. Cal glanced over to his son, checking he was OK. Having found a Santa hat, George was now riding the rocking horse and holding out the hat like a rodeo rider, letting out whoops of 'yee ha' every so often. We watched for a moment as though both trying to absorb George's joy in order to dull our own sadness.

The door tinkled again and a large family hurried in, chill air blowing across the shop as the gusting wind fought to whip the door from their grip. I gave them a practised smile and turned back to Cal.

'I really ought to get on.'

'Yes. Of course.'

George, having now finished his rodeo, came running up to us. 'Lexi. Will Father Christmas know where to find me on Christmas Day?'

I smiled down and ran my free hand over his silky hair. 'Absolutely. I have it on very good authority that he has your address written clearly on his Good Little Boys list.'

'But we won't be at home,' he sighed. 'We're going somewhere else … Anti … goo? What if he can't find me?'

'Oh!' I glanced at Cal but he was looking down at George and doing a stellar job of avoiding eye contact. 'Well. Father Christmas is very good at stuff like that. And if you like, I can get word to him and make sure he knows exactly where you are in …'

I looked up at his father for a confirmation, doing my best to keep my face blank. From the look on his, I hadn't achieved it. A flash of guilt crossed his own. 'Antigua.'

'Right. Of course.'

'It was a spur-of-the-moment thing.'

George's eye was caught by something in the shop and he walked off to investigate.

'Sounds lovely,' I forced out brightly.

This was probably for the best anyway. Mum had invited Cal and George to Christmas dinner and although I hadn't ever thought of myself as a masochist, I'd hoped he wouldn't cancel. I knew Mum's invitation was irrespective of our situation. She adored both of them and hated the thought of them alone in their quiet house while ours rang with noise, laughter, and good-natured arguments.

Last year George and Cal were new to the village and although she'd invited them, she'd accepted Cal's polite refusal; but you didn't turn down a Christmas dinner at Mum's twice in a row with no good reason. It certainly looked like he had a good reason now – several thousand miles of good reasons.

'You've told Mum?' I said, keeping my tone light.

A sheepish look gave me my answer.

'Not yet.'

'You ought to do it as soon as possible. She's already started baking.'

I caught the look he gave me. 'If I tell you I didn't consider coming, I'd be lying. I know it will be wonderful and yes, I feel a pretty shitty dad right now, not giving George that opportunity to spend his Christmas with you all. But like I said, we've been away for Christmas before and he enjoyed it so, although I'm not exactly his favourite person right now, I'm hoping he'll warm to the idea again soon.'

'You're still his favourite person. But you're not coming because of me.'

'No. I'm not coming because of me. Because right now I don't know how to be around you and not feel what I feel for you, and that's not going to make a great Christmas for any of us. I think the break from each other will do us both good, to be honest.'

'Yes,' I croaked out, knowing he was probably right but also knowing that the last thing I really wanted from Cal Martin was space. Keeping my eyes from locking with his, I cast my gaze around. 'I really should go and see if Claire's OK. Have a lovely time in Antigua. Give my love to George too, won't you?' I said, as I began walking away. I knew that if that little boy ran over for a cuddle now, I'd be lost. Cal was right. Space was the best thing for us all.

Pasting on a smile I headed over to the cash desk and began greeting the customers, making small talk about the weather, the season, and the items they were buying. In the background of their hubbub, I heard the doorbell tinkle and glimpsed Cal's large frame fill the doorway as he held the door firmly against the biting wind. George turned and, wiggling his head to try and see me through the people, he then gave me an enthusiastic wave. I waved back and blew him a kiss before turning my attention back to my other customers. The smile on my face might have fooled them, but it didn't fool my head – or my heart.

I wrapped the last of the purchases and laughed with the happy family, their joy filling me with an ache that made me want to run home to my own. I wanted to make the most of their time and their love while I could. Seeing Cal today had made it clear what I needed to do. Deep down I knew it wasn't what I wanted. But it was what I needed and that would have to be enough.

Chapter 20

Not many people in the village owned a matte black Lamborghini Revuelto. In fact, there was a grand total of zero. But I knew one person who did. The bigger question was why it was currently parked in my parents' driveway. Passing the stairs to my own place, I made my way to the back door, getting blown in to the kitchen by an icy wind that was now well on its way to approaching gale status. Sitting there at the table, looking both oddly out of place and yet completely at home, was Marco Benoit. Three of my petrol-headed nephews were opposite him, their eyes wide and their mouths slightly agape as he regaled them with tales of the Formula One track.

'Hello, darling,' Mum said. 'Marco dropped by to see you. I wasn't sure how long you'd be so I've invited him to dinner.' Her tone was entirely casual, as if having billionaire racing drivers sat at your kitchen table was an everyday occurrence. My family had taken my going out with Marco in their stride – as they did everything – and Mum knew us breaking up hadn't been easy on either side. Now she knew the full story, her care for him would have only increased.

'Marco's going to take us out in his car!' My eldest nephew was practically reverberating with excitement.

'Not in that weather he's not,' I replied firmly.

'Exactly what I said,' Marco assured me as he stood and bent to kiss me on both cheeks. 'But I'll come back when the weather is better, yes?'

I nodded acceptance and the boys bounced up and down cheering, before running around making car noises and zipping in and out of the kitchen. Mum eventually sent them into the living room so that she could get on with making dinner. A glance at the stove indicated there was more than just her and Dad and me and Marco eating here tonight.

'What's with all the food?' I asked, shrugging off all the layers I'd put on to walk to and from work today. The weather seemed to be getting colder every day, and the odds of a white Christmas were now only two to one.

'Oh, I thought you might have seen one of the boys at work?'

I shook my head. 'Only briefly but we didn't have time to chat.'

The stream of customers into the shop had been almost continuous today and on the odd quiet moment, I'd taken the opportunity to pack up some online orders and get them ready for collection first thing tomorrow. I was exhausted but I knew it wasn't just from being so busy. Busy was good. Busy kept me from thinking of other things. Like the most gorgeous, interesting, and disturbingly hot man I'd ever met telling me he loved me and me sending him away. Yep, I definitely needed busy.

'Dan asked if we could all get together tonight,' Mum said, interrupting my thoughts as the back door opened again after a brief knock. Cal walked in.

'Oh, Cal, sweetheart. I'm so glad you could make it at such late notice. Is George not with you?'

The warm expression his face held for my mum turned to wary as he looked from me to Marco and back to me again.

'Oh. No, sorry. I should have said. We've been building an army of snowmen this afternoon and he's worn out. I got him to have a nap and he was still out like a light. I didn't really want

242

to wake him, and Martha was happy to come and babysit. Dan's text sounded like it was important though.'

'What's going on?' I asked.

Mum shrugged. 'Honestly, I don't know. I just work here!' she said, laughing. 'Cal, I've only recently made tea. There should be some left in that pot. Lexi, aren't you forgetting your manners?'

I gave her a blank look. Cal Martin had a habit of making a woman forget a lot of things. All I could be thankful for was that I'd never slept with him. I had the distinct feeling that was something I'd never have forgotten. Odd then that despite everything, I was having such a hard time conjuring up any grain of gratefulness for that particular circumstance.

I steered my brain away from that thought with haste. 'Oh! Marco Benoit, this is Cal Martin. Cal, this is Marco.' Mum and I both knew that Cal had recognised the man the moment he'd walked in, but we were British, and there were some things that you just had to do in the right way.

Cal nodded and held out his hand. Marco took it, his mouth smiling but his eyes assessing just as much as Cal's were. The only difference is that Cal didn't even pretend to smile. I prayed that they weren't going to have some squeezy-handshake-until-the-death competition, but luckily they just gave a brief shake and both dropped their hands back to their sides.

'You missed something.' Marco smiled down at me, pulling the hat I'd forgotten off my head and the hair I'd roughly shoved under it tumbled down.

'I so rarely saw you wear your hair loose,' he said, his face thoughtful.

'Not the best idea when you've got your head shoved halfway inside a car.'

'You didn't always have your head in an engine.' He quirked an eyebrow at me and I made a point of ignoring it. And a point of not looking at Cal. 'Still. It suits you.'

'She had it short for a while when she was little,' Mum added as she stirred something that smelled mouthwatering on the hob, 'but it turns out that as much as she declared she wanted to be a boy and do "boy stuff", it irked her to be actually called a boy all the time. She thought if she grew her hair it would stop people doing it. I tried to explain that wearing a dress occasionally might help too but—'

'I'm pretty sure no one's interested in that, Mum,' I said, my insides curling with embarrassment.

'I am,' Cal and Marco both chimed in unison. They exchanged a look and I felt the tension in the air notch up a level. Perfect. Exactly what I needed. A double dose of amped-up testosterone.

'Did you tell Mum you can't make it to Christmas dinner yet?' I asked Cal, dropping him in it in a desperate bid to shift the focus of conversation.

'You can't?' Mum turned, disappointment creasing her features.

Cal gave me a thanks-a-bunch look and set about trying to come up with a plausible explanation that didn't involve the words 'I just need to put a few thousand miles between me and your daughter right now.'

Taking the opportunity of the distraction, I turned to Marco. 'Why are you here anyway? I mean, it's nice to see you, but ...'

'I was passing.'

'Passing.' I raised an eyebrow. Somehow I doubted that.

'And, I wondered if you'd come to a decision yet ... about the things I offered you.'

I could tell that even from the back and involved in another conversation, Cal's body had tensed. I cut Marco a look that told him I wasn't in the mood for him to play games. It was obvious he'd sussed immediately that Cal was the man I'd spoken about meeting and also that we most definitely weren't together. It was hard not to notice that Marco would prefer it stayed that way.

'Don't,' I said, keeping my voice low. The tone was enough for him to raise his hands in submission.

Cal had his arm around my mum's shoulder, hugging her to

him as she patted his arm. 'That's OK, love. You just have a lovely time out there on holiday and perhaps you could pop round when you get home for a meal sometime.'

'That sounds perfect, Annie. Thank you. And thanks so much for inviting us in the first place.'

She patted his arm again and smiled. I could see the disappointment it was masking but I pretended not to notice. The passing glance Cal gave me told me he was doing exactly the same.

'Bloody hell! You traded up your car, Cal?' A still slightly bruised Joe suddenly barrelled in the back door, before opening it wider for more of my nieces and nephews to pile through as the rest of my family arrived in one big influx.

Cal gave a hollow laugh as he shook Joe's hand and then proceeded to do the same to the rest of my brothers, dropping kisses on the cheeks of their various partners. 'Hardly.'

'It's Marco's, Joe,' I called over to him and various glances shot Marco's way. Marco had met my family a few times before when we'd been together, so I left them all to it as Mum asked me to grab some extra napkins from the top of the cupboard. I climbed on a chair. Cal, standing close, automatically put out his hand to help my ascent. I took it without thinking and made the briefest of eye contact with him, receiving the ghost of a smile in return.

I glanced down to check my footing and instead felt Cal's hands at my waist, lifting me down.

'Thank you,' I said, 'but you do know I've been climbing up and down on these chairs since the year dot.'

The smile glimmered again. 'I don't doubt it. And I wasn't suggesting you actually needed help. I just wanted to give it.'

His voice was soft, even though the general noise level of my family having come together was probably way above UK recommendations.

I looked up at him. 'It might be easier for both of us if you don't.'

'I know. And then I see you and I can't help it.'

'Then it's probably a good thing you're going to Antigua.'

A shadow passed across his features. 'And where are you going?' he asked, his glance taking in the additional guest in our kitchen.

I lifted my gaze. 'It's what I'm good at.' Neither of us missed the element of sadness in my voice.

Cal gently swept my hair back over one shoulder. 'So why don't you sound excited about it?'

'I am. I mean, I will be. I've just been really busy with everything else here.'

Keeping myself busy so that I didn't think about you.

'If it's what you want then I'm really happy for you, Lexi.'

I knew what I wanted beyond anything else. He was standing right in front of me, sending my brain spinning and turning my insides to liquid. But I also knew there was something that he wanted too. I chewed my lip and took in the noise and crowd filling the kitchen as my family did what it did best – coming together, laughing, talking over each other, taking the mickey, supporting. Everything he had never had. Everything he wanted. And everything I might not be able to give him. He'd turned now, absorbing the atmosphere. I watched him and I knew my decision.

'Are we late? Did we miss it all?' Giselle rushed into the kitchen, Xander following.

'No, darlings. We're just about to take everything through to the dining room. You're right on time,' Mum said, giving them a flush-faced squeeze as she bustled about.

'Oh good,' Giselle replied, draping her dusky pink wool swing coat over the back of a chair, eyeing the two men flanking me as she did so. 'Hello, gorgeous,' she said, hugging me, 'everything all right?' Her eye contact was direct and her words were loaded.

'Yep. Fine, thanks,' I replied, knowing I wasn't fooling her for a moment. 'How are you?'

She flapped a perfectly manicured hand before laying it on her stomach. 'I'm great. Well, apart from wishing this baby would find somewhere more comfortable to sit than on my bladder. Marco, isn't it? We met at one of the races.' Giselle held out her hand and Marco took it, lifting it to his lips instead of shaking it. I let out a groaning. Marco and Giselle looked at me. Cal and Xander laughed.

'That was out loud, wasn't it?' I pulled a face.

''Fraid so, Muppet.'

'He's being charming.' Giselle laughed her tinkly laugh. There was no way she'd ever cheat on Xander but she appreciated – and knew what to do with – charming manners when she came across them.

'All my charm is, sadly, quite lost on Lexi.'

I rolled my eyes at him and then looked at Giselle. 'Believe me, he isn't always that charming. He can actually be a proper diva at times.'

'Ah! I disagree.' Marco's eyes twinkled with amusement. 'I have been known to be upset ... but I have never slid down the slope to diva-ship. When you have engineers who tell you to stop being such ... what is the phrase you favour again?' He glanced at me, tapping his chin in mock thought. 'Oh yes, "an arse", it is a little difficult to believe that you are particularly special.'

'To be fair, I never said it that much.'

'To be fair, I think I probably deserved it when she did,' he said to the small group we had now formed.

'Right, everyone! Into the dining room please. Cal, Dan, Xander, can you take these please?' Mum directed the boys to the last of the items to be taken through and we headed into dining room, mouths watering with the aromas drifting from the dishes in the middle of the table.

'Thanks for sorting this all, Mum. I know it was all a bit last-moment,' Dan began once we'd all eaten far too much and were sat lounging in our chairs, vaguely wondering how we'd ever move again. 'And thanks to you all for coming. Claire and I have something to share, and we wanted to tell everyone we love all at the same time.'

247

Various murmurs went around the table as glances were exchanged. Marco next to me leant in. 'I feel as though I am intruding.' I laid my hand on his arm briefly and shook my head. He didn't say anything more but it was the first time I'd ever seen him not feel totally at ease.

'And, Marco' – Dan smiled at him – 'you're just as welcome. Everyone knows you might be about to whisk our Lexi away with a much-deserved promotion.' He glanced at me as he made this point. 'But if it makes her happy, then we forgive you.'

Marco smiled and gave an accepting, grateful nod.

'For the most part,' Dan finished, winking at me.

I returned the smile, trying to scrunch down the feelings churning inside of me. I'd made my decision. It was the right one. I knew it was. The sensible one. So why did I have an overwhelming urge to throw myself on the floor and wail like a toddler that I didn't want to go?

'You OK?' Cal, on the other side of me, whispered close to my ear as, momentarily, the others talked around us.

I nodded without turning my head, doing my best to ignore the little rockets of wanting that his warm breath on my skin kicked off.

'So,' Dan started again, 'I expect some of you might have already guessed why we're here. But if you could still act surprised, that'd be great,' he said, taking his wife's hand and laughing. She rested her head on his shoulder and he kissed the top of her hair. 'Claire and I have some news.' We waited as he reached an arm under the table and produced a small, blue teddy bear, which he then sat in front of him. A moment of silence surrounded us as we took in the meaning, smiles forming, tears spilling, and laughter bubbling as we all shared in a joy that had been so wanted and so deserved, and so long in coming.

Beneath the table, Cal's hand slid to mine. He leant closer. 'Are you OK?' he asked, the noise around us concealing his question from the others.

I turned, grateful for his thoughtfulness, and for a moment forgetting that we were supposed to be keeping our distance, being sensible.

'Yes! Yes, I am,' I replied, tears streaming down my cheeks, taking the remnants of the day's mascara with it. 'It's wonderful. Perfect. Oh, Cal, they've waited for this for such a long time!'

Cal nodded, smiling. I knew what he was thinking. That I might find the news hard, and I could understand that. But I also knew the struggle that Dan and Claire had had, the pain, the stress, the disappointments, the heartbreak. It had formed a bond between us that strengthened the joys and deepened the heartaches each of us experienced.

'Do you need this?' he asked, offering me his napkin.

I giggled through the happy tears. 'No, I'm OK for now. But thank you.' He smiled, gave another gentle squeeze of my hand, and then withdrew his own.

'And everything is … OK?' Mum asked the question lurking in all our minds.

'Fingers crossed, yes,' Dan answered. 'Claire's over four months already. We just didn't want to get our, or anyone else's, hopes up too early, which is why we've been a bit sneaky about it – for which I apologise. Had it been summer, Claire hiding underneath big jumpers might not have been such a viable option.' Dan grinned and gave his wife another kiss, the love and happiness beaming out of them like sunshine on a cold winter's day.

'We went for a check-up today and they're extremely happy with the progress and everything's looking great. We're sorry we hid it from you all up to now, but we know you understand. Once we got the news today though, we wanted to tell every special person in our lives as soon as possible,' Claire said, picking up the thread as Dan's eyes shone with emotion.

He wasn't the only one. Napkins had turned into handker-chiefs almost without fail around the entire table. Mum had now appropriated Dad's as well, leaving him to use his sleeve to wipe the tears brimming in his eyes.

'Congratulations!' Marco raised his glass, jerking us all into action, and the sentiment echoed loudly in the large dining room as we all toasted the parents to be and the new life that would be with us before we knew it.

'There's just one more thing,' Dan added, placing another bear on the table beside the first, this one soft pink in colour.

'Twins?' Mum's voice was barely a whisper. It was as though the whole room had stopped breathing.

Dan nodded, the brightest, most beautiful smile I'd ever seen lighting his face. Cal, his own eyes glittering with emotion, turned as I lost it completely and, without a word, held out his napkin to me.

Chapter 21

The room was so full of happiness, it almost felt tangible. Mum had barely stopped crying and the rest of us weren't far behind. Cal was standing chatting with my dad, Dan's arm slung across his shoulder as a bubble of laughter broke from them and I was happy to see him caught up in the joy despite the undercurrent of unhappiness I'd help place in his heart.

'I should go.' Marco leant into me to make himself heard. 'Your fabulous weather is getting worse and I have a flight to catch early tomorrow.'

I laughed, turning to him, the outline of his face seeming slightly fuzzier than it had been earlier. Having a large family, my dad always believed in having a box of champagne in the house in the event that it might be needed for emergency celebrations. This definitely constituted an emergency celebration and as such, he had been circling the room, topping off glasses on every pass. I had the distinct feeling that mine had been topped off more than I originally thought.

'You own the plane, Marco. It's not likely to go without you.'

He made a conciliatory gesture with his hands, lifting his palms. 'True. But still.'

I studied him for a moment, tilting my head to the side before realising that wasn't such a great idea for my balance. Marco steadied me and waited.

'Why did you come?' I asked. 'I mean, here. Tonight. Not that I'm complaining. You're my friend. I love to see you. Obviously …' I struggled with the 's' for a moment, won, and carried on. 'But why tonight?'

Marco lifted the glass from me, and taking a hand that had until moments ago been happily employed in ferrying alcohol to my mouth, led me away from the others and out to the kitchen. Under-cabinet lights cast a cosy, soft glow into the room kept warm by the Aga. On the far side, a net of white fairy lights, like I'd helped Cal put up in his kitchen, twinkled prettily, adding to the comforting feel. Apollo was sprawled out next to the oven, snoring softly. I smiled as we passed him, pausing for a moment and causing Marco to wait too as he kept hold of my hand. Bending, I gave the dog a gentle rub, then leant forward to plop a kiss on his head. I swayed as I overbalanced, and Marco hauled me up.

'I don't think he'd appreciate you flattening him while he's trying to sleep.'

'He does it to me all the time.' I put a finger to my lips. 'But don't tell Mum. He's not supposed to be on the bed.'

Marco let go of my hand and placed his either side of my face, and kissed my forehead. 'I'm fairly sure she already knows. I get the feeling she doesn't miss much.'

I blinked. 'What did she say to you?'

'Actually, nothing. Not like you're implying, anyway.'

'Look, Marco, I know what I'm doing.'

'Do you?'

I squinted, the effects of the alcohol suddenly receding a little. 'Yes.'

'Which is what?'

I pushed my hair back. 'You made me two very lovely offers, Marco. Offers anyone in my position would be stupid to turn down.'

'But you're going to.' A statement rather than a question.

'No.' I saw the flicker of something behind his eyes. 'Well, one of them.'

He gave a small smile. 'I have a feeling I know which one you are turning down.' There was a resignation to his expression. He'd known the answer before he'd even got here. I could see that.

'I am sorry, Marco. I just don't think it's the right thing for either of us.'

We stood together in silence for a moment before Marco prompted me on. 'And the other offer?'

'I'm going to take the job. You and I both know I'm the best person for it.'

'I agree that, for the team, you are definitely the best person. You have talent and I trust you. But I have to say – I don't think this is perhaps the best thing for you. At least not right now.'

'It is! It's the perfect thing, and especially right now! Marco, I need this. Don't you dare change your mind on me.'

'Lexi …'

'Is this because I don't want to get back together with you?'

His perfect teeth showed in a smile, sudden and genuine. 'You really think I would be that petty?'

I blew out a sigh. 'No. I don't even know why I said that. Blame the champagne.'

'I'm not blaming anyone. Or anything. It was a fair question. Yes, I regret that you feel we couldn't make things work between us. And yes, I still think you're beautiful and funny and love that you have no pretensions or airs or—'

'Legs up to my armpits,' I added, remembering that aside from me, he tended to have a predilection for such features in his girlfriends.

'Such legs can sometimes be overrated.'

'Oh really.' My tone was firmly set to 'sceptical'.

'I didn't say always.' The boyish grin he gave illustrated how so many of those endless legs had ended up wrapped around him over the years. He was handsome, amusing, intelligent, and fiercely passionate about the world he operated in. It made quite the package. But it wasn't a package I wanted to open again. I loved Marco, that was true. But not in the way I needed to in order to make things work between us.

I looked up at him. 'Are you really taking back your offer?'

He studied me for a moment then carefully and gently brushed my overgrown fringe back from my eye with his thumb, his hand resting on my face. 'You can't keep running away, Lexi.'

'I'm not running away from anything!' I said, pushing his hand away sharply.

'Aren't you?'

'No! And don't think you can come here, spend a couple of hours with me, and then presume to know everything, because you don't.'

In contrast to me, Marco remained calm, just as he did on the track. 'I'm not presuming anything. And you know I know you better than that. We went through a lot together, Lexi. Good and bad. I know when you're happy and I know when you're sad, however much you disguise it.'

I looked down at my feet, scrunching my toes back and forth on the end of the rug.

'I know it drives you crazy to think there are people who see beyond that tough-cookie shell you try and project.'

Lifting my gaze, I gave him a wary look.

'It's time to stop running, Lexi. It's time to let your guard down and risk everything.'

His dark eyes locked on to mine, as he nodded back towards the sounds of laughter and chatter drifting out from the dining room. 'Do you want to talk about it?'

'Nope.'

'Well, there's a surprise.'

My eyes blazed. 'What's that supposed to mean?'

Marco shrugged. 'You never want to talk about it. You prefer to pack it all away and pretend it's not there, even though it's eating away at you!'

'I do talk about things. Sometimes.'

'So, have you talked about things with Cal?'

'Plenty of things. And what does this have to do with you offering me a job?'

'Because I am not going to be responsible for you running away from something that could bring you all the happiness you've ever wanted.'

I shook my head and felt my insides twist.

'I can't make him happy, Marco.' My voice felt sore and sounded hoarse. The absolute joy of Claire and Dan's announcement contrasted with the perfect misery of how things were – had to be – with Cal. Between all of it, I was suddenly exhausted. To my surprise, Marco laughed. I screwed up my face at him, shocked, but before I could say anything – or do anything – he caught my hands and lifted them as one to his lips.

'Oh, Lexi.' He smiled. 'As much as it pains me to say, that guy is crazy about you. You can see it in every glance he steals at you, every word he speaks to you, every touch. I don't know what's happened between you exactly but at the moment, you both look thoroughly miserable. And thoroughly in love. Whatever it is, it can be fixed.'

I shook my head. Dan and Claire's news this evening had broken the careful dam of protection I kept my emotions behind, taking us all by surprise. I hadn't had time to make sure all the leaks were plugged and now Marco was chipping away at it even more.

'It can't, Marco,' I replied, my voice cracking, 'not this.'

Marco took my hands. 'You know he loves you, right?'

I blinked and a tear breached position, sliding down my face and off my chin, landing on the back of Marco's tanned hand.

'And you love him.' It wasn't a question but I answered anyway. 'Yes.'

'Then you have everything you need. I'll admit I had hopes for us. I've been trying to find the right way to ask you about starting over again for a while. And then I saw those pictures of you. I saw the way he was looking at you. And the way you were looking at him.' He gave me a sheepish glance. 'I'm not accustomed to losing … I had to try. But I also know when I'm beaten. I know I could never make you as happy as he does, no matter how hard I tried. It's clear you do the same for him. Don't waste that, Lexi.'

'I'm not!' I cried, giving up on any semblance of pretence now. 'I mean, I don't want to! Do you honestly think I've not lain awake every night trying to think of a way to change the way things are? Do you think I'd let him go if I had any other choice at all? For God's sake, Marco, I love him! So much that it makes my chest hurt even to think about it, but I have to let him go. For his sake.'

'Why?'

I swallowed, my throat raw and uncomfortable. 'You know why,' I replied, quieter now.

'You've discussed it?'

'Yes.'

'And?'

'And, like the alpha male he is, he thinks that the normal rules don't apply to him. That he can beat the odds! Like you did, and look how well that worked out!'

He gave me a look, and the fight went out of me.

'I saw Cal tonight, just before dinner. He was watching my big, noisy, chaotic family and I could see it in his face – how much that means to him, having that. He's already said that's exactly what he wants for George. And I know he wants it too. Needs it. He had a horrible childhood and he's a wonderful father to George, and would be to any child. I can't be the one to break those dreams. I won't.'

'Lexi, you could never break anyone's dreams. It's just not in you.'

'Marco. This is the way it has to be. I take the job with you, put a permanent distance between us, and give him the chance to find the person he's really meant to be with.'

'Listen to me.' Marco's voice took on a tone that I'd only ever heard him use when he was really, really mad. During all the time I'd known him, he'd never once used it on me. Until now. 'You know as well as me that life can be short. We've seen it. One day you think you have your whole life ahead of you and then, that's it. I missed having that moment by inches and you were witness to that.'

'Don't, Marco. Please! I hate thinking of that day.' I tried to turn away but he stopped me.

'You should think about it. You should think about it every day. I do. It's what keeps me going. It's what keeps me feeling alive and going after what I want, even if I know there's a good chance of me failing. It's what made me kiss you because, even though I pretty much knew you were going to reject me, I had to try. Don't waste something this good, Lexi. Please! You have to try. You have to stop being afraid of taking a chance on love. You're fearless in so many ways, but when it comes to your heart?' His voice was softer now and his smile gentle. 'Not so much. I've seen the way that man looks at you. Hurting you is the last thing on his mind.'

'But what about me hurting him?'

'Why don't you let me worry about that?' Cal's voice from the doorway made me jump. Marco merely turned, calm as ever, accepting the almost imperceptible nod that Cal gave him.

'How long have you been standing there?' I asked, quickly dragging the heel of my hand across my cheeks.

'Long enough.'

'It's rude to eavesdrop. Didn't your mother ever—' I stopped, suddenly realising just how inappropriate my automatic response was. I'd been trying to cover just how excruciatingly awkward I felt and had now managed only to add to it. 'I'm sorry. I didn't mean … I wasn't thinking.'

'It's all right, Lexi.' His voice was soft, and with the way he was looking at me, I knew his response wasn't only in reference to my spectacular foot-in-mouth moment.

Marco broke the spell. 'I should go before this weather really sets in.'

'They're saying there's a big storm headed this way. You going to be OK getting back in that?' Cal nodded at the window, indicating the outline of the sleek Lamborghini parked there, its matte black body slowly being brought into the spirit of the season thanks to the tiny snowflakes now settling gently and decorating the dark paintwork.

'Yes, thanks. If I leave now, I'll be back in London before the roads are too affected.'

Cal nodded, and Marco turned to me. His eyes were kind as he took my hands. 'Thank your family for having me tonight.' We all threw a glance as a big whoop went up from the other room. God knew what they were up to, but from the gales of laughter that followed, it was something fun. A smile tempted my face. How I'd missed the sound of that laughter for all those years. And how I'd miss it if I left again. But I had to. Didn't I?

'I'd say it myself but I don't want to interrupt whatever's going on in there. And congratulations to your brother and his wife. I'm so happy for them.'

'Thank you. Me too,' I croaked, my throat raw from tonight's assault of emotions.

'Have a think about everything I said.' He put a hand to my cheek for a moment. 'The job is still there if you want it. But it's only yours if it's for the right reasons. And I've known you long enough now so don't even bother trying to fool me.' He bent and kissed my forehead and pulled me into a long hug. 'You have to take a chance at some point, Lex,' he whispered. 'And I'm thinking now would be a pretty good time.' Marco let go and stood back. Turning to Cal, he held out his hand. 'I'm fairly sure you overheard me say something about kissing her but as you haven't punched me yet, I'm hoping you've decided not to.'

Cal took his hand and shook it. 'As it's nearly Christmas …' Humour glinted in his eyes.

Marco gave a conceding nod. 'Then I wish you a very merry Christmas. And the best of luck.'

Cal caught the meaning. 'Thanks.'

Marco opened the back door. 'I'll call you soon.'

I smiled. 'Message me when you're home, OK?' I said, glancing past him and looking up at the clouds now sending down larger flakes.

Marco grinned and shrugged at Cal who had now come to stand at my side. 'She's worse than my mother sometimes.'

'And like her, just because you're a world champion doesn't mean I'm going to go all reverential around you. Just send the damn text.'

Marco dashed another kiss on my cheek. 'So feisty.'

He winked at Cal before hurrying out to his car and quickly ensconcing himself inside. The engine burbled into life and, without drama, Marco gently steered the car out of the drive and turned into the road. In the still of the night, we heard the engine open up as its owner drove away from the sleepy village and back to the lights and noise of the city.

I closed the door against the cold and glanced over at Apollo. He'd shuffled himself onto his back and was now lying with all four paws in the air, his front legs loose and floppy, his back haunches folded, and everything overlaid with gentle, contented snores.

'Very elegant, Apollo.'

Cal's gaze followed mine and his beautiful face, moments ago serious and concerned, creased into laughter. I loved his smile, the sound of his laugh, and the way those hypnotic eyes became twinkly and full of joy. I loved the way his long legs covered the distance between me and the dog in a couple of strides and the soft look on his face as he crouched down and carefully lifted Apollo's head from where it was lying at a decidedly odd angle off the edge of his bed. Without waking him, Cal gently manoeuvred him back into a more comfortable position. Standing, he looked back to where I had remained by the door.

'I've never had a dog so I don't know whether dogs can get a crick in their neck or not but …' He shrugged, a slightly sheepish look on his face.

'He won't now. Thank you.' Silence drifted over us. 'Have you thought any more about getting a dog of your own?' I piped up eventually, in order to break it.

Cal shoved his hands in his pockets, dropped his head, and let out a big sigh. Bringing his head back up, he caught me in the tractor beam of that intoxicating gaze. 'Is this the bit where you say everything and anything in order to avoid talking about the things that really matter?'

I pondered a moment. 'Pretty much, yeah.'

He walked back over to where I'd remained, almost fixed to the floor since Marco had left, half of me wanting to get over the fear I had about what might happen next, and half of me wanting to do exactly what Marco had said I always did. Run away. My eyes flicked to the door handle.

'Don't even think about it. Unless it's just to go somewhere else to talk. Which, from the bit I overheard, is something we definitely need to do.'

'Oh, there you are!' Giselle appeared, slightly pink-faced from the warmth and general busyness of the party that was now in full abandon in another part of the house. 'We'd wondered where you'd gone.'

'Marco was leaving. I … We … were just seeing him out.'

Xander wandered up behind his wife and I saw them both look curiously between me and Cal. 'Are you all right?' he asked.

Giselle was next to me now, peering at my face. Without a word, she tugged me over to the light. 'You've been crying.'

'It's nothing. Really.'

The look she gave me showed just how little her kids were

going to get away with if they ever tried it on with her.

'Honestly. It's all … fine.'

Actually, I had no idea what it was, so fine would have to do for the moment.

Giselle was having none of it but she'd known me long enough to know when not to push it.

'OK. Obviously, I don't believe a word but I'll leave you both to it. Are you coming back in?'

'I don't really know, Gis.'

She hugged me. 'Is it Dan's news that's upset you? I mean, I know you're not upset for them but …'

'No! I'm thrilled for them! I'm a bit tearful about it, yes, but it's for all the good reasons. Just like I was with you. I promise.'

Giselle rested her head against mine for a moment. When she'd first told me she was pregnant, she'd admitted that she almost thought about hiding it for a while because she was worried about my reaction. But then she realised by doing that, it would have made it so much worse. And that was true. Life was what it was. I didn't want people treading on eggshells around me. Admittedly, some tact was always appreciated, which even my lummoxes of brothers realised. But apart from that, life was there and you had to deal with it. I could be sad for me, but I would never let that affect the joy I felt for the people I loved.

'We'll leave you to it, then.' Xander verbally nudged Giselle.

She gave me a private grin. 'He's so subtle.' Giving us both a quick kiss on the cheek, she stepped back towards the other room. 'Call me if you want anything. It doesn't matter what the time is.'

'Thanks, Gis. I will.'

'Although, between the hours of nine and five would be— Oww!' Xander teased before getting a whack from his wife. He winked at me over the top of her head. Like Giselle, I knew he was there for me wherever and whenever I needed him no matter what he said. They disappeared from sight and headed back into the throng of the family party.

261

'I'm thinking it might be better to go somewhere else. Somewhere we can talk without any interruptions,' Cal suggested.

Right now I was OK with the interruptions because it stopped me having to face up to him and what that might mean. As if reading my mind, he gave a head tilt.

'Why do I get the feeling you wouldn't mind if your whole family trooped in here right now?'

Even in the low light of the lamp, I knew Cal hadn't missed how I was now blushing as red as the poinsettia Mum had on the windowsill.

'That's what I thought.'

'We can go next door to mine, if you like.'

'If I were a lesser man, the entire lack of enthusiasm in that suggestion might bother me.'

It was my turn to look sheepish. 'I'm sorry. I didn't mean it to sound like that.'

He reached his hand out and warm, long fingers gently laced through mine. It was such a simple gesture but I felt the sparks shoot through me at his touch. He turned, his eyes on mine, and the sparks exploded like fireworks on New Year's Eve.

This wasn't me. I was good at compartmentalising. Or running away, if that's what's Marco wanted to call it. Whatever it was labelled, I did it. I put things in a box. Put them away. Moved on. Done. But Cal refused to conform to my method. His face, voice, body all invaded my thoughts when they weren't supposed to. This wasn't how it was supposed to work. But I couldn't stop it.

'I can practically see the steam from here.' His mouth curved up a little. 'Don't get yourself worked up overthinking. I'm not asking for anything from you, Lexi, apart from for you to let me in. Let me be a part of this decision you're making to push me away.'

'It's not what I wanted, Cal, I promise. I never meant to fall for you. It all just sort of happened.'

'Some things are meant to happen. George wasn't "meant to happen" but I guess sometimes life has other ideas for us.'

Another whoop of cheering and laughter went up from the other room.

'Come on, let's find somewhere a bit quieter. We can always come back later. They'll understand.'

'I don't want them thinking—'

'Lex. It was your mum who told me to come and find you as I was standing in there pretending to join in.'

I looked up at him. 'She's pretty good at that whole mind-reading thing, isn't she?'

'So good. It's kind of disturbing. How did you lot ever get away with anything?'

I shrugged. 'We didn't. We've all had years of practice with her and still can't fool her for more than a minute.'

'I'm glad she insisted.'

'Are you?'

'Yes. Because at least now I know how you feel, which is something you had omitted to tell me.'

I didn't answer and Cal didn't speak, concentrating instead on lifting my coat from the wooden row of pegs on the wall. He draped it around my shoulders before grabbing his own and slinging it over his arm. Opening the door, Cal gripped it firmly as a flurry of snow blew in on the icy draught. We shoved ourselves through the door and quickly closed it behind us, keeping the heat in the house.

Cal took my hand and we half ran through the now-settling snow to the steps, duly gritted earlier, and raced up them. I grabbed the key from my pocket and quickly plugged it in the lock and turned. The cosy warmth from my little flat enveloped us as we stepped in, shutting out the weather – and the world – leaving just me and Cal. The softly changing lights from the small fibre optic Christmas tree I'd chosen provided a gentle, comforting glow.

'I … Can I get you a drink or something?' I asked, suddenly feeling a little awkward as Cal took the coat from my shoulders and hung it alongside his on the shabby chic hat stand behind the door.

'I'd really just like to sit and talk before I explode but if you want a drink, you should have one.'

'I don't really.'

'Stop procrastinating then and get that cute butt over here and sit down with me.'

I hesitated. Cal was doing his best to keep things light, as though coaxing a wary animal towards safety, knowing all the time that it might bolt and shoot straight out into the road.

'Please, Lexi.' His voice was low and his expression looked almost haunted. 'I know what you said, about being friends but it's not working for me, and I don't think it's working for you either.'

'I'll make it work … I have to. It's for the—'

His head snapped up as his brows drew together. He stood and immediately gained the height advantage. I tipped my head back to meet his eyes and almost wished I hadn't. The pain in those grey eyes shot into my chest with a force that felt almost physical. He was done with the coaxing.

'If you're about to say it's for the best, then save your breath. I know it's not and so do you. What's it going to take to get you to realise that? What do I have to do to prove to you that, whatever you think, all I want is you?'

'That's what Marco thought too, at first,' I cried. The guilt at seeing the pain in his eyes kicked me automatically into defensive mode.

'I'm not Marco.'

'Why would you be any different?' I threw up my hands, turning away. I couldn't face him right now because he *was* different. I knew that. I'd never felt like this about anyone and if this was how excruciatingly painful it was to love someone this much, then I was going to make sure I never did again.

'Because everyone's different, Lexi!' I could hear the hurt and the tension in his voice and wrapped my arms around myself to prevent me from wrapping them around him as I turned back to face him. 'And because I bloody well love you more than I know what to do with and I know you love me too. All that put together means that I'm different. That this' – he waved his arm in the air between us – 'is different. And if you'd just give us a chance, we can prove it.'

The silence hung between us. A soft, swishy noise outside signalled that the snow was falling harder, settling quicker. I swallowed the lump in my throat and looked towards the window as thoughts swirled through my head, just as the flakes outside tumbled in the air.

'He'll be OK. He's probably nearly there by now.' Cal picked up on my thoughts about Marco.

Marco was a good friend. Better than I ever knew – his actions tonight showed me that. All everyone saw was the playboy side, a side he admittedly played up to. But there was so much more to Marco than that. I knew that. And tonight Cal had seen that too.

'Call him if you're going to be so worried that you can't concentrate on anything else. It's OK.'

His voice was calm now. Understanding. He'd told me that he'd seen the media coverage of Marco's accident. There'd been a photo of me taken a little after the accident when I'd returned to the garage. Its focus was slightly blurred thanks to the length of the lens used, but there was no mistaking the utter distress on my face. I'd been mortified at the intrusion. At the world seeing my emotions so raw, so visceral.

Marco was used to being in the public eye, but I wasn't. I'd never got used to it. I had no wish to be seen at parties and I'd certainly had no wish to be put on display like that. Once Marco knew about it, he'd put his lawyers on the case and had managed to get hold of the photo, but by then it had already been seen around the world. And one of those people who had seen it was Cal Martin.

Whatever Marco said, I knew there was someone better for

him, more suited to that lifestyle he favoured. But I still loved him, like family now. I'd never forget that day or the fear, and with Joe's recent accident still in mind, I was on edge.

My phone let out a soft ping, signalling the arrival of a message. I walked over to the tiny console table near the door where I'd left my mobile earlier this evening.

Home. So you can stop worrying now. Talk to him!!! xxx

'He OK?'

I replaced the phone on the table and hovered there for a moment, my fingers fiddling with the petals of the impossibly real-looking cream silk roses displayed in a cut glass vase.

'Yes. Thanks.'

'Good.'

'He told me – again – to talk to you.'

'And are you going to take his advice?'

I let my hand drop to my side before I risked destroying the flower display entirely.

'I'm scared, Cal. And I'm not used to that. I never baulked at going for the biggest jumps on my mountain bike, or following my brothers to the highest branch in the tree. That was just a challenge to me. And I like challenges. But this feels like so much more. And, honestly, I'm not sure if I can do it.'

'Because you might risk your heart?'

I shook my head. 'No. Because I might risk yours. And your son's.'

Cal held out his hand, and I looked at it, wanting to take it. I wanted to take his hand and I wanted so much more but—

'Lexi, stop thinking for a moment and just listen.'

Lifting my gaze to meet his, I saw the faintest of smiles shadow his lips as he wiggled his fingers towards me. Reaching out, I took his hand and as he pulled me close, his arms wrapping tight around me, one large hand cradling the back of my head.

Immediately, I felt some of the knots begin to loosen. This was where I should be. In my heart, I knew it. But the problem wasn't

266

my heart. I'd always been sensible and practical and overruled the silly whims of my heart. The one time I hadn't, it had ended in pain on both sides. And this time would be so, so much worse. The question was whether I was willing to take that risk again. To take a chance on Cal Martin. On myself.

Cal gently pulled us both down onto the well-loved sofa and we sunk into its comforting depths. He kept his arms around me and leant his head gently on mine.

'Lexi, do you really think I haven't thought this over a million times?' He breathed a kiss into my hair. 'I grew up protecting myself from anything and anyone that could hurt me. I swore to myself I'd never let anyone in enough to risk my feelings, and when George came along, I knew that I'd do everything I possibly could to give him a happy home and would never do anything to risk his happiness, or put confusion into his life.'

Cal sat up a little and turned me, so that I was facing him. 'The only thing you'd be risking, if you let yourself, is adding more happiness, more joy, and more love to both our lives.'

I met his eyes and saw the honesty in them. He believed every word and I knew that I did too.

'But what about …'

'More children?'

My gaze dropped to his chest, and he hooked the side of his finger under my chin, bringing it up. He waited until I met his eyes before speaking.

'If it happens, I'll be incredibly happy. But if it doesn't, I'll still be incredibly happy because I'll have you, which is more than I ever thought I'd find. I love you, Lexi, and so does George. I will always love you, whatever happens. And I will be right beside you, always. For the good times and the bad. That's what love's about. Whatever happens, we'll be in it together, and being together is already more than enough. I meant everything I said before. I want you in our lives. That's the most important thing to me. Anything else is a bonus.'

He brushed back a lock of my hair that had tumbled forward. 'I love you.' He gave me the smile that had caused my stomach to do backflips from the very first time. 'You have no idea how much! If you give me the chance, I promise to show you every day.' He took my hand. 'But I can't do this alone, Lexi, and I know it's scary. I've never done this before either – given my heart over to someone so utterly and completely – and it scares the life out of me, if I'm honest, but it also feels like the only thing I should be doing. It feels more right than anything I've ever done in my life.'

I leant forward and kissed him, feeling the hesitation in his body. Pulling back, I met his eyes, wary.

'Please don't tell me that was a goodbye kiss,' he whispered.

I shook my head, the smile spreading on my face. 'No. It wasn't. It was a time-to-be-brave kiss.'

'So, you're saying yes?' The surprise in his voice tore at my heart. He'd opened himself to me, laid himself bare, knowing, even expecting, to be turned down. His honesty and bravery breached my emotional dam entirely.

'I am. I want this. I want you, and whatever does or doesn't happen. I want it all.'

Cal touched my face gently, his long fingers sliding back and entwining themselves in my hair, his eyes never leaving me.

'I used to be a daredevil as a child.' I began. 'Nothing fazed me. But somewhere along the way, something happened; I lost some of that bravery. I lost some of that self-belief. Now it's time to get it back. It's time be brave about something that really matters …'

I barely had time to take a breath before Cal's mouth was on mine, his arm wrapping around my waist, as the other cupped the back of my head, his fingers splaying as his mouth delivered a kiss that stopped me thinking about anything other than how good it felt to be here, being kissed by this man, and feeling his solid, broad body pressing close to mine as his mouth moved and began trailing down my neck …

Chapter 22

Outside the snow was already half a foot deep at least.

'Are you going to be all right getting back?'

'That's why I wore these.' He wiggled his feet like a clown in funny shoes, but the expensive hiking boots were far sexier. Although to be fair, everything Cal wore was far sexier, precisely because it was him wearing it.

'Good thinking. I guess you won't be needing them in Antigua.'

He pulled a face. 'No. Probably not. I'm kind of wishing I hadn't booked that now.'

Giving a shiver, he turned his collar up against the snowflakes sneaking their way down his back. I reached out and grabbed a scarf from my coat stand.

'Here,' I said, wrapping and knotting it around his neck.

'Thank you.' His voice was so soft it almost drifted away on the gust of wind that blew across the steps, adding to the snowdrift building up against the side of the house. 'I'd better go.'

I nodded. 'Can you let me know when you're in, just so I know you didn't turn into Mr Frosty on the way home?'

'If you promise to go right to sleep straight after.'

'That sounds like a bribery line you'd use on George.' I smiled.

'I employ it whenever and wherever I need to. So, do you promise?'

'I do.'

'Good.' He swooped in for another kiss and my hands slid behind his neck, resting on the scarf, pulling him closer.

'I wish you hadn't booked it too,' I said as we broke from the kiss.

Cal rested his forehead against mine. 'I'm pretty sure it's going to feel like the longest week ever. Especially as George still hasn't forgiven me for us not getting to spend Christmas at your parents' place with his friends.'

'He'll be fine once he gets caught up in all the holiday excitement, I'm sure.'

Cal pulled a face. 'We'll see. I'm not about to place any bets.' He gave another yank at his collar as the wind blew across the steps.

'Go on,' I said. 'Before you let all the snow in.' The last thing I wanted right now was for Cal to leave but we both knew staying wasn't really an option tonight, not with little George at home and them heading off to Antigua tomorrow.

'I'm going.' He threw me that grin that always turned my insides deliciously liquid as soft laughter bubbled from him, its sound being absorbed into the landscape now muffled by its thick layer of soft white.

Cal half slid down the banisters, lifting his legs and letting the muscles in his arms support his weight until he got to the bottom where his feet landed with a soft squish in the snowdrift that was building at the foot of the steps. He turned, raised a hand, and then trudged off towards the gate. As he got to it, he waved again and blew a kiss.

I closed the door, gave a quick shiver, and then threw the double lock before hanging the key on the hook next to the door. Resting my head on the solid oak of the door for a moment, I knew I had to keep my brave pants on and take another risk.

Checking the clock on my dresser, I picked up my mobile and dialled. It rang twice before being answered.

'Hi, Marco. I have an answer for you.'

For the first time in weeks, I woke without a knot in my stomach and smiled to myself at the lack of tension in my shoulders as I moved. Rolling over, I grabbed the remote control from the other bedside and aimed it roughly in the direction of the TV. The red light went green and then BBC News came up.

'*With the worst snowstorm to hit the south-east for several years, people are being advised not to attempt travel, with airports and many roads being closed.*'

The reporter was in the standard North Face jacket with a woolly hat and full make-up. Frankly she looked like she was freezing her arse off and that her first call, when she got the feeling back in her fingers, was going to be to her agent.

'*Now back to you, Ariana, in the studio.*' She didn't exactly say 'you lucky bleep' but the suggestion was definitely there.

'*This is BBC News. It's eight forty-seven. Here are the headlines. A major snowstorm has engulfed the south-east of England with falls in some areas of at least …*'

I had a day off today and although we'd all eaten enough for the entire village last night, astoundingly my stomach was now grumbling and requesting to be fed. I kicked my feet out from the covers and headed into the bathroom, running the toothbrush around my mouth in an attempt to get rid of the dried-up bird-cage feeling.

Shoving my feet into my Ugg boots out of habit, I quickly remembered what lay outside, and instead rammed my pyjamaed legs into wellies and layered my cosy down-filled coat over my dressing gown. I wasn't going to win any fashion awards but that was the last thing on my mind right now. Admittedly, that was never the first thing on my mind but even less so today. Opening the door, I scooted down the steps and tramped through snow

271

that hovered dangerously close to the top of my wellies before almost tumbling in the back door to the kitchen.

'Hello, darling,' Mum said, looking up from where she was stirring something on the hob. 'Would you like a cup of tea? I've just boiled the kettle.'

'I'll make it. Do you want one?'

I saw her give me a little sideways look. 'I'm not sure there's enough water in there for three.'

I frowned. 'Three?'

Mum lifted her head as she tasted whatever was emitting the most delicious smell from the pot in front of her. She didn't say a word but her eyes spoke volumes.

'Cal is not in my ...' I stopped just in time before the word 'bed' popped out '... flat,' I finished.

Mum tilted her head. 'And yet you seem different. Relieved. Happy.'

I handed Mum her cup of tea and kissed her on the cheek before taking a chair at the table. Apollo stretched on his bed by the Aga, lifted his head and, in a tangle of long legs, righted himself and plodded over to me. Sitting with his hip against the chair, he doinked his head against me. I rubbed his head and dipped down to plop a kiss on the solid, warm bulk of it.

'Maybe that's because I am.' I took a sip of the tea and felt it rush warm and soothing through me. 'Actually, I have something to ask you.'

Mum put the spoon down and faced me, a cautious smile hovering around her mouth.

'How does one go about applying for a permanent position at The Four Seasons?'

Apollo hadn't been enthused about this walk. In fact, his excited dance when I picked up the lead stopped almost immediately the moment I opened the door, and he looked out at the alien landscape. Smothered by snow, everything looked different, softer, curvier, and most of all, as far as the dog was concerned, colder. He gave me a look and then scooted back to his bed by the nice warm Aga, trailing the lead across the kitchen. I toed off my boots and tramped across.

'Come on, lazy bones. We have to catch them before they leave. It'll be fine once you're out there. You'll enjoy it.' I bent and picked up the lead and waited. Apollo gave me another look. I wiggled my fingers in my jacket pocket and his ears perked up. 'There's a treat in it for you if you do.'

He appeared to consider this for a moment and then scrabbled up, his nose immediately prodding at my pocket.

'All right, hang on. I can't get my hand out with your big beak in the way.' I laughed. 'Here,' I said, holding my hand flat with the piece of sausage on it. Apollo hoovered it up and looked up at me for more, ever hopeful. I laughed again. 'In a bit. Come on.' He followed me and I shoved my double-socked feet back in my wellies and headed out the door.

The snow was a little deeper than I anticipated in places and I was inordinately glad we had a Great Dane and not a Chihuahua. Once he'd got over his initial sniffy disdain about coming out with me, Apollo had decided that actually, this white stuff was pretty fun and had spent the entire walk charging about through snowdrifts, more often than not showering me with overspray as he made himself into a doggy snowplough.

Thankfully the weather had changed this morning. Above us stretched a beautiful cobalt blue sky, the sun hung bright within it, although with more show than function. It was still bitterly cold and I'd lost all feeling in my face within minutes of leaving the house. We made our way to our intended destination and I was relieved to see Cal's car still in his driveway. Of course, he could have arranged a cab. Caught up in the emotions of last night, I'd forgotten to ask how he was getting to the airport, or what time he was even leaving. He'd told me he'd call when he was there though as I hadn't had a call yet, I just had to hope I hadn't missed them.

I rang the doorbell and quickly set about drying off Apollo with the little microfibre towel I'd stuffed in one of my pockets. The fabric quickly wicked off the moisture from his shiny, caramel coat and he dutifully lifted each paw without any fuss for me to give it a wipe. Just as I was finishing the last one, the door opened and I straightened, shoving the towel back in my pocket as I did so.

'Hi!' Cal smiled down, evidently surprised to see me.

'Hi, I …' My words faltered a little. God, he was gorgeous. The smile tilted a little more as he waved us in through the door. Wearing a black cashmere jumper, dark-wash jeans, and – thanks to the underfloor heating that ran throughout his house – bare feet, he looked relaxed, understated, and sexy as hell. I stepped in, unclipped Apollo's lead, and told him to stay as I accepted Cal's assistance with the removal of my coat. As I did so, I caught sight of myself in the large, ornately framed full-length mirror that took up a portion of the wall in his hall. I, most certainly, did not look sexy.

'Oh my God, I look like Rudolph!' I said, my hand flying to my nose.

Cal let out one of those deliciously deep laughs and turned me to face him.

'You look lovely. Like always.'

I peered over my shoulder at my reflection again. Resting his hands on my shoulders, Cal gently turned me back again. 'I said you look lovely.' His hands went to my face and he bent his head down towards me. Sinking into the kiss I sighed, and I felt him smile against me. Pressing myself as close to him as I could, I wanted to make up for all the weeks I'd wasted. Time that I could have spent in far more enjoyable ways, like this …

Eventually we broke apart and Cal grinned, then pointed at my hat. I frisbeed my hat over to him and he stuck it over my jacket. Having pulled off my boots, I was finally done.

'I won't stay long. I know you've probably got to leave any time for your flight. Actually I wasn't sure if I might have missed you, but—'

'Lexi! Apollo!' George came hurtling down the corridor, sliding on his socks and careering into me. Apollo, being a bright dog, did a neat little sidestep to avoid the small child-shaped projectile.

'Hi, chilli bean!' I said, hugging him and dropping to my knee. 'You all packed for your holiday?'

George gave me a quizzical look, looked up at his dad, then back at me. 'We're not going to Antigoo, Lexi. Didn't Daddy tell you?'

'Oh!' I said, standing back up. 'How come?'

Cal pointed outside. 'That has cancelled our flight.'

'Oh dear. That's awful,' I said, feeling the biggest grin I owned slide onto my face.

'I know. It's really terrible,' Cal replied, his smile as wide as mine.

'George, why don't you take Apollo into the living room. I'll be there in a second.'

George charged off calling the dog who loped lazily beside him. Moments later, peals of childish laughter rang out from the other room. George popped out of the doorway, his face shining with laughter. 'Apollo just farted really loudly!' he informed us with glee before disappearing again, more giggles drifting out almost immediately.

Cal smirked. 'It has to be said that the bar for humour is set quite low in this house.'

'That's OK. When it happens while we're at the table, you'd think we were all George's age. And that includes my parents.'

Cal grinned.

'I really hope it's just noise and that my dog isn't actually gassing your child.'

We walked up the corridor and stuck our heads into the living room. Apollo seemed unfazed by his behaviour and, luckily, hadn't seemed to have left too much of a pong.

'All clear.' Cal chuckled and led me through to the kitchen side of the bright, open-plan room.

'Coffee?'

'Thanks,' I replied and Cal started moving around grabbing mugs and coffee pods from the cabinet.

'So, I hope you don't mind but I called your mum earlier to see if that offer for Christmas Day dinner was still on.'

'I'm guessing by George's happy little face that it is?'

Cal stepped towards me, closing the gap until there was none, his large, warm hands resting on the curve of my hip as he drew me closer still.

'It is. And George has been invited to go and help Harry and the gang make iced biscuits to hang on the tree. Matt's coming to collect him in about half an hour. And then I've got some ideas that might lead you to getting to see my happy little face …' His smile was an enticing combination of desire, teasing, and pure mischief. And I loved it.

Chapter 23

The Christmas Village Festival was a big event in our little corner of the world, and I had wonderful memories from my childhood of the parade and getting to stay up late, not to mention all the goodies being sold in the stalls in the tiny market square. Each hut was topped with a white waterproof felt covering, giving the impression of a snow-covered roof. Tonight, however, nature was giving a helping hand. Gentle snowflakes fluttered down, catching on everything, including the long, dark eyelashes of the man currently standing next to me.

Cal and Dad were stood chatting away beside me, stepping back as some shoppers took advantage of the little slices of free Christmas Delight Toffee I was holding as a promo for the shop. All the shops closed tonight, allowing their owners to enjoy the parade, but that didn't mean we were going to miss out on squeezing in a bit of advertising. Thankfully, Mum had let me off wearing the elf costume tonight, something I was grateful for.

One of the passing women, now chewing on the toffee, surreptitiously eyed Cal before raising her eyes at a friend and giggling. Probably the most popular stand at the fair was Edna's Excellent Eggnog. I knew from experience it truly was excellent, and I had a feeling that this particular group of ladies might have come via that same stall. Caught up in conversation, Cal didn't notice the admiring glances being thrown his way. One arm rested around my waist as he stood chatting, his free hand snaking down occasionally to pinch a square of toffee. The third time he did it, I tapped him on the knuckles and he burst out laughing.

'Think yourself lucky,' Dad said, taking two pieces from the tray and handing one to Cal, 'normally you get rapped on your first attempt.'

I felt a blush shadow my cheeks. 'He's new to the village. I'm being nice and making allowances.'

'Oh!' Dad nodded thoughtfully. 'That's what it is.'

Cal grinned widely and squeezed me close, his lips pressing gently on the top of my head.

'Dad!' George's voice carried over moments before he and my nephew appeared through the milling crowd, people parting before them like the Red Sea. Matt moseyed after them, his wife's hand in one of his and an extra-large eggnog in the other. The children arrived laughing and out of breath, and George stopped by bumping into his dad's leg and wrapping his arms around him.

'Having fun?' Cal asked.

'Yes!' George's face was beaming, his nose pink from the cold. 'Hi, Lexi!' George transferred his cuddles, sharing me with my nephew who already had his arms wrapped around my thighs. I cuddled them close, bending and dropping a kiss on both their heads, laughing at the bad cracker joke they shared and feeling happier than I'd ever thought would be possible just a few short days ago.

'Now that's a lovely picture!' Mum called, holding up her phone in front of her. 'Now everybody say, "Christmas Pudding!"'

Laughing, we all did as instructed and I snuck a glance at Cal as she beamed at us, having taken the shot. His eyes were already on me, shining with laughter.

'Mum always thinks saying "cheese" around this time of the year isn't very festive. We had a whole debate about it one year, putting forward our argument that it was still appropriate because it's traditional to have a cheese board and so on, but she wouldn't have it. Mum cooks the dinner so it's often a good idea to let her win these arguments if we want to eat.'

'I'd have thought you'd all be mucking in together,' Cal said, peering at something sticky on the end of George's mitten. 'What actually is this?' he asked, bending closer. George studied it for a moment before shrugging.

'I think it's probably candyfloss,' Matt's wife offered. 'They only had a tiny bit each. I hope that was OK. George got a bit excited and forgot to take off his mitten first when he put his hand in.'

Cal nodded, enlightened, then gave a shrug of his eyebrows and smiled. 'No problem. Thanks for treating him.'

'Our pleasure. Those two are joined at the hip these days. It's lovely.'

Cal's smile widened. 'They are. It's been so good for him coming here. He's really come out of his shell. He was so shy before and found it a bit difficult to make friends, but he has some great ones now. It's definitely made me worry less about him.'

'He's part of the family.' Matt smiled, his grin widening as he looked between us.

We all turned to where the boys were now playing hide-and-seek with each other, using Matt as a hiding place. Like all of my brothers, Matt took after Dad's side of the family: tall, broad, solid, and good for playing hide-and-seek around.

As we stood in a group talking and laughing, I mentioned to Mum that Cal thought we were bad children as we left her alone to do the dinner on Christmas Day. Mum's momentary horrified look made me smile.

'Oh no! The kitchen is definitely my domain on Christmas Day, Cal,' she explained. 'The last thing I want is a whole bunch of my offspring coming in and telling me I'm doing it wrong.' She winked at us before hugging his arm. 'I'm afraid I'm a bit of a diva when it comes to Christmas dinner. My children have learned not to get in the way and just come when they're called for certain jobs, like carrying things to the table. Other than that, I thoroughly enjoy it all. I know that's probably not very PC or whatever these days but I'm afraid I don't take a lot of notice of all that. I do what I enjoy and taking care of my family is something that brings me a lot of joy, just as they do.'

Cal brought his other arm round and hugged her. 'They're very lucky to have such a fantastic mum.'

Mum pushed herself up on her tiptoes, and with the help of Cal bending somewhat, planted a kiss on his cheek.

George was now looking a little worn out from all the excitement. Hopefully he'd manage to stay awake long enough not to miss the parade. He leant against me and I put my arm around him, stroking his hair. I felt his weight increase a little and glanced down. He looked up and gave me a tired smile. Reaching down, I hauled him up onto my hip and he cuddled into me as I wrapped my arms around him, revelling in his snuggles.

'You OK?' Cal leant towards me. 'He's getting quite heavy.'

I smiled up at Cal, cuddling his son a little tighter as I did so. 'I'm fine. Don't forget I'm used to lugging racing car wheels about.' I jiggled George a little and kissed his temple as he giggled sleepily. 'This one is light as a feather compared to some of those.'

A flash went off, making us look up. 'So cute!' Mum grinned, tapping at her phone. 'You don't mind if I pop this on our socials, do you, Cal? George's face was tucked into Lexi's shoulder so he can't be seen, in case you're worried.'

'Fine by me.' He smiled at her.

'Ahem?' I raised an eyebrow.

'Oh, I know you don't mind, darling,' Mum replied, planting a big kiss on my cheek before beginning to tap away on her phone.

'I think we might have created a monster introducing Mum to social media.'

I could feel Cal's laughter as he stood close to me. 'You're not helping.'

'You love it.'

I looked up, meeting his eyes, and I couldn't deny it. I did love it. All of it. But especially him.

As the sound of the parade drifted down, the children began jumping excitedly. Almost as one, Matt and Cal each lifted a small boy onto their shoulders, enabling them to see over the crowds as carefully decorated Christmas floats drove slowly into view, their costumed occupants dancing along to the music and waving to the crowds that lined the village high street.

Bringing up the rear was Santa's sleigh with a well-padded Father Christmas at the helm, and a very glamorous Mrs Christmas next to him. The ornate sleigh body, crafted by Matt, hid something that sounded suspiciously like an old Mercedes.

'Sounds like she's running all right now, thanks to you two.' Dan appeared next to us, directing his comment at Cal, a niece perched happily on his broad shoulders, her little hands firmly grabbing two handfuls of hair. Claire was his other side, bundled up against the cold in a warm puffy coat and looking healthy and happy. 'Make quite the team, don't you?'

Cal looked down at me. One arm rested on George's leg, as he balanced on his shoulders, but the other was wrapped around my waist, holding me close. I met those stormy ocean-grey eyes that tonight were filled with laughter and joy that perfectly reflected my own.

He let that almost illegally sexy smile slide onto his face. 'I think we make the perfect team.'

Epilogue

One Year Later

I sat back, Apollo at my feet and beside me, the man I woke up with each day, who I was still amazed, and incredibly proud, to call my husband. Christmas dinner was over for another year and the noise and laughter surrounding the table made me smile. It had been a year full of surprises from Cal's unexpected proposal on this day last year in front of the family he was now lovingly a part of, to the perfect, quiet wedding. Cal had been worried when I'd told him I'd turned down Marco's generous job offer – he'd been incredibly supportive of me taking it, if that was what I had wanted, knowing that we'd make it work somehow.

But I'd known it wasn't what I wanted. It was an amazing opportunity but it was time to make a change. Time to be brave. I looked around at my large, noisy family, now with the addition of three more: Giselle and Xander's baby daughter, plus Dan and Claire's twins. I wanted to be here. With Cal and George and with my family. My enjoyment of travel was still fulfilled by having taken over liaising with our international suppliers. But now the travel was on my terms and I loved it. I loved being part of my family again in a more meaningful way.

I only wished that I could have avoided picking up the kids' stomach bug for Christmas.

'You OK?' Cal leant over, our goddaughter's chubby arms flailing about as she sat on his lap and did her best to upend anything within her short reach, giggling with every attempt.

'Yeah, just a bit tired.'

'Did you make an appointment with the doctor?'

I moved my water glass further away from the baby's reach and shook my head.

'It's just a bug. They can't do anything about that anyway. It'll pass soon enough. Everyone's had it practically.'

Cal smiled at me. 'Right.'

I gave him a tired smile. 'What?'

'You're right. Everyone has had it. And everyone else only threw up for one day and recovered in three. You've been sick for over a week now.'

'Maybe I was run down.'

'I thought you said you've felt better this year than you have in ages.'

I sighed and leant my head against his arm, the baby catching on to my finger and giggling as she played. 'I have really.'

Cal moved closer, his lips brushing my ear as he spoke, sending hot, delicious tingles throughout my body. 'That's what love – and lust – can do for you.'

I laughed, knowing he was right. In the past couple of years, my life had taken directions I'd certainly not planned for or expected. But in the end, I was exactly where I was supposed to be. Cal and I both knew that the likelihood of any more additions to our family was low, but we had acquired a couple of four-legged ones several months back and he'd been right. We did have the most wonderful, full, and happy life. We accepted how lucky we were to have what we had already been given. And that was enough.

'Anyone want tea?' Mum said, rising from her chair with her party hat slightly askew and a definite rosy bloom to her cheeks.

'Not for me, thanks. It's really weird but I've gone right off tea lately.'

Without exception, every adult in the room turned their heads to look at me.

I met the smiles with confusion. 'What?'

Cal, the baby still on his lap, placed a kiss on my temple. 'I have an extra Christmas present for you. You don't have to open it now. Later is fine.'

'Cal, no. You've already given me so much!'

Giselle leant over and took the baby back onto her lap, her face beaming. 'I think he might have given you something else, if we're all reading the signs right.'

I switched my shocked gaze from her to Cal, who laid a thin box in front of me.

'When you didn't shake off the bug, I got to wondering …'

I knew the shape. I'd bought enough a few years ago to recognise one from fifty paces. My fingers laid upon it, its contents holding so much promise … but also the possibility of so much disappointment. Cal and I hadn't been trying for a baby consciously. We were enjoying our life together with George and travelling. Cal had promoted Xander, lessening the pressure on himself and allowing us more time together. We'd both been brave and it had paid off.

Two minutes later it proved to have paid off in more ways than we could ever have allowed ourselves to believe.

Loved **The Best Little Christmas Shop**? You'll love…

The Christmas Project

When professional organiser Kate Stone is asked to declutter Michael's home in time for Christmas, she's happy to help.

He may be gorgeous, but Michael might just be the grumpiest, rudest man she's ever met. If he wasn't her best friend's brother, Kate would never have hung around!

But underneath Michael's icy exterior, Kate is surprised to find a caring man who has struggled since his wife left. While she is more used to sorting messy sock drawers than messy love lives, Kate can't help making Michael her secret Christmas project.

With the big day only a few weeks away, can Kate and Michael put aside their differences to make his house a home again? And will they find love along the way?

Out now!

Dear Reader,

We hope you enjoyed reading this book. If you did, we'd be so appreciative if you left a review. It really helps us and the author to bring more books like this to you.

Here at HQ Digital we are dedicated to publishing fiction that will keep you turning the pages into the early hours. Don't want to miss a thing? To find out more about our books, promotions, discover exclusive content and enter competitions you can keep in touch in the following ways:

JOIN OUR COMMUNITY:

Sign up to our new email newsletter: http://smarturl.it/SignUpHQ

Read our new blog www.hqstories.co.uk

https://twitter.com/HQStories

www.facebook.com/HQStories

BUDDING WRITER?

We're also looking for authors to join the HQ Digital family!

Find out more here:

https://www.hqstories.co.uk/want-to-write-for-us/

Thanks for reading, from the HQ Digital team